TRICKSTER'S GIRL

BY HILARI BELL

Houghton Mifflin Harcourt

Boston New York

4722 7599 11/11

www.hmhbooks.com

The text of this book is set in Garamond.
Book design by Susanna Vagt

The Library of Congress has cataloged the hardcover edition as follows:
Bell, Hilari.
Trickster's Girl / by Hilari Bell.
p. cm.
Summary: In the year 2098, grieving her father and angry with her mother,
fifteen-year-old Kelsa joins the magical Raven on an epic journey from Utah to
Alaska to heal the earth by restoring the flow of magic that humans have disrupted.
[1. Adventure and adventures—Fiction. 2. Shapeshifting—Fiction.
3. Magic—Fiction. 4. Environmental degradation—Fiction.
5. Grief—Fiction. 6. Family problems—Fiction.] I. Title.
PS7.B38894Tri 2011
[Fic]—dc22   2010006785

ISBN: 978-0-547-19620-6 hardcover
ISBN: 978-0-547-57724-1 paperback

Manufactured in the United States of America
DOC 10 9 8 7 6 5 4 3 2 1

4500321396

To my mother,
who drove with me
from Denver to Alaska and back,
and watched this book
being born.

PROLOGUE

RAVEN HAD SPENT TOO LONG on the hunt. He cocked his head, beady eyes fixed on the sweating girl. In this form, his vision was sharp, but he'd perched near enough that even with weak human sight he could have observed the curious weave of the girl's black suit. The stark color wasn't becoming, but something about this girl spoke to senses that went beyond a bird's vision. She hadn't the luminous dimensionality of his own people, yet she was rooted in her reality. It wasn't much, but no human he'd encountered in this incarnation of the world had shown even that much promise. He'd already spent too long on the hunt. His time was running out. He had to try.

CHAPTER 1

"FRIENDS, WE ARE GATHERED HERE to commemorate not the death of Jonathan Peter Phillips, but his life."

They even got the name wrong.

Though given how much else was wrong, Kelsa supposed she shouldn't complain about that. It was the name on her father's birth certificate. And his life did deserve celebration. She pushed her bangs off her sweaty forehead, wishing that the tempcontrol in her formal jacket worked better. At least she'd been able to braid her long, frizzy hair off the back of her neck. Her mother's stylish cut, the same kind of haircut she'd so often tried to talk Kelsa into, clung damply to her neck under the hot late-May sun.

Kelsa's mother had insisted on having the formal service at graveside—even though no one was actually buried anymore and as per the cemetery contract, the urn would sit on its granite pedestal for only sixty years. Her father wasn't there, so it probably didn't matter that his life was being recounted by a minister who might not even have met him.

It should have been a gathering of his friends, telling stories about the times her father had helped them or made them laugh. About his passion for the living earth he'd studied and taught. About the time he'd taken his nine-year-old daughter on a hike up a desert canyon to a hidden waterfall, where butterflies danced between the shining curtains.

The memory glowed, jewel bright. So many memories. Fifteen years of them. It wasn't enough.

Oh, Pop.

Kelsa had vowed to get through this without crying, but the tears welled up anyway. Her mother had been crying quietly since the service began, Joby sitting in her lap, even though his five-year-old body must have been both heavy and hot.

". . . the many years he taught biochemistry at the University of Northern Utah," the minister droned.

Kelsa blinked hard and sniffed. This wasn't her father's real funeral, and she'd cried an ocean over the last few months. She was tired of grief, tired of the whole damned mess. The simple facts the minister recited, *graduated from, worked as a park ranger, met his wife in,* didn't begin to encompass the reality of her father's life. Any more than the graceful black granite urn held his real ashes.

Kelsa lowered her gaze, hiding a fierce smile that no one would have understood.

◦ ◦ ◦

Eventually the service ended, with a modern blessing on her father's soul and all those he had loved. No words of ashes and dust; very little about death at all. Death wasn't fashionable. Kelsa had to admit that it was the ultimate grind, but when someone died you really ought to talk about the "dead" part. The minister had done his best, she supposed, given that the man he was eulogizing had never set foot in a church in his life.

"I like the churches God made better," he'd told Kelsa one autumn afternoon, gesturing to the towering peaks around them, the sweep of meadow and sky.

But none of this was the minister's fault, so Kelsa shook the man's hand and accepted his condolences with a polite mumble of thanks. He wasn't sweating, which either meant there really were miracles or the tempcontrol in his black coat worked better than hers.

Her mother was sweating, and she was so pale that despite the thorny wall of her anger Kelsa felt a flash of concern.

The minister must have shared it. He picked up Joby, handed him over to Kelsa, and had her mother separated from the crowd and headed toward the waiting cars of the funeral cortege in short order.

Their car had a driver supplied by the mortuary, which was just as well. Kelsa wasn't sure her mother was up to driving.

As soon as they were aboard, the repulsers lifted the car off the pavement and the chiller kicked on, ruffling Kelsa's damp bangs with a burst of cool air.

"Thank God that's over," her mother murmured, sinking back in her seat.

Kelsa was suddenly furious all over again. *You were saying goodbye to your husband! How can you be glad it's over?*

But they'd both been saying goodbye throughout the last four horrible months, ever since the doctor pronounced her father's cancer too far advanced for even modern medicine to cure. And Kelsa knew her mother had loved her father.

She just hadn't loved him enough.

∘ ∘ ∘

One of the good things about her mother's faith was that neighbors were there for each other in bad times. When someone died, that translated to a refrigerator full of casseroles, salad, and bread.

It also meant babysitters. When the car reached their house, Mrs. Stattler was waiting to take Joby off to play with Mike. Kelsa's mother took two aspirin, since the Reformed Church didn't approve of stronger drugs unless they were necessary, and lay down for a nap.

Kelsa, with nothing to do till dinnertime, fought down an unjust desire to be angry with Mrs. Stattler too. Mrs. Stattler's willingness to add Joby to her own gaggle of boys was one of the things that made her mother's excuses such carpo.

I can't take care of a five-year-old boy and a dying man, Kel. And you have to go to school, though Kelsa knew—both of them knew—that the school would have let her skip classes for months to nurse a dying father. She could have homeschooled while she did it. She wouldn't have quit. Kelsa *always* finished what she started.

But her mother had refused even to ask the school. Even to try. That was what Kelsa couldn't forgive. Just as her mother couldn't quite forgive her for siding with her father when he refused to give in to what he called "the great irrational." Because he wanted to spend the final months of his life with his family, instead of being prayed over by strangers.

It was his choice.

And it wouldn't have worked, anyway.

Kelsa watched as her mother brought Joby home from the Stattlers' and programmed the multichef to heat their supper.

She banished the sneaking sympathy as her mother picked at her food, and forced herself to respond to Joby's chatter about the mud city he and Mike were making. Mr. Stattler was an enthusiastic gardener, and his yard contained things that weren't often found in this suburban neighborhood, including old-fashioned dirt.

Including, Kelsa suddenly remembered, an old-fashioned posthole digger. Mr. Stattler always let neighbors borrow his tools. Would he be willing to lend Kelsa his posthole digger for this?

No, he'd be horrified by what she'd done, the lies she'd told.

Yes, he'd understand.

Or he'd think she was traumatized by grief and forgive her.

Kelsa knew that Mrs. Hennesy, her guidance counselor, had already told her mother that Kelsa "needed to talk to someone."

This wasn't so much because Kelsa's grades had fallen—no one expected your grades to be perfect when your father was dying. It was because when Mrs. Hennesy had taken her mother's side, Kelsa had stopped talking to Mrs. Hennesy.

Kelsa's mother had suggested several times that Kelsa talk to the grief counselor at the hospice. But Kelsa had hated the hospice, hated everything about it, and she'd refused.

Of course her furious refusal made her mother, and everyone else, even more concerned about her emotional stability.

If I'd agreed, if I'd appeared more stable, would they have let . . .

No, she knew they wouldn't. And it was too late to change anything now.

If prayer could have saved him, Kelsa's would had done the job.

Dinner lasted far too long.

Her mother put Joby to bed, reading aloud to him as she'd once read to Kelsa. It made Kelsa's heart ache, despite everything.

She was letting her mother down. But her mother had let her father down too, so life was tough all over, wasn't it?

Eventually her brother went to sleep. Not long after that her mother went to bed, exhausted by the stresses of the day despite her nap.

Kelsa lay in her own bed, waiting as the distant hum of traffic tapered off, as the breeze through her open window began to cool. She'd planned to wait, dramatically, till midnight. But by eleven fifteen she was certain her mother was sleeping, and if anyone else saw her it wouldn't matter. She'd gone on so many late-night walks with her father, eluding the heat of Utah's summer days, that even if the neighborhood patrol spotted her they'd only wave.

She dressed in dark jeans and a plain cotton stretchie—tan, not suspicious burglar-black. Then she reached up to the top shelf of her closet, feeling behind her winter clothes till her fingers located the thick plastic bag that held her father's ashes.

They were heavy. So much heavier than the flour she'd substituted for them in the granite urn, that she'd raided her father's tackle box and thrown in half a dozen weights to make up the difference. The ashes were a different color as well, grayish, so she'd gone up to the attic and swept up a pan of dust to mix into the top layer of flour. It was still too white, but her mother never opened the urn to look, and Kelsa didn't think anyone else would either.

Her father might have. He'd had a scientist's curiosity about most things, and he'd been too logical to care how he was buried.

Kelsa cared.

She put the plastic bag into her day pack, and in case she was stopped by some patroller who didn't know her, she folded a light jacket over the top. Water, because her father had insisted she never set out on any hike without it, and rain gear too, no matter what the weather report said. In case her mother woke up and checked on her, Kelsa left a message on the house com board saying that she couldn't sleep and had gone for a walk. Her personal ID card would identify her to the house security system, so she could lock the back door and leave the system on behind her. Kelsa might be angry with her mother, but she wasn't about to take chances with her family's safety—not even in a quiet neighborhood like hers.

The night air was rich with the smell of petunias, and the moonlight was so bright she could almost see their colors. Kelsa's house backed onto an urban greenbelt, with a rubber-crete path running down it. Their fence was so low she simply swung her legs over it. The Stattlers' fence, five houses down, was almost as low, but pulses of red light flashed along its base, prepared to offer a discouraging shock to wayward rabbits—and if Kelsa shook the fence on the way over she might get shocked as well. The rabbits eventually tunneled under the barrier and ate Mr. Stattler's lettuce anyway, but at least, he said, they had to work for it.

In the end Kelsa climbed into a neighbor's yard, up into an old fruit tree, and then leaped over the Stattlers' fence. The Stattlers' trees would let her depart the same way, but for now . . . she'd remembered correctly; the tool shed wasn't locked.

It was so dark inside that Kelsa couldn't see a thing, and she knew the cluttered tools could make an incredible racket. She frowned, and after a few seconds managed to focus her eyes in the way that brought up her night vision, her tense shoulders relaxing as the stacked tools, boxes, and sacks emerged slowly into sight.

She'd had to get her vision corrected in second grade. The Reformed Church felt the same about mechanical vision enhancements as they did about unnecessary drugs, but her mother was moderate enough not to argue when Kelsa's father said that as long as they were messing with her eyes she might as well get the standard package.

She used the enhancements so seldom that she sometimes had trouble bringing them up, and even with her ability to see what she was doing, one of the shovels clanked against a laser trimmer. It wasn't loud enough to wake anyone, and Kelsa finally extracted the posthole digger. Its cylindrical blades were attached to a shaft over four feet long, with a plain wooden bar crossing the top. Wood and steel—the old-fashioned tool felt right to her. You should have to dig to make a grave, metal carving the earth. She hoped she'd raise a sweat, that her hands would blister, her muscles ache.

She tossed the awkward tool over the fence and climbed out of the Stattlers' yard. She didn't see any patrollers on the familiar walk down the greenbelt, down two streets, while moving in and out of the street lamps' coppery glow. She did swing wide around the traffic lights. Their cameras generally came on only if someone ran the light, but the police could set them to continuous wide scan at will, and you never knew.

The quiet was soothing. Kelsa was almost sorry when she reached the willow-lined creek that flowed through this part of Springville, a tiny strip of brush and weeds in the midst of the urban world. If you got off the rubbercrete pathway, you could see the tracks of magpies, cottontail rabbits, coyotes, and even deer in the mud of the meandering streambed.

It was her father who had taken her off the path, who'd taught her to identify both tracks and scat. This scrap of undeveloped land wasn't the vast, open wilderness he'd loved, but it was their favorite city hike—as close to rightness as Kelsa could get.

She walked for twenty minutes, crossed the footbridge, and then cut off the pavement onto a dirt trail the local kids, and possibly coyotes and deer, had beaten upstream to the place where the queen cottonwood loomed over a shallow bend.

Leaves rustled a welcome. Kelsa dropped her pack and pressed her palms together as if in prayer, then swept them up into a wide circle that ended with her hands folded at her waist. She bowed, finishing the whimsical homage to trees her father had taught her.

"Greetings, your majesty."

Kelsa had always had a sense of the presence that lived in trees. Not aware, exactly, but old and patient and very alive. The bioplague that had wiped out so much of the South American rain forests hadn't even begun to come this far north. Its first traces were only now appearing in Mexico, and reporters on the holovid, and in the online papers and magazines, were certain it wouldn't spread outside the tropics. Of course, five years ago they'd been certain it would never spread out of the small corner of the Amazon where it had been released. Certain that even the trees there would fight it off eventually.

The scientists who published in scholarly journals, which her father had allowed her to read despite her mother's protests, were a lot more worried. Her father had gone to the

Amazon to study the plague himself, as soon as the infected zone had been declared safe for humans. Sometimes Kelsa felt that his cancer, diagnosed over a year later, was an extension of the bioplague—as if he'd caught it from the trees.

But that was impossible, and her mind knew it. It was her heart she couldn't convince.

She set the point of the posthole digger against the earth and turned it. She'd never used this tool before, but it was easy to master. The dry clay near the roots was hard going, but about four inches down it grew damp and began to soften. Soon every few twists of the handle allowed her to lift out a scoop of earth, which she shook onto the growing pile.

Eventually, the handles brushed the ground. Kelsa emptied the last scoop, laid the digger aside, and reached into the hole. Cold dirt grated against her arm, but her stretching fingers couldn't find the bottom. It was deep enough. And so much better, truer, than the manicured grass and lifeless stone of the cemetery. This place, where foxes and raccoons still left their tracks, where the remains of his body might lend a bit of strength to the towering ancient whose leaves whispered in the moonlight—this was what her father would have wanted.

She hadn't been able to let him die the way he wanted to, but at least she could bury him that way.

Trying not to think, because if she started to think she'd start crying—again—Kelsa pulled out the plastic bag and ran the slider down the seal. The ashes thumped into the bottom of the hole. She felt odd about throwing the bag in the trash with traces of ash still clinging to it, so Kelsa went down to the stream and captured some water in the bag, which she then poured into the hole as well.

"Here lies Johnny Phillipini," she said defiantly, "who took back his great-to-the-fifth-great-grandfather's name when he was in college, even if he never did get around to changing it legally."

His wife had preferred Phillips, despite the awkwardness of Dad's colleagues and students asking for Professor Phillipini when they called the house.

He'd been a good teacher. A good husband. Such a good father.

There was nothing more to say and she was crying. Again. She should be used to it by now.

Kelsa dropped to her knees and pushed dirt back into the narrow hole, the muddy clay cold and soft on her bare palms. She hadn't worked long enough to raise blisters, but she could feel it in her muscles, in her hands—the simple reality of a grave in the earth.

Ashes to ashes, dust to dust. All part of the cycle, her father would have said.

After she'd patted down the last of the dirt Kelsa wiped her hands on her jeans, dug a tissue out of her pocket, and blew her nose. She rose to her feet. The tree's quiet spirit, the rustling darkness, comforted her more than any human presence, soothing the raw pain. But nothing could fill the aching emptiness left by her father's absence. There was one more thing to say.

"Goodbye, Dad."

She was reaching for the posthole digger, turning to go, when a man stepped out of the shadow of the tree trunk, almost as if he'd stepped out of the tree itself.

Kelsa started back, stumbling, almost falling. The man— no, boy, for he looked only a few years older than she was— moved forward into the moonlight.

His face was round, but with high cheekbones, and his straight black hair was perfect for the asymmetric wedges of his fashionable haircut. He wore jeans and gel-soles, like Kelsa did, but his round-collared shirt had buttons like a dress shirt, though the sleeves were fuller and the cut was wrong.

He was one of the best-looking guys Kelsa had seen outside of a fashion ad, and his cocky smile told her he knew it.

"Relax," he said. "I think you'll do. I've been looking for you for a long time. I wouldn't dream of doing you harm."

Kelsa picked up the posthole digger. "I don't know who you are or what you're doing here, and I don't care. I want you to leave. Now."

His smile never wavered. "But I've only just found you. I can't let you go yet. Besides—"

He stepped forward so quickly she had no chance to back away, and he brushed the ball of his thumb over the flat spot between her eyebrows. He stepped back just as quickly, at the same time she did, and raised his thumb to his lips. "Yes, you'll do. So I can't afford to lose you. Sorry," he added with another charming smile. "But there it is."

Kelsa raised the posthole digger, prepared to swing it if he took another step. "Look, mister, I don't know where you come from . . ." His faint drawl didn't sound quite like any accent she'd heard before, and his skin had a swarthy cast. ". . . but Utah takes statutory rape seriously. So back off and get out of here, or I'll start screaming."

The creek might feel like a slice of wilderness, but there were houses only a few hundred yards away and the night was quiet. If she screamed, someone would wake up and report it. For all his creepy weirdness, she didn't feel like he was hitting on her. But if it wasn't that, what was he doing? She didn't lower the digger, even when his smile faded.

"I'm not trying to . . . What's the phrase? Hook up?" The amusement in his voice was clear. "Or in a way I am, though not for the purposes you think. I want to . . . recruit you? Yes, that's the right way to put it."

"A pimp's even worse than a pervert," Kelsa told him, though she didn't think he was a pimp, either. His English was fluent, but something about the phrasing didn't sound right. Maybe this was all some sort of linguistic misunderstanding.

"You have a very dirty mind," he said. "Not that I object to that. It's the fact that you don't believe in magic that's going to make this difficult."

Kelsa snorted. "I haven't heard a lot of lines, but that's got to be one of the worst. What part of 'go away' do you find so mysterious?"

He shook his head sadly. "You don't understand."

"Oh no, I got it. We'd be magic together. Or maybe it's just you that's magic, with any girl you meet. But you were right the first time. I don't believe in magic."

The smile came back, crooked now, but still annoying.

"Then why don't I show you some," the young man said. "It will probably be quicker than arguing."

Kelsa stepped back once more, but he didn't move toward her. Instead . . .

He began to shrink, not crouching, but actually growing smaller. His swarthy skin darkened, his whole body crumpling like a piece of paper laid on a bed of embers. His skin shredded into blackened strips. His clothes folded into a messy pile, restraining a tattered writhing thing that suddenly extended two ragged protrusions and shrieked in a voice so rough it held no humanity at all.

Kelsa's mind was screaming, but her tight throat emitted only a strangled squawk. She threw the posthole digger at the dark shape and ran, feet pounding on the packed dirt, moving even faster when she reached the rubbercrete path, though she'd have sworn it was impossible to run any faster.

When she reached the first streetlight the stitch in her side forced her to stop, but she didn't bend over; she spun wildly, trying to peer into the darkness in all directions at once, trying to hear over the beat of blood in her ears. She was back on the grid now, in view of the cameras whether they were scanning or not, so she should be safe. But . . .

What the hell was that thing?

She had read that people once took drugs that gave them hallucinations, long after the intended effect of the drug had worn off—and if this was what drug users saw, then they had to be even crazier than she'd thought! But one of the things Kelsa agreed with her mother's church about was avoiding drugs, so why was she seeing . . . whatever it had been?

The darkness no longer seemed peaceful. Kelsa took the streets back to her house, jogging from one circle of light to the next, her every sense alert for some sign that the *thing* might be following her.

Assuming he was still alive after . . . after being burned to charred rags, in a lightless, heatless fire, in front of her eyes.

Kelsa began to run again.

The PID card in her pocket unlocked the front door as she approached it, and she burst into the house and gasped, "Lights!"

The hall lights responded, filling the room with a harsh glare.

"Kel?" Her mother's voice came from the kitchen. "Is that you?"

Kelsa dashed for the safety of her mother's company as if she were Joby's age.

Her mother's hair was tousled, and she was wearing her husband's well-worn bathrobe. She frowned when she saw Kelsa in the doorway. "I didn't know you'd gone out. I don't think it's safe for you to go out at night without"—she took a breath and finished it—"without your father."

The annoyance in her eyes deepened as they ran over Kelsa—Lord only knew what she looked like—and the words *grief counseling* hung in the air between them.

If she told her mother what had happened tonight, it wouldn't be grief counseling. Her mother would have Kelsa sitting on the steps of a psychologist's office before the secretary opened the door in the morning. Unless she just called for the men with the tranqs and skipped the intervening steps.

"I couldn't sleep," said Kelsa. "So I went for a run. Sorry if I worried you."

Her mother shook her head, guilt replacing the angry concern in her expression. "I didn't even know you'd gone out."

Kelsa couldn't deal with it now. "I'm going to get a shower. I'll see you in the morning."

∘ ∘ ∘

She left for school earlier than usual, and she was probably going to arrive late; the cottonwood bend was almost a mile out of her way.

In the early-morning sunlight it was hard to believe that . . . whatever-it-was had happened the night before. The guy was probably some sort of magician, Kelsa thought, who got his kicks out of terrifying strangers. In a couple of days she'd see an ad for the great Creepo, Master of Illusion, performances every day at three and seven.

She was still going back to check it out.

The glade looked as it always did in the daylight. The post-hole digger lay in the dappled shade where she'd thrown it. How was she going to get it back to Mr. Stattler's shed? The flickering light made it difficult to see details on the ground behind the tree, and the dry mud was too hard to take an impression. There were a few scuff marks, but that proved nothing except that someone had been there. And Kelsa and her father weren't the only people who hiked down the creek bed.

Maybe she'd imagined the whole thing. Though if she had, she'd better take her mother up on that grief counseling! If she was hallucinating something like that, she really was crazy.

Kelsa didn't think she was crazy. If she was going to hallucinate anything it would be her father, or at least his spirit. But he was gone.

Should she put some stones on the grave to mark it? Stones weren't common in the flats around Utah Lake, but she could find some. Or perhaps she should just smooth some wet mud over the top, scatter a few of last year's dead leaves, and let nature reclaim it?

She was looking for stones as much as at the grave, so it took her several seconds to realize that the circle of disturbed earth was larger than the neat hole she had dug. What in the world . . .

She fell to her knees and brushed away a handful of leaves, revealing the circumference of this much-wider hole. Outraged fury welled up in her heart, blunted by confusion. Kelsa could think of no reason why even the burned-up creep would have dug into her father's grave.

CHAPTER 2

SHE WAS LATE FOR SCHOOL, barely reaching the building before the automated security gates closed. Closed gates meant she had to check in through the office, and too many tardies counted against your record.

As it was, she was able to slip into the classroom and log on to her deskcomp in time to keep from generating an official notice. Her teacher frowned at her, but having to go to your father's funeral in the middle of finals week earned you a little slack. After this weekend there were only two days of "school spirit" activities before the summer break.

Before her father's illness, Kelsa would have gotten sympathetic glances from several students to make up for the teacher's frown, but in the stresses of the last year she'd pretty much abandoned friends. No one wanted to hang with someone who was more involved with dying than with dates. Kelsa planned to pick up those friendships again, eventually, but she didn't have the emotional energy to work on it now. She'd be lucky to pass today's tests.

She managed to focus on the life studies final because she liked biology. The human studies teacher (whose classes the students called history about half the time) was still trying to help some of the slower kids understand the political tangle that had led to two Asian wars, so Kelsa's mind was free to wander. Only now, for the first time in months, she found it straying not to her father but to the creep. Had he really dug up her father's grave? Why?

If she kept the main window on her deskcomp open to the lesson, she could launch a side window to the greater net without its showing up on the teacher's board as a turnout—which was why some teachers powered off all the deskcomps and resorted to old-fashioned lectures rather than try to compete with v-chat.

According to the net there were several stage magicians in the greater Provo area who could be hired to perform at parties and business openings. None of them bore any resemblance to the guy she'd seen last night—who hadn't looked much older than her own fifteen. Too young to be a professional magician. Kelsa was searching through various magic tricks, hoping to find the one he'd used on her, when the chime sounded for class change. For her number studies final (which even the teachers still called math), she had to go to her locker to get her notes.

The halls had been tiled and painted in relaxing earth tones, but the students who flooded down them in their neon-trimmed stretchies more than made up for the put-students-to-sleep atmosphere the architects were trying for. Kids with long hair had braided flashing neon-cord into it, and one boy had glued rippling red and silver strips into his eyebrows.

Kelsa had cut one of those sticky strips out of Joby's hair and knew how effective that adhesive was. She was still smiling when she reached her locker . . . and found the creepy stranger leaning against it.

"What are you . . . How did you get in here? This is supposed to be a secure building!" Though once he got past the scanners, no one would have questioned him. He looked like a student, though he still wore the same retro cotton shirt he'd had on last night. The crumpled fabric made Kelsa wonder if he'd slept in it. In the daylight he wasn't frightening; just another teenager in the crowd. But there was something in his expression, as he looked over the surging mob, that had Kelsa upping her estimate of his age.

"With everyone dressed the same, isn't it hard to tell boys and girls apart?" he asked.

Kelsa blinked in surprise. "No." In truth, there were times when she had to look closely to determine a person's gender. Where did a question like that come from? Was he from some foreign country after all? But even in places like India women wore stretchies and jeans as often as they wore saris. His skin tone might have been Indian, but the bone structure didn't seem quite right.

"Are you from some other country?" Kelsa asked.

His curious expression grew more guarded. "You might say that. On the other hand, you might not. Are you ready to believe in magic yet?"

"Ahhh!" Kelsa buried her hands in her frizzy hair and tugged, a gesture of frustration she'd inherited from her father, along with the hair. "You're not supposed to be in this building! Get out, now, before I—"

"How do you know that?" he asked.

"What?"

"How do you know I'm not supposed to be here? If I was a new student who'd just moved to the city, I could be enrolled in this school."

Kelsa frowned. No one would come in this late in the year, but it was a big school. She'd been so caught up in family traumas over the last few months, she might have missed any number of new students.

"Are you enrolled here?" she demanded.

He hesitated so long the warning chime sounded. "No."

"Then you shouldn't be in the building," Kelsa repeated. She punched in the numeric code, and her locker door opened. The hall was emptying, the noise diminishing so rapidly she could hear his exasperated sigh.

"I've told you nothing but the truth. Doesn't that count for something?"

Kelsa found her note chip in the clutter of readers, book cards, and batteries, and closed her locker before she turned to face him.

"Did you dig up my father's grave?"

His dark eyes shifted. His lashes were very long. A couple of the girls who were hurrying past seemed to have noticed that too. They whispered to each other, and one turned to stare at him before they vanished into their classroom. He really was gorgeous. If Kelsa hadn't just buried her father, she might have cared. Right now grief was using up so much of her emotional energy she couldn't even maintain friendships— let alone fall madly in crush with some strange guy.

"I can explain that," the stranger said. "Look, we got off to a bad start, but I was so happy to find you I didn't think it through. My name is Raven, and I didn't mean to frighten you, but I really need to talk to you. I need your help. I need you to trust me."

He met her gaze now, eyes full of pleading sincerity. But he hadn't explained, and Kelsa had never met anyone she trusted less.

"No," she said. "I don't trust you, and this magic you keep talking about is pure carp! Get out of here, or I'll call one of the teachers and have you thrown out."

The hall was empty now, all the teachers in class, and in the safety of a populated place she hesitated to interrupt them—though you should interrupt a class to report someone stalking you! But weird as he was, she didn't feel stalked. Not exactly.

His shoulders sagged. "All right. I'll go. For now."

He turned and walked away, trailing his hand over the long row of lockers . . . and every door he touched popped open down the length of the hall.

Kelsa's math final was a disaster.

○   ○   ○

Those lock pads were so old, they didn't open half the time even when you punched in the right code!

Kelsa rolled over in bed and thumped her pillow into a more comfortable shape.

After struggling through dozens of equations, which never added up the same way twice, Kelsa had spent every free moment of the rest of the day studying magic tricks—the art of illusion, magicians called it. Most of the tricks were clever, and some were totally 'treme. Some could even be performed on the street, without the props filled with hidden compartments or holo shields that most "magicians" relied on.

But not one of those tricks would enable someone to open a whole row of cranky lock pads—locks that usually failed by stubbornly refusing to let even their owners open them.

No, not magic. Not even a magic trick. But there were ways to do what he'd done. There were burglar tools that would bypass a cheap lock pad, some of them small enough to strap onto your wrist under a rumpled cotton sleeve.

Of course, lock trippers, particularly the small ones, were illegal. And they were reported to be horribly expensive even on the black market, which was the only place you could buy one. They were also hard to make, according to the respectable net sites, not something an amateur electro-geek could cobble up in his basement.

According to the nut-net sites you could build one with old transistors and rubber bands—well, not quite, but the nut-net's claims were almost that wild. On the other hand, if it was easy to put one together would the authorities admit it?

Either way, that Raven creep was not only a creep but a criminal. And crazy too. He probably made a habit of digging up graves! Kelsa rolled over again. It was warm, but she'd still shut her door against the air chiller and opened her windows to catch the natural cooling of the night.

She hadn't felt threatened by him today—mostly he was annoying. That was it. An annoying guy, putting on some sort of mystery act to try to pick up girls! Forget the way those lockers had opened. In broad daylight. No, don't forget it! Anyone who owned a lock tripper was—

Because her window was open, she heard the flapping wings and the rustling in the ancient crab apple tree. It grew so close to the house that she could leave her curtains open in the summer and still have privacy from the neighbors.

A bird perching in that tree wasn't uncommon, though this one sounded larger.

The wings flapped again, right up to her window, and something rapped sharply on the thermopane.

Kelsa sat bolt upright and stared as a big black bird hopped back into the branches. Soon a large pale shape emerged from the shadows. The leaves rustled furiously as he struggled into his shirt. Of course, Kelsa thought dazedly, his clothes wouldn't come with him when he . . . No!

The stranger was up to his tricks again. Illusionists had been using trained birds for centuries, but using one to terrorize women was vile. The oversize stretchie she slept in fell to midthigh, so she didn't bother to grab a robe when she stalked over to the window and whispered, "What the frack are you doing? You're trespassing! Get off our property right now, or I'm calling the police!"

"I'd be gone by the time they arrived." His voice was barely louder than the shaking leaves as he shifted position—the leaves were pretty noisy. The branches he perched on bobbed under his weight, and although the old-fashioned shirttails were long enough to preserve his modesty, he wasn't wearing jeans. Was she supposed to think that he'd flown his shirt up into the tree as a bird, then put it on? He was an idiot! A half-naked idiot, sitting in the tree outside her window. She really should call the police. But he clung to the quivering branches with a desperation that was more comical than threatening.

He muttered something that sounded like "gee-so-fat," which made no sense at all, and braced one foot cautiously against a thicker branch.

"Look, we got off to a bad start. Let me try again. My name is Raven—"

Kelsa snorted. "Yeah, right."

"And I need your help. Will you just listen? That's all I ask." He sounded serious, for once, but he must have worked for years to train that bird. Or maybe he used sound recordings and some sort of holo projection. Whichever it was, he was lying to her in every way, and she'd have to be an idiot to listen.

"No," said Kelsa firmly. "If you're not off my property in three minutes I'm calling the police. If I ever see you again, I'm going to report you as a stalker. You leave me alone! Got it? Good!"

She slammed the window shut and drew the drapes before going back to bed. She'd check in five minutes, and if he was still there she would report him!

But he was right; he'd be gone by the time they got there, and her mother didn't need the stress of her daughter being stalked along with her other problems. Neither did Kelsa!

He's just some lunatic, she told herself firmly. *A grave-robbing nut!*

She was pulling the blankets over her head only because he weirded her out, not at all because she didn't want to hear the sound of wings flapping in the darkness.

o   o   o

By breakfast, Kelsa had realized that she should have called the police even if he would have been gone when they arrived. Stalkers weren't harmless, no matter how often they said they wouldn't hurt you. It wasn't only in vids that they sometimes raped or murdered their victims. And in real life, Kelsa thought soberly, their victims were less likely to heroically escape at the last minute.

She took her vita-juice out to the backyard and looked around the base of the tree for evidence, but grass grew right up to the trunk so there were no footprints. He hadn't scraped the tough bark when he climbed it. There was no evidence but her word, and if Kelsa described the tricks he'd played the police would think she was crazy.

The next time she saw him, if there was a next time, she'd pull out her com pod and record everything he did and said. And why hadn't she done that earlier? Because she was stupid, that's why.

Kelsa sighed. With luck she'd never see him again—and if she did, she'd be ready.

She half expected to see him leaning against the lockers every time she turned a corner, but he didn't reappear for the rest of the day. Kelsa managed to get through her history final in reasonable shape, though the number of questions she had no memory of made her realize how much her father's illness had distracted her.

The soft fog of grief threatened to close down again at the thought, so Kelsa opened a side window on her deskcomp and looked up some statistics about stalkers—which convinced her that she really should have recorded him and called the police.

She added the name Raven to her stalker search. If he'd murdered a dozen teenage girls in some other city, she'd call the police without a recording.

She found no mention of a homicidal maniac calling himself Raven, which lightened her mood considerably. On impulse, she ran "Raven/illusionist/magic," even though he was too young to be a professional performer. She didn't find him with that search either, though she did come across several hits on the Native American trickster spirit Raven, who was also a shapeshifter.

So that's where he got the shtick from.

Or that was the form his psychosis had taken. Kelsa shivered and closed the window. She knew what she had to do if she saw him again.

But he didn't come popping out at her as she walked home, and nothing flapped up that night to tap on her thermopane behind the closed curtains.

o   o   o

"Have you thought about our summer plans?" Kelsa's mother's voice was filled with the kind of fake cheer that didn't belong at the breakfast table, even at the best of times. "I was thinking, maybe we should do something different this year."

With her father gone, neither of them had the heart to go camping—and Kelsa had no desire to do anything with her mother, anyway.

"I might take Aunt Sarabeth up on her offer," Kelsa said. Aunt Sarabeth lived in an apartment in downtown Chicago, and Kelsa had always thought that she wanted a teenage niece to visit her as little as Kelsa wanted to waste a summer in a city. But her aunt renewed the offer every year, and there was nothing else she wanted to do.

Her mother frowned. "Are you sure? I was thinking maybe you and Joby and I—"

Kelsa pushed her chair back from the table. "I've got homework."

Her mother knew she didn't. Her scowl was designed to trip Kelsa's guilt switch, but Kelsa didn't apologize.

She wanted to go for a walk, but she was afraid that Raven guy would be waiting for her—though as the day wore on, being terrorized by a stalker began to look good compared to the sagging depression that saturated the house. In the last few months her mother—who had once despised d-vid and had strictly limited the amount her children watched—had taken to shutting down in front of the screen for hours on end, watching nothing but comedy and old flat-vid movies with happy-happy endings.

Kelsa understood her mother's need to escape, but by Sunday morning she would rather have hung around with Jack the Ripper than go to church with her mother and Joby and then spend the afternoon listening to canned laughter. Besides, Sunday was Kelsa and her father's hiking afternoon, and she wasn't going to let either grave-robbing sickos or her mother keep her from honoring that tradition.

Kelsa knew her mother was still angry with her, but the expression of relief that flashed across her face when Kelsa said that she'd be gone for the rest of the day was annoying.

Her mother and Joby had departed by the time Kelsa topped off her hiking pack: a sandwich, an apple, a handful of energy bars, and several bottles of water, since it would be hot in the canyon. She always took her com pod on long hikes, in case she needed to call her mother and tell her she'd be later than expected, or in case of emergencies. But her mother would have been surprised when Kelsa snapped it onto a lanyard and hung it around her neck. People who wanted to have their hands free often wore their pods that way, but when she hiked Kelsa usually kept it in her pack or her pocket.

Not today. Her crazy stalker had probably given up, but if he hadn't, she'd be ready for him.

She took the city shuttle out to the canyon trailhead, and even on a hot Sunday morning both the shuttle and the first mile of trail were crowded. Most of the nature lovers were couples or parents with young children. Once she and her father had been part of that group, and Kelsa felt her throat tighten.

But most of the young kids dropped out after the first mile, where the trail steepened and the real canyon began. Her father had said it was debatable whether this was a "real" canyon.

It had been created seventy years ago, when a series of droughts convinced the Provo planners that both their growing city and the nearby farms needed more water than could be sucked from Utah Lake. They'd built Paradise Dam, which soon created Paradise Reservoir. And to bring the water down to the city, instead of laying eighty miles of expensive pipe, they'd chosen to run it through a series of mountain valleys. With a river roaring down them, the valleys were slowly eroding into canyons filled with tumbling rapids and a series of spectacular waterfalls—if you viewed them in the spring, when the farmers most needed water. In winter only an icy trickle flowed through the boulder-dotted streambed, and even now, at the end of May, the flow wasn't the roaring cataract it had been the last time her father had enough energy to hike this trail.

He'd been feeling the effects of both the cancer and the treatment drugs by then, his steps slowed, his face and body sweaty with effort—forgetting, sometimes, to smile for his daughter's sake and pretend that nothing was wrong. Would that memory fade someday, and the memories of her father striding up the trail as if it was his natural habitat come to the fore again?

It wouldn't have worked!

"You have to believe in faith healing for it to have any effect," her father had said. "I don't."

And Kelsa had agreed with him.

Now she transformed her grief, her anger, into energy to climb. By the time she reached the next milepost she was drenched in sweat, her muscles moving as if they'd been oiled.

It was nearly noon; the intense sunlight cast stark shadows and flashed on the rushing water. For most of its length, the trail ran roughly ten feet higher than the river it followed. Air scented with hot dust and pine filled her lungs as Kelsa climbed carefully down the steep rocky bank. After looking around to be sure no one was in sight, she stripped off her stretchie and soaked it in the river. It ran deeper than she'd thought, maybe three feet deep, and cold. Even after she wrung out her shirt the fabric clung clammily to her skin, but as she hiked up the trail, she now wore a tempcontrol shirt that cooled her more efficiently than the high-tech ones worn by several of the red-faced hikers coming down the trail.

Her shirt was nearly dry, and she was looking for a shady place to stop for lunch, when she saw Raven. He sat on a rock at the edge of the steep bank, wearing the same clothes as before. They were beginning to look grubby. Didn't whatever hotel he was staying at have a laundry?

She set her com pod to "record," twisting the focus to the widest possible scan. The edge of the images would be distorted, but anything that happened in front of her would be preserved. That knowledge alone should have sent him running—he had watched her adjust the pod—but he remained seated on the rock as she approached.

"Are you following me?" she demanded, though only an idiot would give her a confirmation on record.

"Of course I am." He shot her that glowing, untrustworthy smile. "How else can I talk to you? Are you ready to believe in magic yet?"

If he had followed her, how had he gotten ahead of her on the trail? He must have realized where the shuttle was going and hiked up before her. But Kelsa hadn't been on this trail for months. Had he been watching her, stalking her, for that long?

A shiver that had nothing to do with her damp shirt ran over her skin.

"I don't believe in magic," she said. "I've told you before that I want you to leave me alone. And I'm going to enforce it. I'm going to the police."

The smile still lingered, though his eyes had grown serious. "This little thing, it makes a record of our conversation?" He gestured to the thumb-size pod.

"Of course." Kelsa frowned. There was no place in the world so backward that people wouldn't know what a com pod was!

He may not have known much about tech, but the clasp on the lanyard was simple enough for anyone's understanding. He rose to his feet and reached out—she'd forgotten how quick he was—and pinched the catch open, dropping the com pod into his hand.

Kelsa had stepped back, but now she lunged forward, snatching at the pod as he twisted aside. "Give me that! It's mine!"

He threw it into the river.

Kelsa had never before felt the kind of fury she did then; it surged through her blood, whiting out rational thought.

"You bastard! My father gave me that!"

She pushed him.

She hadn't thought it through. She was sure, almost sure, that she hadn't intended to kill him. But they were standing at the top of the riverbank, and Kelsa put the full weight of her body and her anger into that shove.

He stumbled back and fell over the edge.

She heard him hit several rocks on the way down, heard the splash as he hit the water. She reached the edge just in time to see him sink.

It was only a few feet deep, but the channel here was narrow, the current hard and fast. One white sleeve splashed to the surface, but his face didn't emerge. Why didn't he stand up? Start to swim? Had he hit his head? Whatever the problem, he'd be too far downstream for her to reach him if she took the time to scramble down the bank.

Kelsa knew this river, this trail. She ran down it, keeping one eye on the shimmering white of his shirt and another on the rough surface. If she broke an ankle, he might die!

The few minutes it took her to reach the bend where the river spread and slowed, where the trail dipped down to the water, seemed an eternity. Kelsa rushed into the river, stumbling on the slippery rocks, feeling the chill soak through her jeans, into her shoes. Her eyes were fixed on the patch of white floating just below the surface, and she managed to position herself in front of it. Plunging her arms and face into the water, she fisted both hands in the fabric as the current whisked it past.

Even before she hauled it out she knew the shirt was empty.

A scream rose in her throat and she stared frantically, trying to catch a glimpse of a body beneath the rippling surface, a hand breaking free, anything—

The silver fish that leaped out of the river was the biggest she'd ever seen, easily four feet long. Larger than anything that could survive in a creek that vanished every winter. Kelsa's jaw dropped. She was already clambering toward the shore when it jumped again, out of the water and into the muddy shallows.

Kelsa struggled up beside it, close enough to see each gleaming scale and the seep of blood from a gash over one round fishy eye, before it began to change.

In the full sunlight, the stretching skin and warping bones should have been even more horrifying. But the fish was turning into something human, instead of a human dissolving, and perhaps that made it less shocking—it could never be less than grotesque. His skin still had a silvery cast when his features became clear enough to be recognized, and a gash over one eye oozed blood. Then he began to cough—hard, rasping coughs, like someone who really had almost drowned. Living color flooded his face, and the last of the silver sheen vanished.

"Jehoshaphat! You almost killed me!"

Kelsa's mind began to function, and she realized that the terrible transformation had taken only a handful of seconds. Even as she watched, the bruises on his temple faded and the cut healed—but the blood was still on his skin. Kelsa reached out and touched it. His skull was firm; his flesh held only the normal cold of someone who'd been swimming in a freezing river. His clothing had not magically reappeared with his human form, but Kelsa was too shocked by the rest of it to care.

"Could I have killed you?" Her voice was too calm. She should have been screaming. Part of her was screaming, but either she was crazy, or she had to accept the evidence of her eyes.

She didn't *think* she was crazy.

He coughed again before he answered. "Yes, you could have killed me. Transformation takes time, and I have to be conscious to do it. I can be killed. I can be hurt too!"

He rubbed his temple and glared at her, and for some reason the simple human irritation in his expression brought the world back into focus. The sun was warm on her back, birds twittered in the brush, and Raven had no clothes on. She tried to keep her eyes on his face, but they crept down anyway. He *looked* human.

Kelsa yanked her gaze up again and handed him his shirt. Her cheeks were hot.

"I didn't mean to kill you. Though you probably deserved to get hurt. But now . . ."

She took a deep breath. If she was crazy she was crazy. She might as well go with it.

". . . I'm ready to listen."

CHAPTER 3

"You want me to rob a museum?" Kelsa asked incredulously. "No way!"

Raven had put on the cotton shirt she'd retrieved and the rain pants Kelsa kept in her hiking pack. The combination looked a bit odd, but not enough to draw the attention of passing hikers to the shade of the tree where they'd settled. Because, Raven said, it was likely to be a long discussion.

It was going to be shorter than he thought if he didn't say something more sensible than that.

"It's not really robbery," he told her. "They don't even know—"

"Is the museum going to be locked?" Kelsa demanded.

"Well, yes. But I can take care of that."

"Are we taking something without permission, and with no intention of returning it?"

"Yes, but they won't care—"

"Then it's robbery. And no way."

The dark eyes met hers directly. "Not even to stop the tree plague?"

"There's no excuse . . . The tree plague?"

It had begun over two years ago, when a small group of terrorists had released a mutating bacterium into the South

American rain forest, promising to provide the antidote when their demands were met.

Given the importance of the rain forest to the planet's slowly recovering ecosystem, the authorities had taken them seriously: they'd captured the terrorists' compound and all their scientists' notes, along with the scientists themselves, and offered them a chance of parole—someday, maybe—if they produced the antidote right now. And the terrorists had. But it hadn't worked.

"Only about a third of the trees have been affected, outside of the initial kill zone," Kelsa told him. "And it was just detected in Mexican forests a few months ago. They still think some trees will develop natural defenses and fight it off. And every botanist on the planet is looking for a cure."

"Only a third of the trees in the Amazon rain forest have died," Raven corrected. "They're all infected. And they're not fighting it off, and no one's going to find a cure, because the real source of the problem isn't that vicious little bacterium at all."

Because of her father's interest in the tree plague, Kelsa knew more about it than most, and she'd heard nothing of this. "Then what is the source of the problem?"

The dappled sunlight leaking through the pine boughs cast irregular patches of light over Raven's face and hair. "Magic."

"That's ridiculous!"

He said nothing, but a not entirely suppressed smile tipped up one side of his mouth.

Kelsa had seen him change from a fish into a man. *Seen* it. In a place and from a distance that left no possibility that it had been faked. Still . . .

"That's crazy! It was started by bioterrorists!"

"Oh, the bacterium's exactly what you think it is," the dark-haired boy told her. "But the reason the trees aren't fighting it off—as they should, and your scientists are right about that—is because the leys have been so badly weakened they can't support the forest."

"The *laze*? What—"

"*L-e-y*. That's the English word for them. Or at least, the word that comes closest. Leys are . . . think of underground rivers of natural and magical energy running through the surface of the world. Most humans don't even know they exist. Though there have always been a handful of exceptions, hence a name for them in English. In other languages too. Unfortunately, the fact that most humans aren't aware of them hasn't stopped you from mucking them up."

Humans. You. Kelsa wished her com pod wasn't at the bottom of the river.

"What *are* you?"

She was half prepared to run if he took offense at the question, but he only smiled.

"In this part of the world, I'm Raven."

"Raven." If you were crazy enough to accept magic, the logic was inescapable. "The Native American trickster spirit, Raven? But he's been here for hundreds . . . thousands . . ."

He looked like a teenager, but he'd never talked like one. Nor quite like someone for whom English was a first language.

"Not thousands," he said. That smug smile was beginning to annoy her. "And we've strayed off the subject. The weakening of the leys, which is what's keeping the trees from fighting off this bacterium, was caused by human interference with nature and magic, and it's going to take human magic to fix it. That's why you have to steal the medicine bag from the museum."

Kelsa's head was spinning. "Medicine bag? Like pills and stuff?"

"No, a medicine bag that a Navajo shaman named Atahalne made back in 1897."

"A shaman?"

"I told you some humans understood the leys. The leys were becoming fouled, even back then. Now, of course, the problem is critical. But Atahalne," Raven rattled off the choppy syllables fluently, "saw the problem at the very beginning, and he knew how to fix it. One of the last humans who possessed that knowledge, I might add, and a man of considerable courage, whether they admit it or . . . Anyway, he put together a medicine bag strong enough to heal the leys. Do you know what that is?"

Given the context, she did have a vague idea. "It's a small bag full of pollen and . . . and things, isn't it? Navajo people used them"—she'd seen the phrase on a card in a tourist trap—"to keep the person who wore it in harmony."

"Exactly," said Raven approvingly. "This one is mostly filled with sand from a place where several of the leys that run through this continent meet. But there were other things mixed in, things that tied him into its power. Atahalne set out to deliver the dust to nexus points all along the ley that runs from Colorado to Alaska."

"Nexus points?" Kelsa asked dazedly. Half her mind was still trying to take in the fact that the kid sitting in front of her was hundreds of years old. And by his own admission, not human.

"A nexus is . . . think of it as a valve along the ley line. Power can flow through and be strengthened, or it can be weakened and choked off. Atahalne set off in 1892 to revitalize the nexus points. But before he reached the first point he caught small-pox, near Salt Lake City, and died. His possessions—"

"He set out for Alaska, from New Mexico, in 1892? *Walking?*"

"He was in his fifties," Raven said. "It would have taken him years. And illness wasn't the only danger he faced along the way."

Kelsa wasn't a history geek, but she could see that a lone Na-tive American trying to cross a large stretch of territory that was still being conquered by white people had faced a *lot* of danger.

"And you won't even rob one little museum." For once, Raven sounded like a teenager.

"His medicine bag ended up in the museum?" Kelsa asked.

"It did. So it's up to you . . . ah . . ."

"Kelsa Phillips," she supplied. He was asking her to com-mit a felony, and he didn't even know her name?

"It's up to you, Kelsa Phillips, to take up Atahalne's medi-cine pouch, journey to Alaska, and complete his quest. Will you do it?"

"No way."

He had argued as she hiked back down the trail. He'd claimed that the fate of the whole planet was in her hands, because they had to start at the edges of the disruption, where the leys weren't so badly damaged, and work back toward the source. If this ley wasn't healed first, the rest couldn't be healed at all.

"Then why don't you do it?" Kelsa asked. "Turn into mist and flow through the keyhole or something?"

"I told you, humans did the damage, so humans have to fix it."

"Why? Is that some sort of magical law or something?"

"Or something." But his mobile face had closed.

"Fine," said Kelsa. "If it's a magical law, then you can magically change it."

"It doesn't work that way."

He didn't board the bus with her. The backwash from its stabilizing jets kicked up a puff of dust and ruffled his thick black hair. He was still standing there, scowling at her, when the bus pulled away.

But even if she believed him—which she didn't!—she was only fifteen! She had a bereaved mother and a brother who needed her. She couldn't even rob a museum, much less take off for Alaska by herself!

To tell her that trees weren't the only living things whose immune system had been weakened by the corruption of those so-called leys was a low, dirty blow. Even if the doctor had admitted that cancer rates were on the rise, and the medical community didn't really understand why.

o   o   o

Her eyes were dry again by the time she reached her shuttle stop, but she knew they were still red, and that her mother would see it and be concerned.

Kelsa was hoping to sneak up to the bathroom and apply cold water before her mother saw her. So when she let herself in and heard the silence that meant no one was home, her first reaction was relief.

Then she realized that her mother should have been home from church several hours ago.

First, she checked for a message on the com board. Nothing, but her mother had probably sent the message to Kelsa's com pod—which thanks to that lunatic whatever he was, was now at the bottom of the river.

The house com board had been programmed as a backup for all their pods, so after running her fingers through the menu for a few moments Kelsa was able to check her pod's messages. Only there weren't any messages.

She called her mother's pod and got the signal that it was turned off or out of range, so she left a message for her mother to call home and signed off, trying not to panic.

Kelsa had always known, abstractly, that anyone could die. Levcars crashed. Planes malfunctioned. But when her father died, her subconscious conviction that the universe couldn't do that to her, to her family, had shattered. Her family could be taken from her. Even Joby, young as he was, could be snuffed out, and she wouldn't even know about it till the hospital called. Till the police came to knock on her door.

Her mother must have gotten stuck in traffic on the way home from church . . . for almost two hours? OK, then her com pod was out . . . and she hadn't been able to borrow someone else's or find a public board?

Kelsa paced between the kitchen and the front door, arms wrapped around her body to keep the seething emotions in check.

Of course, her mother might simply have forgotten to call and leave a message. And if that was the case, then Kelsa would simply kill her when she got home and solve the problem for good!

After her father became ill, the rule that if you were delayed coming home you always called to let the family know where you were had become ironclad.

Which must mean that her mother *couldn't* call.

That didn't stop Kelsa from calling again—still off/out of range. Or smashed in some horrible car crash?

Kelsa was pulling up the contact button for the nearest hospital when her common sense kicked in. Her mother was less than two hours late. It was too soon to start calling hospitals, and the police would laugh in her face.

Anyone could be delayed for a couple of hours.

Kelsa went back to pacing. And it wasn't really a coincidence that when the security system finally chimed to signal the approach of a card it was programmed to accept Kelsa was bringing up the hospital's contact button—she'd brought it up six times in the last half-hour.

She paged out to the welcome screen and turned to face the front door, her heart drumming with anger and relief. She would wait on the anger, because her mother might have a good excuse.

The door opened and Kelsa's mother came in. She was smiling down at Joby, the sunlight shining on the neat straight hair her son had inherited. She still wore her church suit, and she looked tidy, healthy, and happier than she'd been when she left that morning.

At least she wasn't stupid. She took one look at Kelsa's face, and horrified guilt wiped away her smile.

"Oh honey, I'm so sorry. I forgot. I turned off my pod because I was talking with Jemina, and I just forgot to call. I'm so sorry."

Her mother hadn't called her honey since she'd come home two months ago carrying the brochure for the Healing Hands Wellness Retreat. And Jemina Judson was the church's grief-support-group leader. But that was no excuse.

"It wouldn't have taken you thirty seconds to call in and leave a message." Kelsa tried to sound cool and controlled, but her voice shook.

"I know." Joby was looking from one of them to the other, a worried frown wrinkling his forehead. "I'm sorry," her mother went on. "We'll talk in a minute. Joby, why don't you find a vid you like, and I'll make you a snack. PB crackers?"

Peanut butter was one of Joby's favorites—an excellent bribe. Kelsa had no desire to let her anger spill onto Joby.

She stalked up the stairs and paced in the hallway while her brother settled in front of the d-vid.

Her mother had apologized. She'd been talking to Jemina, gotten involved in the conversation, and forgotten the time. Forgotten to call in, even though she was the one who'd declared the rule ironclad. Even though Kelsa had *never* forgotten to call if she was delayed.

This wasn't some sort of subtle revenge against Kelsa for supporting her father when he'd refused to go to the retreat. Her mother wasn't cruel. She'd simply forgotten.

"Come on down, Kel," her mother called from the foot of the stairs. "You might as well have a snack too."

Kelsa's stomach was in knots, but when she reached the kitchen, her mother was setting out a plate of crackers and slicing some cheese. As if she thought Kelsa could eat. As if she cared.

Because if she cared, she'd have called home!

"One of the things I talked to Jemina about was your idea of going off to visit Sarabeth," her mother said. "We figured it had pros and cons."

She pushed out a chair for Kelsa and seated herself at the kitchen table.

Kelsa remained on her feet. "And that kept you from calling in?"

Her mother sighed. "I've apologized for that three times already. I'll apologize again if you want. But I'm not going to apologize for letting your father go to the hospice. It was the right decision for all of us, and—"

"Not for me," Kelsa hissed. "I told you—"

"Your father agreed." Anger dawned in her mother's eyes. "He knew perfectly well he'd need more nursing than I could provide, and the hospice is there to care for the dying. You're the one who said we had to do it all his way. To let him make the choices."

"He only agreed because he knew it was what you wanted," Kelsa said. She'd once considered those words unspeakable. Unforgivable. But she'd used them before. Used them when she realized how miserable her father was in the hospice, how much he wanted to be home with his family, no matter what he said.

Her mother had ignored her. And that was something Kelsa couldn't forgive. No more than her mother had been able to forgive her for not insisting they try *everything*.

Kelsa's mother took a deep breath and ran a hand through her hair, disarranging the neat wedges.

"I told Jemina that we'd work through it, but maybe she was right. Maybe some space between us, for a few months, would be a good idea. For both of us."

"Getting rid of family when they become inconvenient is your system, isn't it?" Kelsa demanded bitterly. "Well, I certainly don't—"

Her mother's hands slammed down on the table. "I'm sorry!" Her voice was as loud as it could be without disturbing Joby. "I'm sorry I forgot to call, all right? I'm not perfectly reliable, like you. I'm not perfect! And you're going to have to learn to live with that."

"Fine." Kelsa turned and stalked up to her room. She didn't slam the door, because she didn't want to upset Joby any more than her mother did.

But part of her wanted to. Part of her wanted to scream, to smash things, to bring the whole world down in flames.

Perfectly reliable.

"Go to hell."

∘ ∘ ∘

She had no way to contact Raven, but whatever else he was, he didn't strike Kelsa as a quitter. She left her bedroom window open, and she wasn't even surprised when she heard leaves rustling in the tree outside.

A lot of rustling. He climbed the tree in human form, stopping several feet short of the branch he'd perched in so precariously the other night.

"Well?" he asked. "I should have told you that I can help. Not just with the robbery, but with the whole journey. I'll have to, since you can't find the nexus points without—"

"I'm not going all the way to Alaska," said Kelsa. "That's just crazy. But if you need a human partner to get that medicine pouch out of the museum, you've got one."

° ° °

She hadn't expected it to happen that night. Maybe he didn't want to give her a chance to change her mind.

Kelsa had to admit she might have changed her mind. Her counselor had warned her that a death in the family could change people, make them do things they ordinarily wouldn't. She'd added that Kelsa should think carefully before doing anything she might later regret.

Maybe her counselor was right. Maybe this dark desire to break the old patterns of her life was a product of grief and loss, and one day she'd be sorry.

But right now, Kelsa didn't care. She was ready to walk on the wild side.

She left a message for her mother that she couldn't sleep and had gone out. The last thing she wanted, as she set out to commit her first felony, was for her mother to call the police and report her missing.

The rumble of the rising garage door would certainly have awakened her mother, but her motorbike was narrow enough to fit through the side door.

The old-fashioned rubber tires made the bike a bit conspicuous on city streets, but there were a lot of off-roaders in Utah. And her helmet would make her anonymous, even to the thousands of security cameras that made up the grid.

Of course, the numbered plate hanging from the back of the seat would erase that anonymity in an instant, but Kelsa had some ideas about that. Her father had claimed that if he wanted to use it, he had an excellent criminal mind, and that Kelsa had inherited that, along with the hair.

A roll of white adhesive tape and a few snips of the scissors transformed a three into an eight. A few more snips, and a tiny triangle of dark electrician's tape turned a *D* into a reasonably good *B*.

The best computer in the world wouldn't trace the license number BAF-482 back to Kelsa's bike. Assuming the police had any reason to try to track her down, which Raven had promised they wouldn't.

Raven, whom the Native Americans had named Trickster. If he was who he said he was, which she still couldn't believe. Even if she had seen him change from a fish into a man.

She grabbed her father's helmet for Raven, wheeled the bike out to the street, straddled it, and punched in the start code.

Raven met her at the corner of the next block, as they'd agreed. He looked at the bike with more interest than he'd ever looked at her.

"Why does this have wheels still, when other vehicles fly?"

"They don't fly." The hum of the electric engine was softer than their lowered voices, nothing to draw attention. "They levitate on a magnetic current between their generator plate and the road. So if you want to go where there's no pavement, you've got to have tires."

She handed him her father's helmet, trying not to imagine what her father would have said about this. She'd have been grounded into the next century! She still would be if her mother caught her.

Raven fumbled a bit with the helmet straps, but he flung his leg over the bike and settled himself behind her as if he knew what he was doing.

"The museum is affiliated with that big university in Provo," he said. "Do you know where it is?"

"Of course. My father worked there."

Kelsa took off down the quiet street, her heart hammering as if she was already committing a crime. But even if one of the street cams happened to be on—or more likely, someone who knew her mother was looking out the window—all she'd done so far was set off on a bike ride. With a strange boy. A *really* strange boy! That would get her grounded for only a year or two.

And at least her mother would never call her "perfectly reliable" again.

Kelsa ran the bike's speed up a bit in celebration, though not enough to trip a traffic sensor into report mode.

o o o

They reached the campus in about twenty minutes; traffic was light this late on a Sunday.

Kelsa even remembered where the museum was, though having little interest in the history of the Southwest, she'd never gone there. It was in the oldest part of the campus, housed in several well-remodeled buildings that had been built as private homes a few centuries ago.

"Take your bike into the alley between those houses."

She was driving so slowly that Raven hardly had to raise his voice to be heard through the helmets. "There are no cameras back there."

The alley was only four feet wide, and very dark. When Kelsa turned into it, the bike's headlight illuminated several trash cans, and trash cans usually meant . . .

The door was just in front of the cans. Kelsa pulled the bike past them and made sure it couldn't be seen from the street before shutting it off.

In the absence of the headlight the alley became very dark. She removed her helmet, then took a few seconds to bring up her night vision, running her fingers through her flattened hair.

"I'll let you in." Raven dismounted and handed her his helmet. "It will only take a few minutes."

"What about the alarm?" Kelsa murmured. "And the security cameras?"

"It won't be a problem."

Even with her night vision engaged, she couldn't make out the details of the transformation. Perhaps it was too horrifying for her to want to watch closely. But only moments later a huge black bird struggled out of a pile of cloth and flapped upward.

Kelsa shook her head. Either she was completely deranged, or the world was even more full of wonder than her father had taught her. And if she wasn't crazy . . .

If the Native American spirits were real, what about other mythical creatures? Was she about to encounter dragons and vampires? And werewolves, oh my?

She reached down and picked up the discarded clothing. The fabric felt real, with the rough softness of cotton and denim, the heat of his body still lingering in the folds.

If she wasn't crazy, did the power to stop the tree plague really rest in her hands?

Kelsa's heart was pounding. When the door opened, she jumped and barely suppressed a yelp.

"That was fast!" She handed Raven his clothes and stepped inside, averting her gaze from his nakedness. "How did you get in so quickly? In fact, how did you get in without tripping the alarm?"

"The same way I did the other night, when I first located the medicine bag." His voice held none of the fear that tightened her throat. "Someone who works in one of the upstairs offices likes fresh air. They leave the window open about three inches."

"Even at night?" It was embarrassing listening to him dress. They were standing in a narrow hall, which led to what had once been a kitchen and now looked like some sort of workroom. A security camera hung from one corner of the ceiling, but its power light was dark. He must have handled it, just like he'd promised.

"The window's fastened so it can't rise any higher," he told her. "And it's not in a place a human could reach without a ladder. But I had to tear the screen again, and that may raise questions, so I'd like to finish here tonight. This way."

Alarms on the screen were unlikely. Kelsa followed him down the hall, through the workroom, and into a room filled with cabinets of pottery and informative signs. It should have felt reassuringly mundane, but . . .

"This is creepy," Kelsa whispered. "Everything's so old."

"Not all of it." Raven drifted over to a display of shiny black pottery. Kelsa had once been told the name, but she'd forgotten it. "Much of this is modern. Beautiful, though."

Maybe he had reason to be a history geek, but still . . .

"Shouldn't we get this over with?"

"You're right, of course." He turned away from the pottery and led her through another room, where the walls were covered with maps and flat panels that contained clothing, jewelry, and small artifacts. Nothing looked like you could black-market it for millions, so maybe this museum didn't have high-tech security. Kelsa relaxed a trifle.

In the next room a case of kachinas caught her eye—one in particular.

"Was that you?" She gestured to a small statue of a dancer, masked in black, with black feathers dripping from his arms.

Raven barely spared it a glance. "That's Crow Mother. She's not a bad woman, but she hasn't yet made up her mind."

Hasn't *yet?* Kelsa's sense of reality fractured once more. "Hasn't made up her mind about—"

Every com board in the building chirped at the same moment. Kelsa almost jumped out of her skin. "What the—"

An eerie glow shone through the doorway to another room as a com board on the desk activated.

"Museum of the Southwest." The woman's voice was crisply professional. "This is Tri-metro Securicorp, and we have an alarm activated in your building. Please give us your security code and password."

"I thought you took care of the alarm!" Kelsa whispered furiously.

"I did." Raven sounded concerned, but not nearly as panicked as he should have. "The big red bell by the front door hasn't—"

"The silent alarm, you—"

"Please, get on a board and give me your security code and password." Professionalism was giving way to impatience. "If you'd repaired your security cams, as we requested two days ago, I wouldn't need confirmation. But this is the third time in four months you've forgotten to notify us when someone was working late, and I must remind you that according to your contract one more false alarm will result in a raise in your rates. So if you're still there, you'd better get on and verify immediately, or I'll be forced to call campus security. Which, as you know, means an automatic fine."

It had happened three times in four months? Kelsa took a deep breath to steady her nerves.

"Don't do that!" she called. "I have Professor Hammond's permission to be here, and everything."

"Who is this, please? I don't have a Professor Hammond on my staff list."

"Well, he let me in," Kelsa said. "He said it would be OK. He had a key card."

"It must have malfunctioned," the woman said. "But I still have to verify that he has access. Tell him to get to a com board, please, and give me his security code and password."

"He's gone now." Kelsa took Raven's arm, pulling him back toward the door, but he didn't budge. "The professor just let me in to work on the signs. Extra credit."

She pulled harder, scowling. Raven shook off her grip.

"It's this way." He strode quietly through the doorway at the far end of the room. Kelsa glared after him.

"Well, someone has to give me a security code in the next two minutes, or I'll have to call campus security," the woman said. "It's procedure. Would you come to the com, please? If you have a student ID, at least I could identify you."

"I can't," said Kelsa desperately. "I'm, uh, I'm holding some glued stuff. If you'd just call Professor Hammond . . ."

"I'm calling campus security. Now."

The light from the com board winked out.

Kelsa raced through the doorway where Raven had gone. "She's calling security! Where are you?"

"Down here."

She followed his voice into another narrow hall, and down a set of steep, winding stairs. The basement was clearly used for storage, and Raven was standing beside a pile of boxes.

"It's in this one." He pointed to the second-lowest box in the stack.

"I don't care about your stupid medicine bag," Kelsa snarled. "She's calling campus security! They'll be here in minutes!"

"Then we have only minutes," said Raven. "So you'd better get started."

"I'm leaving," said Kelsa.

"I'm not." There was no yielding in his face or voice. "Not until we've got what we came for. And if I get caught, I'll name you as my accomplice."

"You wouldn't. I can't turn into a crow and fly out the prison window, like you can."

"Then you'd better . . ." He sighed, his shoulders suddenly slumping. "No, I wouldn't. But we can get it now if you'd just get a move on. I won't let you get arrested. I promise. Please!"

Kelsa took one step toward him, then rushed across the basement and dragged the first box off the stack.

"You said you'd taken care of the alarm too," she grumbled.

"And the alarm didn't ring," Raven said. "I still don't know how that woman knew we were here."

He took the second box off the pile and put it on the floor. "It's in this one. In a tin box, in the front right corner near the bottom."

When Kelsa raised the lid, the box was filled with other boxes and objects, probably priceless irreplaceable artifacts, swathed in ordinary bubble wrap. She plunged her hands through them with ruthless haste.

"Why couldn't you do this? You could have had it out by the time I got down the stairs!"

"I told you, humans caused the problem, humans have to fix it."

"But this isn't magic! It's just moving a couple of—"

Her groping fingers touched a metal corner.

She had to lift out half a dozen anonymous bundles to extract it, and when she did the tin box rattled. It held several bits of worked flint, an old pipe, a sheaf of faded photos of people wearing the long hair and loose jeans of the mid-1900s, and a soft leather pouch about the size of a flattened golf ball. It was tied shut, the rest of the cord forming a loop designed to be worn around the neck. The few beads still stitched to its surface were about to fall off. This was clearly far older than the photos. Kelsa was afraid to touch it.

"Come on!" Raven was looking at the ceiling, as if he could see what was happening above them. "I did some work on the leather when I was here before. It won't fall apart on you."

Kelsa picked up the bag and squeezed it gently. It squished under her fingers, but the leather felt fairly sturdy. Still . . .

"It's too old. It's probably valuable. We shouldn't handle—"

The sound of a door opening in the building above wasn't loud, but it froze her in her tracks.

"Tarnation," Raven muttered. "Nothing else for it."

"What are we going to do?" Kelsa whispered. Visions of handcuffs and barred windows flashed through her head, even though in modern prisons the windows were covered with steel-threaded tempra glass.

"Don't look so panicked." Raven was repacking the box. "We'll have some time before they get down here."

Footsteps crossed the floor above them. The old boards creaked.

"Can you shapeshift me into a raven too?" Kelsa asked, though remembering how horrible that had looked, she'd almost rather go to jail. "Can you—"

"No," said Raven. "And a huge bird flapping around in here would make them a lot more suspicious than a false alarm with nothing out of place. Help me get these boxes back together."

Kelsa flung the cord over her head and helped him replace the artifacts. Then they restacked the crates.

"Now what?" she demanded.

"Now we hide."

Raven went over to an old closet and opened the door. Despite the long rolls of plasti-board, and more stacked boxes and bins, there was room for a couple of people inside. He bowed and gestured for her to enter.

"They'll look there," Kelsa said.

"Not if it's locked and they don't have the key."

There was an old-fashioned keyhole under the doorknob.

"You don't have the key either! Even if you did, you couldn't lock it from inside."

Raven scowled. "Do you always argue like—"

He stopped, listening. Footsteps started down the stairs.

Kelsa shot across the room and into the closet, even though it was stupid, even though it would delay their discovery by only a few more minutes.

Raven stepped in after her and closed the door. Even enhanced night vision needed a bit of light to work with. She couldn't see what he was doing, but he bumped into Kelsa several times as he knelt in front of the door.

She didn't dare speak, even in a whisper, so Kelsa laid a hand on his shoulder. The muscles under the cloth of his shirt were tense, which meant he wasn't as unconcerned as he pretended. Which didn't exactly reassure—

A soft click came from the lock, and the tension in his shoulders eased.

How did he do that? Even if he'd had the key, closets weren't designed to be locked from the inside. Was she going to have to cope with even more magic than shapeshifting? The sound of voices came through the door, and Kelsa stopped caring about magic.

"Nothing down here either." The woman sounded irritated. "I told you. Just some grad student coming in without the code. I bet she freaked when the desk paged in."

"Then how did she get out?" a man's voice demanded.

"Out the back door," the woman said. "She probably left it wide open. These kids don't give a carp about the trouble they cause for other people. All they care about is picking up their study notes, or their com pod, or whatever they left behind."

"But Nadine's board shows the door closing after the alarm went off," the man protested. "It's logged as closed when she talked to the intruder at—"

The door rattled as someone tried the handle. Kelsa's heart tried to batter its way out of her rib cage.

"Eleven fifty-two. It hasn't opened again."

"So maybe the sensor on the door is glitched," the woman said. "It wouldn't be the first time. I don't care what Nadine's board says. We've been through the whole place. There's no one here."

"I suppose." The man's voice was growing fainter. "But it's weird."

The voices receded into silence.

"You might as well sit down," Raven said softly. "We should give them time to get away from the building before we leave."

Kelsa was glad to sit down. Her knees were shaking. "Suppose they find my bike in the alley?"

Raven shrugged. "Then someone must have left a bike there. There's nothing to say it's yours."

There would be if they peeled the tape off her license plate. But someone who didn't know about silent alarms probably wouldn't know about license plates either, and Kelsa had tucked it out of sight behind the cans. They might well miss it.

"How did you lock that door?" she asked.

His laugh was warm and deep in the darkness.

"You'd call it magic. But it didn't take much. The lock is designed to open, so it wants to."

"But if you can do that, why didn't you get the pouch out yourself, the first time you broke in here? And don't give me that carp about magical rules, and a human having to do it. What's the real reason?"

"The rules are the real reason." There wasn't enough light coming under the door for her to see his face, but he sounded serious. "I'm bound to them, or it all fails. Why do people these days swear by a fish?"

"By a fish? Oh, carp."

"A carp is a fish."

"Not really. It's a euphemism. About sixty years ago, the people who didn't want anyone swearing on vid, or anywhere, really, got a law passed that you couldn't use bad language on the net either." Kelsa squirmed away from a box corner that was poking into one shoulder blade. "They got the software companies to put in a program that whenever someone typed in profanity, it changed a few letters. Which was stupid, because it still means the same thing."

"It is stupid," said Raven. "But it's not new. They used to say 'tarnation,' but 'damnation' was what they meant."

He'd said "tarnation," she remembered. And Jehoshaphat. Was he really that old?

"It didn't work either," Kelsa told him. "Because people started using *carp* or *carpo,* and *frack* to swear. So then the people who believe in dirty words decided those were dirty words too and tried to ban them. But by that time there was a new government in office, and they haven't been able to get the software companies to change their program again. They're still trying."

"You're a stubborn folk." Raven's voice was full of amusement. "That will be to your advantage, on the way to Alaska."

"I'm not going to Alaska," Kelsa said. "I told you I'd help you rob the museum, but that's it."

"But you owe me. Because I kept you from getting arrested, just as I promised. The least you can do now is finish the job."

"I owe . . . You're the one who got me into this!"

"Deeper than you know." Raven reached out and lifted the pouch, then let it thump down on her chest. "You're bound into the healing magic now. I mixed some of your father's ashes into the dust."

"You what?"

"I'm sorry if you're upset." He didn't sound sorry. "Atahalne would be appalled. The Dineh won't have anything to do with dead bodies. They—"

Kelsa didn't care about the Dineh, whoever they were. "You mean my father . . . his ashes are here?"

"And that matters to you," Raven said calmly.

"You bet it does!"

"Which is why those ashes bind *you* into Atahalne's magic. Which will make it possible for you to use it."

"You're crazy."

But if he wasn't . . .

She'd seen him lock a door without a key. She'd seen him shapeshift too, but somehow the small click of that lock had convinced her of his reality, of his magic, in a way that seeing him change hadn't. Perhaps because the lock was something real, something from her world. She didn't owe him anything. That was outrageous. But he had kept them from getting arrested. Maybe . . .

"Where is the first nexus?" Kelsa asked cautiously.

"It's in TuTimbaba," he said. "The lava fields north of here. Craters of the Moon, they're called now. There are lava tunnels there, perfect for an earth nexus."

Craters of the Moon was in Idaho. "If all you need is a cave, how about Timpanogos. It's only about an hour's ride. We could do it tonight if you could find some way to get us in."

Raven shook his head. "It has to be in the lava tunnels at TuTimbaba. It's not that far. Little more than a day on that bike of yours."

Craters of the Moon National Monument was just over the state border, but it would be a full day's ride and a full day back. And she'd need to find an excuse to get away from her mother, and . . .

"One nexus," said Kelsa, making up her mind as she spoke. "After that, you'll have to find someone else."

CHAPTER 4

She wasn't going all the way to Alaska. Kelsa made that clear to Raven again when they parted that night—after *she* had found a narrow bathroom window that wasn't linked to the alarm system and bruised every inch of her body squirming through it.

"Remember, I'm only going to do that first nexus." She'd pulled over at a corner near her house to drop him off. Where was he staying? A hotel? A nest in a tree?

"Why say that so firmly?" Raven swung off the bike and removed his helmet. The half-flattened, half-spiked hair would have looked ridiculous on anyone else. "You don't even know where the second nexus is. Once you've done the first, you might want—"

"I don't make many promises," Kelsa told him. "Because if I promise, if I start something, I'll finish it. So I'm careful about commitments."

He raised his brows at the grim certainty in her voice. "It's your decision. I can't make you do anything. If nothing else, it would be against the rules."

"What are these rules of yours, anyway?" Kelsa asked. "You said they were magical? Like laws of magic?"

"No, I didn't," Raven said. "I said they were 'or something.'"

"So what are they?"

"I'd like to tell you, but it's against—"

"The rules," Kelsa interposed dryly. "Why am I not surprised."

She was beginning to suspect he was making up those rules as he went along, and his smug smile was really starting to get on her nerves. But she wouldn't be dealing with him for much longer, so it hardly mattered. Because Kelsa finally knew what she wanted to do next.

o   o   o

She set the alarm to wake her half an hour early, and in the morning she went down to talk with her mother while she fixed breakfast. They both agreed that it would be good for Kelsa to go away for a while.

"Start your vacation with a vacation!" The forced perkiness in her mother's voice put Kelsa's teeth on edge.

A board call to Aunt Sarabeth's apartment caught her aunt dressed in a sleek suit on her way to work. She looked a bit startled, but hesitated only a second before saying that of course she'd be delighted to have Kelsa stay with her for several weeks. For the whole summer if she wanted to.

Kelsa gave her full points—the dismay hardly showed at all.

They settled on Kelsa's departure date, June fourth, just four days from now. She still had two days of school spirit activities to get through, but that proved less boring than she'd expected because she could slip away from the basketball game, or the vid club's presentation of "2093–94 in West Springville High," and find a vacant deskcomp to do some research.

There were plenty of myths about Raven, stretching from Northern California through most of Canada and into Alaska. Had this ley he was so concerned about been his? Or in his territory?

But the Native American myths were clearly myths, not history. Kelsa might have been forced to wrap her mind around shapeshifting—although if matter couldn't be created or destroyed, then how did something the size of a teenage boy shrink into something the size of a very large bird? And how did it become not denser, but light enough to fly?

But even if Kelsa accepted some form of magic, there was no way Raven could have found the sun—which had been hidden by gods, giants, or evil chiefs—and swallowed it to return it to the sky.

That part was clearly myth. But some of the rest . . . If the stories were even half true, then Raven lied a lot. But so did the rest of the spirits. What was it he'd said about Crow Mother? *She hasn't* yet *made up her mind . . .*

Kelsa shivered. At least Raven had helped the humans he encountered, most of the time. And that couldn't be said of some of the other spirits.

In truth, the Native American spirits reminded Kelsa of the ancient Greek gods—quarrelsome, selfish, greedy, and jealous. Way too "human" for comfort, if you were forced to admit they might not only exist but really have some kind of supernatural power.

She also tried to research leys and promptly found herself deep in the nut-net. If Raven wanted her to sacrifice a rabbit and examine its entrails, he was going to get a very rude refusal.

But she did find some sort of reference to magical currents flowing through the world in almost every human culture. So maybe those leys of his really did exist.

Her foray into the nut-net destroyed any impulse she might have had to talk about this to Carmina or Andi or any of her old friends. If she started sounding like the people whose sites she'd seen . . . well, she wouldn't have any sane friends, that was certain.

Wasn't isolating their victims from others one of the techniques abusers used to control them?

She wasn't a victim, Kelsa told herself firmly. She was going to run up to Idaho, do what Raven wanted with the first nexus, then take two weeks to camp in the wilderness her father had loved.

She hadn't realized how exhausted, how drained she'd become until the possibility of two weeks' camping on her own had occurred to her. Now that it had, she craved the healing peace of the open places like a drought-stricken plain craved water. Peace to mend her tattered heart. Peace to say goodbye.

After she got home, Kelsa waited till her mother had gone to bed, then she went on the airline's site and canceled her ticket. Transferring the money into her own debit account took a bit of work, but her account was a subset of the family's master account. She had all her mother's account numbers and knew the answers to all her security questions, even the name of her first pet.

Her father's com pod was still in the box of his possessions the hospice had packed for them. Neither Kelsa or her mother had wanted to deal with it, but she needed a pod—and explaining how hers had ended up at the bottom of the river was *way* too complicated.

Her father's pod was a bit big, and the matte black finish too masculine. It took only a few moments' work on the house com board to make sure all calls sent to her pod would now come to this one, though changing her father's ID to her own made her heart ache. After a moment's hesitation, Kelsa clipped her father's pod onto the cord that held the medicine pouch, which Raven had insisted she wear. Two talismans, one of which she might even be able to keep.

Next morning she made a board call to Aunt Sarabeth's office from school. Kelsa managed to catch her aunt between meetings on the second try, but Sarabeth was clearly in work mode and a bit distracted—just as Kelsa had hoped.

She managed to sound genuinely disappointed when Kelsa said she'd changed her mind, that it was too soon for her to leave her mother and Joby now.

The genuine sympathy in her face when Kelsa said that her mother wasn't up to dealing with her late husband's family right now made Kelsa feel guilty—but not guilty enough for her not to cancel the trip to visit her aunt.

She had two days to pretend to pack everything she'd need for a trip to Chicago, while really packing for solo camping in the wilderness.

If her mother hadn't been avoiding her it would have been a lot harder, so Kelsa did nothing to ease the stiff formality between them.

She still couldn't talk her mother out of driving her to the airport.

"I can get on a plane by myself." She got out of the levcar and dragged her bag off the back seat.

"All right." Her mother got out and came around to the curb.

She looked like she wanted to hug her daughter, but didn't quite know how.

Kelsa's throat tightened. "I'll be fine."

She picked up her bag, holding it between them, and her mother's arms fell back to her sides. "All right. Take care. And say hi to Sarabeth for me."

Her mother and her father's sister had never been close.

"I'll be fine." Kelsa turned to go.

"Kel . . . All you can do is the best you can do. You can't do more. No one can."

Was that an offer of forgiveness? Or a plea for it? Either way, Kelsa couldn't deal with it now. "I'll call you when I get in."

She went into the terminal, and her mother got into the car and drove away.

She ate lunch in the airport and spent an hour trying to read some of the zine flimsies scattered around the waiting area. Then she put her bag into a locker, paid for a month, and boarded a shuttle bus headed home.

Her timing was perfect. As the bus pulled up to her stop she saw her mother in her car, taking Joby to his play date with the son of one of her closest friends. Her mother didn't even glance at the bus as she drove by.

Kelsa entered the house and went up to her room to fetch her pack. The empty silence was soothing, and she'd be home again in a few weeks.

She went into the garage and pulled her bike out from under the storage shelves where she'd parked it. Then she maneuvered her father's bike, which had been parked behind hers, forward so her bike's absence wouldn't be obvious unless someone looked closely.

Her mother paid no attention to the bikes, anyway. It was her father who'd taken Kelsa up the wilderness trails to camp as soon as she was old enough. Her father who'd taught her to drive his bike before it was strictly legal, helped her get her probationary permit, helped her buy her own bike—used, but still serviceable—the day she turned fifteen.

"I'll take Joby," she promised him aloud. "As soon as he's old enough to enjoy it. We won't forget. Either of—"

"Who are you talking to?" Raven's voice made her jump.

"How did you get in?"

"The door was open." He looked around the garage curiously.

"No, it wasn't."

"It wasn't locked. Are you ready to leave?"

"Yes." Kelsa unplugged the charge cord, and it coiled back into its socket. "Are you riding with me? I thought you'd . . . I don't know. Fly?"

"Flying for a long distance at the speed your bike travels would be very tiring. And if I travel with you, there's less chance we'll be separated."

And less chance she'd change her mind?

"I don't mind your coming along," she said. "But my tent's not big enough for two."

It had been big enough, barely, for her and her father. It wasn't big enough for her and a strange boy. A too-good-looking boy, who according to the old myths had no scruples about seducing human women.

"That won't be a problem." Raven's face was grave, but a cocky smirk lurked in his eyes.

Kelsa handed him his helmet. "Then let's ride."

。 。 。

Just passing through the greater Salt Lake metro area, which extended from south of Springville to Ogden, took the rest of the afternoon.

It was dinnertime, and the bike's charge was running low, when she pulled into a flash charge center.

"This will take about twenty minutes," she told Raven, running her account card over the scanner, then pulling out the retractable plug. "We'll have plenty of time to go to the bathroom and see what kind of flash food they've got for dinner."

She nodded toward the service center—she could see signs for only McPlanet and Go-food. Her favorite flash food was Green Machine, but she didn't spot their swirling logo on the building's ad run.

"It doesn't seem to take other vehicles that long." Raven gestured to a levcar that was now pulling out.

"They have a different kind of battery," Kelsa told him. "It's faster, but if they run out of juice they can't fill it with a solar charger, like I can."

The ability to take a solar charge was optional in off-road vehicles, especially the older ones, and her father had insisted on it.

"A solar charge," said Raven slowly. "If you can run it on sunlight, why pay here?"

Kelsa, who'd been about to explain what a solar charge was, took a second to change gears. He might be ignorant about some aspects of modern technology, like silent alarms, but he wasn't stupid.

"It takes about eight hours, on a very sunny day, to get a quarter charge," she told him. "If it's cloudy, forget it. A solar charger is for emergencies, if you get stranded. Or you can use it to keep your charge topped up if you're spending the day in camp. But when you're traveling long distances it's not practical."

The big trucks' stabilizing jets buffeted them as they went into the service center. Raven, Kelsa was interested to note, headed straight for the bathroom. So he did have some human weaknesses.

She needed to go too, but she could wait for a few more minutes. She didn't want him interrupting this.

She chose her backdrop carefully. A rack of zine flimsies and small bags of candy and nuts. Enough like an airport that no one would be suspicious.

She'd hoped her mother wouldn't be home, that she could leave a message, but her mother's face appeared in the pod's small screen seconds after the first chime.

"Kelsa! Are you in Chicago?"

"Landed safe and sound," Kelsa confirmed. "Aunt Sarabeth wanted to hit the bathroom before we leave for her place, but she said to say hi, and I thought I might as well check in now."

"That's great. Are you—" The oven buzzed, and her mother's head turned toward it.

"I'll let you go," Kelsa said swiftly. "I'll see you in a couple of weeks, anyway. Bye!"

She cut the connection and headed for the ladies' room. In a few hours she'd have to change her com pod's ID to match her aunt's, and text her mom a message that Kelsa had arrived and that Sarabeth had lots of plans to keep her busy. Her aunt often communicated by text, so it wouldn't arouse suspicion.

Then, after she'd taken care of Raven's first nexus, whatever that entailed, Kelsa would have the better part of two weeks all to herself. The ache in her soul eased a bit at the thought.

∘ ∘ ∘

The sun was setting as they approached Honeyville, and Kelsa stopped at a commercial campground. She winced at the fee—fifty dollars for one night.

Between her own meager balance and the refunded round-trip ticket, she had more than six hundred dollars in her account, but after the charge, dinner, and tonight's camping, she'd spent over eighty dollars in her first day on the road. Of course, camping in the national monument would be cheaper, and this campground included a slow charge port as part of the site services, so she'd save a bit there.

She resolved to ask Raven if he had any money, but by the time she got out of the office he had vanished.

Kelsa snorted. He wouldn't get out of it that easily.

∘ ∘ ∘

"Do you have any money?" Kelsa demanded when he sauntered up to her camp next morning. Her tent had just deflated, and she smoothed the rest of the air out of its ribs as she folded it into a compact bundle to stow on the bike.

"I can get some if you need it," he said. "But it won't last long. Why?"

Get some? It wouldn't *last long*? And how had he been getting food and clothing without it?

"Not yet." Kelsa would be rid of him in a few more days. She didn't need to know. Especially if knowing made her an accessory after the fact. "We'll reach the Idaho border before lunchtime. Earlier if we don't waste any more time getting on the road. You've got your PID card ready to show at the border, right?"

The curious expression that was becoming all too familiar swept over his face. "Pee-idy card?"

"Personal identification card," Kelsa told him grimly. She should have known. "They'll check it at the border and at any hotel we stay at. If the police stop us—and they'd better not!—they'll also check our DNA against the card strip and our record to be certain the cards are really ours."

Raven's mystified expression deepened. "What does all of that mean?"

"It means you're flying across the border," Kelsa told him. "I'll stop and let you off several miles before we get there."

∘ ∘ ∘

She had to pull off on a back road that led into the low hills to find privacy for him to change without being seen—by her, as well as the traffic.

He made his way into the low scrubby pines till he couldn't be seen.

"Where can we meet?" Kelsa asked.

"I'll find you." His helmet came flying over the brush. "I've got a clear enough feel for Atahalne's magic by now. I could probably sense it anywhere within fifty miles. More if I concentrate." The bushes rustled and his jeans and shirt followed the helmet.

"Is that how you found the pouch in the museum?" Kelsa asked. "By sensing its magic?"

"Sort of." Shoes, with socks and briefs rolled neatly inside, sailed out of the bushes. "Before I knew what I was looking for it was a lot harder."

Then he stopped talking.

As Kelsa packed his clothes hastily in the bike's saddlebags, she heard the rush of flapping wings and looked up in time to see him flapping off to the north. This was too weird!

She was glad to be alone on the bike as she got back onto the highway and weaved through the low hills that took her up to the border station. There was too much wind to talk while the bike was moving, so he hadn't bothered her much, but it wasn't the same as being alone.

On the other hand, it would have been nice to have a chance to ask some questions.

She'd been through this station once or twice, and through the stations between Utah and Colorado and between Utah and Arizona or Nevada more times than she could count.

She waited patiently in the vehicle line while the levcars ahead of her paid the crossing tax and drove slowly through the scanners. The only thing she carried that was at all suspicious was a single set of boy's clothes, which weren't all that different from hers and wouldn't show up on a scanner anyway.

The line for trucks, which were not only scanned but visually inspected, was a lot longer. The shortest line was for walkovers—people who crossed without a vehicle to avoid the tax.

When her turn finally came, Kelsa handed the guard her PID and waited while he scanned it, making a record of the fact that Kelsa Phillips crossed into Idaho at that date and time—if anyone cared. At least the charge for taking a bike across was minimal. He also checked her probationary license to be certain she was old enough to drive legally. Soon after that she was on her way through the green agricultural valley between two mountain ridges, which ultimately emptied into the drier upland plains of southern Idaho.

She'd gone only a few miles when a huge black bird swooped across the road in front of her.

Kelsa turned off at the next side road, and kept going till a low hill concealed her from the highway's teeming traffic.

There were no trees nearby.

Raven flapped down and perched on the bike's handlebars. His beady black gaze was too intelligent for a bird. He was almost two feet long from tail tip to beak, and his talons looked sharp and formidable.

"This is too weird," Kelsa told him.

He let out a squawk, which could have meant anything, and hopped down to the ground.

Kelsa unpacked his clothes, peeking surreptitiously as the black form began to grow in ungainly bulges and spurts. The feathers flattened, melting into oily-looking skin that slowly faded from black to warm tan. The strong beak receded into a lipless gaping mouth before the lips ballooned and a human nose sprouted above them.

By the time the transformation was complete goose flesh had broken out all over Kelsa's body. "I've got to stop watching that. Doesn't it *hurt*?"

"Not much. It's not pleasant though, and it takes a lot of energy." He picked up his clothing and began to put it on.

Distracted from trying not to notice his body, Kelsa saw that the golden skin was paler than usual, and there was a hint of strain around his eyes.

"I'm sorry," she said. "I'll try to avoid making you do that in the future. But unless you can get a PID, which you can't—"

"Don't worry about it." The charming smile flashed. "You do your part. I'll take care of everything else."

"Sure you will. How does this magic of yours work, anyway?"

"It's different from yours," Raven told her. "Do you have anything to eat in that pack?"

"I don't have any magic at all. Different how?"

"I'm not sure I could explain it," Raven said. "It's like . . . like a cat trying to tell you how to purr. You don't have the ability to do it, so—"

"That doesn't mean I couldn't understand what it . . . Wait a minute. Have you *been* a cat?"

"I can be," he said. "But one thing I can tell you about magic is that it uses energy. So I really hope you packed something to eat, because I'm starving!"

          ∘ ∘ ∘

They ate breakfast there, breaking into Kelsa's packed supply of apples, crackers, and peanut butter, then returned to the main road. They reached Pocatello too early for lunch, but stopped and ate anyway, and on Raven's advice picked up some sandwiches and energy bars for dinner.

Kelsa saw his point when they turned off the highway onto the state road. She'd been on many roads like it, and food and charge ports were few and far between.

"This used to be near the Shoshone-Bannock Reservation, didn't it?" Raven half shouted over the wind of their passage.

Since there wasn't anyone behind her, Kelsa slowed the bike to answer him. "I don't know. The reservations were disbanded about twenty years ago."

"They were?"

He sounded startled. It had probably been a big deal, back when he was learning words like *tarnation*.

"The government said it was time for Native Americans to become first-class citizens," she told him. "The Native Americans called it the final land grab, and are still furious about it, even though the government did pay them for the land. My father said it was because the casinos were making so much money, the government wanted to tax them."

Raven asked no more questions, so after a moment she kicked the bike back up to speed.

Away from the bustle of the highway, the silence of the empty places began to seep into her soul, soothing the raw anguish that had been with her, she realized, ever since the doctor had pronounced her father's illness incurable. It wrapped her in a fragile bubble of peace that wasn't disturbed even when the huge motor homes lurched past, though the wash from their jets made the bike swerve, and Raven's arms tightened around her waist.

They were nearing the monument, the long dark snakes of lava ridges disrupting the flatness of the plains, when an old-fashioned painted sign with a boxy building a few blocks behind it caught her attention.

"ERB-1?" Kelsa let the bike slow to a crawl so she wouldn't whisk past the sign before she could read the smaller print. "What's ERB . . . Oh."

ERB-1 had been the first nuclear power plant built in North America. The arms around her waist fell away, but Kelsa could feel the angry stiffness in Raven's body.

"You people really are lousy stewards." His voice was calm and very cold. "Only a handful of miles from a major nexus too."

"They're all shut down now," Kelsa said defensively. "Even in Europe, finally."

It was a hard thing to defend. Her father had described nuclear waste as "an ecological catastrophe in the making that would make global warming look like a child's prank."

"The ice sheets are beginning to refreeze," she added. "They say that in as little as a century the Florida islands might be land again. But you're right. We were lousy . . . Wait. Is this why the first nexus to be healed has to be here? Because of that?" She gestured to the utilitarian building and the chunky machines crouched beside it.

"In part. A large part. It will be late for the nexus ritual by the time we get in. You'll have to camp there tonight."

The angry tension had left his body, and Kelsa decided to take the hint and set her bike in motion.

Soon the winding lava ridges drew closer to the road, and a volcanic cone loomed off to the left. The sun was getting low when she entered the monument, and she decided to pick out a campsite first, but at the campground entrance Kelsa stopped the bike to stare.

"This is surreal."

Everything was black. The flowing stone had crumpled and cracked like drying mud, breaking into ragged heaps and plates and piles. The campsites had been carved out of the bends in the stone's flow, each site a separate alcove with walls of stone that were often higher than Kelsa's head.

Blotches of lichen discolored the dark basalt, but it was also being colonized by the hardy desert scrub and a few gallant pines.

"Does it bother you?" Raven asked. "It makes a lot of people nervous."

"I'm not sure," Kelsa admitted, gazing over the blasted landscape. "But . . . I know it's Saturday, but the parking lot by the ranger station was almost full. Isn't this an awfully public place for a nexus?"

"A lot of them are," Raven told her. "The power of a nexus sometimes manifests itself in natural phenomena. The old shamans considered many of them sacred sites and made sure their beauty was protected."

Kelsa laughed. "That's pretty much what the Park Service does."

About half of the campsites were occupied. Kelsa chose a site, and after unpacking her gear she rode the bike back to the ranger station to pay for the night and to plug her bike into one of the slow charge ports available in the lot behind the building.

The trails tempted her. This ecosystem was unlike anything she'd ever seen. But by the time she got her tent inflated and camp set up, the sun was going down, and she had no desire to risk those rocks in the dark.

The unearthly landscape still looked strange to her, but her subconscious must have known that there was nothing to hurt or threaten her in this sea of twisted stone. She slept peacefully, until the light of the rising sun on the walls of her tent teased her awake.

Raven rejoined her for another breakfast of peanut-butter crackers, then they went back to the ranger station and picked up a trail map.

"This is a nexus of earth." Raven sounded like he was trying not to seem nervous. "You'll have to be completely surrounded by earth for the magic to work. That's what makes these lava tunnels so perfect."

An older woman coming out of the restroom stared at him, and Kelsa took his arm and dragged him out of the building. "Keep your voice down. I can't believe there are this many people here at nine thirty!"

"They aren't kidding about your needing a flashlight either," Raven went on. "It's going to be dark down there."

Leading him around the building to the charging rack, Kelsa checked to make sure there was no one within earshot before asking, "Don't you think it's time you told me what I'm supposed to be doing?"

"It's simple," said Raven. "All you have to do is go into one of the lava caves till you're completely surrounded by earth, then drop a pinch of dust from the medicine bag and say the words that will activate the interaction between its magic and the ley."

Kelsa blinked. "You couldn't have done that?"

"I told you, a human—"

"I know, I know." She unplugged her bike and punched in the start code. "A human has to fix it. That's the rule, right?"

He swung himself onto the bike behind her. "It's more than that. The dust in that pouch is your magic, not ours. I'm not even sure I could activate it."

"Activate." Kelsa swung them out of the parking lot and started back to her camp. "You sound more like a scientist than a . . . what are you, anyway?"

"Raven."

She waited.

"That's the truth, as much as you can understand it. I've never lied to you."

She wondered if he heard the unspoken "yet" as clearly as she did.

By the time she packed up her tent and biked out to the lava field that held the tunnels, there were even more tourists.

"This is crazy." Kelsa stared at the clumps of people wandering around the asphalt paths that covered the ragged dark rock. "A . . . a magical ritual should take place in the wilderness. In private."

It was Sunday morning, but three school buses were parked at the far end of the lot. A church group? Kelsa wondered if she was more afraid of being reported to the park police, or of looking like a total idiot.

"Not many of them will go down into the caves," said Raven. "You'll manage."

"The kids will go in the caves," Kelsa told him. But she set off down the trail, anyway.

The black asphalt blended perfectly with the black basalt, and the informative signs weren't obvious. The wind was chilly, but the sun was bright. If Raven hadn't been so tense about the whole thing, she would have enjoyed it.

Shortly after they left the parking lot, the trail split into two branches.

"Which way?" Kelsa asked. "Indian Tunnel's that way, the other two are down there." She gestured to the longer of the two paths that twisted across the lava field.

"I don't know," said Raven. "Whichever way works best for you."

"All three caves are linked to the nexus?"

"In a sense," said Raven, "every cave near this ley is linked. But it has to be a cave that *you* can use."

"So which way do we go?"

Raven shrugged, which was even more unhelpful than usual. His shoulders were hunched against the cold breeze, though Kelsa had offered to loan him her jacket. His expression was indrawn, and for once, unreadable.

Kelsa, perfectly comfortable in long-sleeved therma knit, looked at the flock of kids scattered along the longer trail and took the path that led to Indian Tunnel.

Most of the tourists they passed were retired couples, but there were a few families with toddlers in tow. Indian Tunnel, when they reached it, was accessed through a rugged break where the rock plate had collapsed into the tunnel beneath. A party of adults was climbing up the combination of rock and concrete steps, with a hand rail to assist them. The steps went down at least twenty feet, and probably more.

Kelsa and Raven waited till the tourists had climbed up before they started down, and at the bottom Kelsa strode eagerly into the cave. It was much larger than she'd expected a lava tunnel to be, and rounder. The crumpled flowstone of the floor was amazingly level for a natural surface, but it was by no means smooth—a sprained ankle begging to happen. Kelsa kept her eyes on the ground when she was walking and stopped to look around.

Ragged holes in the ceiling, almost thirty feet above her head, lit piles of rubble below them. They'd gone several hundred yards down the tunnel when they confronted a rock pile more than twice Kelsa's height that completely filled the lower half of the cave. No one else was in sight.

"How about here?" Kelsa asked. "We're certainly surrounded by earth."

Raven shook his head. "It's too open. There's too much of the world above."

Kelsa looked around. She could hear pigeons cooing in a crack in the basalt where they'd nested. Water dripped. Although the light had dimmed in the middle of the tunnel, she hadn't turned on her flashlight—her night vision had more than compensated for the darkness.

"Onward, then."

Sunlight poured over the collapsed rock, showing the slightly worn places where other people had climbed the barrier. Kelsa chose a path and worked her way up the rock fall without much difficulty.

"I can see the exit from here," she told Raven, who was clambering up behind her. "It gets even more open."

"One of the other caves then."

By the time they scrambled up the final slope and out the exit, Kelsa was feeling the pull in her calf muscles.

"This is fun!"

Raven scowled at her.

"Oh, come on, there's no reason not to enjoy this. I'm on vacation!"

She led him back to the fork in the trail. Hiking out the other branch, they passed several groups of children being herded back toward the buses by harried adults. Only a handful of tourists remained.

"That helps," Raven commented. "A little bit."

"What are you so nervous about?" Kelsa demanded.

"Nothing. I'm certain this will work."

He didn't sound certain. She raised her brows and waited.

"Almost certain," he admitted. "This is more important than you know."

"Well, that makes me feel better." In truth, she didn't much care. She would drop a pinch of dust, say the words he told her to say, and then he could go find another human to finish what's-his-name's quest. Preferably an adult who had the whole summer off and enough money to travel all the way to Alaska.

The much narrower collapse of stone that led down into Boy Scout Cave was blocked with a neat sign, Closed Due to Ice/Snow Hazard.

"Lovely," Kelsa said blankly. The brochure on the back of the trail map said that ice remained in some caves all year long, but this was the beginning of June!

"We'll try the next cave" was all Raven said.

Several hundred yards later the trail ended at the entrance to Beauty Cave. The opening was huge, but unlike the entrance to Indian Tunnel, there were no steps. And when Kelsa made her way to the bottom of the rock fall, there was no light in the tunnel beyond.

"Better?" she asked.

"We'll see."

Kelsa wasn't ten yards into the tunnel when she switched on her flashlight. The cold made her grateful for therma knit. The tunnel was huge, the walls and ceiling beyond the reach of Kelsa's solar-charged light. Without enhanced night vision, she could barely have seen the floor.

She'd been in caves before, and should have expected it. Still . . . "This is dark."

"According to the map, the tunnel curves up ahead." Raven's voice was hushed, as if he didn't want to disrupt the cave's stillness. "If we go around the bend, we shouldn't even be able to see the entrance."

"Wonderful."

Kelsa moved onward, both her light and her attention fixed on the rough floor. The glitter of crystals around its edge warned her about the first ice patch, but she slipped a little anyway.

"To the right," Raven murmured. "The floor rises. There's no ice there."

They picked their way between the frozen puddles for another dozen yards before a long stretch of floor coated with a thin gleaming skin brought Kelsa to a stop.

"I can't see any way around it."

"We haven't passed the bend yet," Raven protested. "We can still see light from the entrance."

Kelsa looked back. The white circle behind them looked plenty far to her.

"This is deep enough."

Raven stirred restlessly, but made no further protest.

Kelsa pulled the medicine bag out from under her shirt. Warm from the heat of her body, it felt as if it belonged to her—which was probably why Raven had insisted she wear it.

She sat the flashlight carefully on the floor and began untying the cord that closed the bag. "All right. What do I say?"

She only hoped she could say it in English instead of Navajo, though if it had to be Navajo he could probably coach her through it.

"You'll have to figure that out," said Raven. "It's your magic."

"What? You said all I had to do was drop a pinch of dust and say the incantation to activate it."

"That's exactly what you have to do." Raven's tone was utterly reasonable, though his teeth were beginning to chatter.

"But I don't know any incantations! This is crazy! You—"

"Don't get upset," Raven snapped, "or you won't be able to focus, and this is important! You were reaching out to the tree spirit when we first met. That's how I knew you could do this. Just reach out to the earth in the same way and tell it, persuade it, to heal!"

He sounded all too serious. Kelsa gazed around in exasperation. Even with her night vision and the flashlight, she couldn't make out more than a small portion of the floor and a bit of the wall beside her. But she could sense the space around her and the rock enclosing it, old and solid. The bones of the earth itself.

She didn't need to see. This wasn't a place of seeing.

Taking care not to spill the pouch, Kelsa sank down to sit on the cave floor. The stone was rough and cold under her butt— not at all comfortable. But that was part of this place too.

She let the cave seep into her senses: silent blackness and the scent of damp stone. It had a different aliveness from that of the trees, from anything in the world above. He'd been right. They hadn't been deep enough before.

She took some time to assemble all the words, but they felt right. Real.

"Bones of the earth, flowing liquid to the surface, crumbling to form the flesh of the world. You are so strong, nothing but time defeats you. Be strong now. Strong enough to forgive." ERB-1 loomed in her mind, in her heart. She'd been calling it dust, but what the pouch really held was sand, gritty between her fingers. Her father's ashes were mixed in with them. "Be strong enough to heal. Be strong!"

She scattered a pinch of sand over the cave floor as she spoke. The moment of stillness that followed was just long enough for her to feel monumentally silly—then all thought was wiped away by a shattering blow that set every bone in her body vibrating like a mallet-struck gong. The vibration went on and on, receding into darkness, pulling her with it.

Kelsa was lying on the tunnel floor when thought returned, lumps of stone pressing into ribs, hip, temple, and one sore knee. Her head ached fiercely.

"Ow! What the hell was that? Did you hit me?"

"No." Raven sat cross-legged beside her, looking far too comfortable on the hard stone. "You had a good connection to the ley, and some of the power lashed back through you. You were right. We were deep enough."

The smug smile was back.

"Frack you." She picked up the light, pulled herself to her feet, and started unsteadily out of the cave. Her headache lessened with each step, which it wouldn't if he'd hit her hard enough to knock her out. She was done with him, anyway.

Kelsa felt almost normal by the time she climbed back to the surface of the lava field, more shaken and angry than hurt. It took her several moments to notice that no one was on the trail anymore. The tourists were milling around the parking lot, waving their arms as they talked.

"What's going on?"

"I told you that nexus power frequently has physical manifestations." Raven was retying the cord around the medicine bag's neck.

She glared at him, then started back to the parking lot.

"Did you feel it! Biggest I ever—"

"Thought it would knock me right off my feet," an elderly woman was saying. "Would have, if I hadn't had my walking stick."

"I wonder if it did any damage."

"I wonder how big it was, on the Richter scale. Must have been at least a two."

Kelsa stared at the chattering crowd. Then she turned and waited for Raven. He was only a moment behind her.

"There was an earthquake? While we were in the cave? Why didn't I feel it?"

"You more than felt it." He took her arm and led her over to a picnic table. "Sit down. You're still pale."

"Did I . . . Did we . . . You're kidding!"

"I doubt it did much damage," Raven said. "Healing magic almost never does."

"But that's crazy!"

"You know, one of the main symptoms of crazy is denying or ignoring what your senses perceive. You can hardly deny you perceived that."

She couldn't deny it. Any more than she could deny she'd seen him shapeshift. Which meant . . .

"I could heal the tree plague? For real?"

"Not heal it," Raven admitted. "That will take a lot of people doing the same thing you're doing all over the planet."

"Is that what the other shapeshifters are doing?" Kelsa asked curiously. She had a lot of questions about shapeshifters, and he'd evaded most of them.

"No," Raven told her. "This is our first attempt. In fact, this is the first proof we've had that humans can heal the leys at all! But if you can strengthen and open this ley, all along its length, when the plague reaches the forests of the Northwest it will stop. And then, maybe, we can start pushing it back. If you succeed, your scientists will probably claim the bacterium couldn't survive outside the tropics. But if this ley isn't healed, strengthened, if the power doesn't flow along it like it does now in the nexus point you just blew open, then that plague *will* move out of the tropics."

"So." He held out the medicine pouch, dangling from the cord around his fingers. "For the final time, Kelsa Phillips, will you take up Atahalne's quest and finish the healing he started?"

She didn't have enough money to travel to Alaska. She didn't have time to get there and back before her mother missed her. She was only fifteen . . .

"Yes." Kelsa took the medicine bag and hung it around her neck once more. It felt right there. "But first, you're going to answer some questions."

CHAPTER 5

IT WASN'T TILL AFTER LUNCH that Kelsa set out for the Saw-tooth Mountains. She was getting tired of peanut butter.

She thought Raven had genuinely tried to explain the exact nature of the leys. The problem was, the leys weren't an exact sort of thing.

"How much do you know about acupuncture?" he'd asked.

She'd blinked in surprise. "Not a lot. There are currents of energy in the human body. They've photographed them, you know. Just eight years ago, on a full-spectrum electromagnetic scanner."

He looked startled. "They can see chi now?"

"If they use the right scanner they can," Kelsa confirmed. "They still don't know why stimulating particular points . . . Oh."

"Exactly," Raven said. "What you're doing with the leys is planetary acupuncture."

That almost made sense, sort of. But when she'd asked him where the next nexus was, the analogy fell apart. Acupuncture points were always in the same place, and the nexuses . . .

"It's sort of like plumbing." Raven gestured with half a peanut-butter cracker. "A clog can occur anywhere in the pipe, and the flow through the pipe is weakened. Clogs might be more likely to occur where the pipe bends or there's a valve or something, but they can happen anywhere. And sometimes running a lot of water through the pipe is enough to ease the constriction, but sometimes, like here, you have to be right on top of the clog and break it apart."

Kelsa had grasped that, mostly, though she didn't like hearing that he couldn't tell her where all the nexuses would be, or even how many there were. His best guess was a vague "certainly fewer than a dozen." Between Craters and the end of the ley. In Alaska.

"I can call Mother and ask if I can stay with Aunt Sarabeth a few more weeks," Kelsa told him. "I think she'll agree. And if I call home on a regular basis, Mom probably won't call my aunt."

In fact, her mother would be as glad to have Kelsa out of the house as Kelsa was to be gone. A small part of her heart ached at that thought, so she pushed it aside.

"But how can I plan our route if I don't know where the nexus points are? And what are we going to do for money?"

This was her third day on the road, and by her rough tally she'd spent over a hundred and fifty dollars.

Raven's gaze shifted aside. "Why don't you leave that to me?"

"Why don't you find some brainless groupie to complete your quest? I want to know where I'm going."

The school counselor had told Kelsa that becoming an "overcontroller" was a natural response to the chaos and disruption caused by a death in the family. She said that as long as Kelsa recognized where her need to control her life and the people around her was coming from, she probably wouldn't become too big a pain in the ass.

Her counselor had some good moments, but Kelsa wasn't about to let someone else take control of her life right now. Especially not someone whose handsome dark eyes weren't meeting hers.

"I can tell you roughly where the next nexus will be," he said. "It's somewhere around Flathead Lake."

Kelsa had never been that far north. "That's in Montana, isn't it?" She unclipped her father's . . . her new com pod and brought up a road map. His screen was bigger than hers had been, but not by much, which was why people used boards for detailed work. "We'll have to go back to I-15," she said. "But after that it's a straight shot—"

"I want you to take a different road," Raven said. "Through the Sawtooth Mountains."

Kelsa squinted at the small map. She could see that route, but . . .

"It would keep us from backtracking, but it would probably take more time than just getting back on the highway."

"I've been in the Sawtooths," Raven told her. "They're beautiful."

Kelsa laid the com pod aside. "What aren't you telling me?"

"Well, mostly, I want you to follow the Salmon River. It starts in the Sawtooths and runs right beside the road most of the way to Flathead Lake. By the time you get to its end you'd have a real affinity for the river, and you could call on water to open the next nexus."

"Call on water? I thought the nexus here was an 'earth nexus.' "

"It was," said Raven. "This time. But the part I wasn't telling you is that I'm going to send you through the mountains on your own. If I fly by the shortest route, I should reach Flathead Lake around the same time you do."

"And that way," Kelsa said slowly, "you wouldn't have to worry about the Idaho-Montana border. You do realize that I have to be granted government permission, which I don't have, to exit the U.S. and enter Canada? And that in Canada, as foreign nationals, they'll be checking our PIDs—which you don't have—all the time?"

"I'll take care of it."

Kelsa had serious doubts about that—and he still wasn't telling her everything. But short of quitting the quest and walking away there wasn't much she could do about it. And she couldn't quit.

She'd seen pictures of the kill zone in the Amazon, not only in her father's journals but in d-vid on the news.

The tall dead trunks were already decaying, because several other bacteria, which had burgeoned naturally in the wake of the first, were eating them away. In the heavy tropical rain it looked like the forest was melting, as if it had been sprayed with acid.

She hadn't been able to stop the cancer that had killed her father. Faith healing wouldn't have worked. Nothing she could do would have saved him, no matter what her mother believed.

If she could do something to stop this corrosive cancer from spreading through the world, she had to try.

o o o

The flatlands before she reached the Sawtooths held grazing cattle, then turned to farmland. One of the farms she passed raised llamas, and the babies danced clumsily around their mothers like knitted puppets.

Kelsa stopped at a flash station and topped up her charge before heading up into the Sawtooths—more expensive than an overnight charge, but a lot less time-consuming than stopping to spread out the solar sheets if she ran out of juice. Solar sheets that wouldn't have done any good today, anyway, since clouds were gathering over the peaks.

The Sawtooths were beautiful: jagged volcanic crags with snowbanks on their highest slopes. It was spitting snow on Galena Pass, and Kelsa turned up the heat control in her biking jacket and pants. Those tempcontrols worked better than those in most of her coats because her father had paid for quality.

"You may not need good tempcontrol outerwear often," he'd said. "But when you need it, you need it."

Of course once she'd gone over the pass the sun came out, and she had to turn it all off and unzip for a while to let the fresh mountain air blow through.

The Salmon River started as a tiny, chuckling creek. Kelsa wouldn't have noticed it if not for the sign on a bridge where the road crossed over. But as the sun sank and the road swerved gently down, more creeks and streams flowed in.

By dusk the Salmon was a rushing cataract, huge by Utah standards, and the road ran right beside it down the valley it had carved.

Kelsa found a fishermen's campground that didn't charge too much for a night's camping, and she pitched her tent there, falling asleep with the roar of the river in her ears.

She was so tired of peanut butter that she splurged on breakfast in a small café near the campground—cheaper, when she wasn't feeding Raven. Whatever he really was, he ate like a teenage boy.

She made up bits of river incantations as she rode down out of the mountains.

Rolling water, carrying life with you. Carver of mountains.

It was still fairly early when Kelsa reached the flatland and joined state road 93. The rocky, wooded slopes of the mountains gave way to volcanic soil, whose colors reminded her of the red-rock deserts of southern Utah, though these crumbling slopes were completely different geologically. It was still before lunchtime when the road emerged from the technicolor buttes, and the broad valley that held the town of Salmon opened up before her.

In town, she discovered she'd come far enough north to catch up with spring. Lilacs and fruit trees that had stopped blooming weeks ago in Provo were in full blossom here.

If she reached Alaska, when she reached Alaska, would she catch up with winter again? The prospect was both enchanting and scary.

Kelsa stopped at a small grocery store and bought a stock of energy bars, protein sticks, and heat-in-can soup—though she knew from experience that she'd get tired of these foods even more quickly than she tired of peanut butter.

The storage space on her bike was limited, but she added a couple of plastic-wrapped sandwiches for future meals and a premade salad for today's lunch. She was beginning to hunger for fresh food, and the lettuce in these grocery-store salads was less dubious than the ones they sold in flash centers.

She got back onto 93 and went north toward the lake, with the Salmon River racing beside the road. Kelsa had ridden for half an hour and passed through the small town of North Fork, when she realized that the river looked much smaller.

Were they pulling out water for the farms? But the Salmon now appeared to be running in the other direction, back toward town.

You can follow the river all the way to Flathead Lake.

Frowning uneasily, Kelsa turned her bike and rode back to North Fork.

It was hard to follow a river through a town, even a river the size of the Salmon in a town that was relatively small. The streets followed their own straight grid, and the river kept swerving away from them.

But soon she found the place where the main branch of the Salmon flowed out of town . . . to the east, followed by a small county road.

Did it curve through the hills and valleys and rejoin the main road later?

Kelsa pulled off the road into a shaded glade, took out her com pod, and pulled up a map. The long straight rift that held the road leading to Flathead Lake certainly looked as if the Salmon flowed along it. There was even a note in very fine print that said the river she'd followed to the north was the Salmon. What was going on here?

She closed the road map and went into the net. It took some wading through the data pools, but she finally came up with a river runner's map of Idaho and Montana. The river that ran along 93 north of town was the North Fork of the Salmon River. After this it continued flowing east, and then south through an area where there were no roads at all, and eventually it emptied into the Snake River near the Oregon border. It never even came close to Flathead Lake.

Raven had lied to her. Lied about the river's course, at the very least. But something had happened at Craters of the Moon. Something that was neither a lie nor a crazed hallucination on her part. According to the news-net, that earthquake had scored a 2.7 on the Richter scale and been felt for hundreds of miles. And when reporters asked geologists why no one had predicted it, the geologists had been very defensive about how reliable their equipment usually was.

He'd said he would meet her at Flathead Lake, so Kelsa decided to go there. And see what he had to say for himself. Then she would decide if—magic or no magic—she wanted to do something as big and crazy as biking to Alaska with a partner who lied.

Back on 93, the Salmon grew smaller and smaller and then disappeared as the road climbed into the high mountains once more.

The Montana-Idaho border station was at the top of Trail Pass, and Kelsa's fantasy of catching up with winter stopped looking so unlikely. Snowdrifts dripped, and meltwater ran down the ditches on either side of the road. The long white streaks of ski slopes decorated nearby peaks.

Kelsa was so angry with Raven that she presented her PID and crossed the border with barely a thought for the record of her travels being created.

It was only 4 p.m. when she saw the campground beside Bitterroot Creek, but the name struck her as appropriate and she was tired. She might have reached Flathead Lake before dark, but why should she put herself out to be on time for someone who lied to her?

The next morning, still seething, she ate a leisurely breakfast of energy bars, and then she packed up and pulled out onto the road. It was midmorning by the time she came over a hill and around a bend, and Flathead Lake burst into view.

Kelsa had grown up only a few miles from the marshy shore of Utah Lake. Camping with her father, biking with him, hiking together—she'd seen dozens, maybe hundreds of mountain lakes. Flathead took her breath away.

She could see only one end of it, for it stretched around a curve in the mountains that ringed it. Bluer than the sky, dotted with tiny tree-furred islands, it was the most beautiful lake she'd ever set eyes on.

She was so busy gawking that she missed the scenic turnout, placed there to allow drivers to pull off and gawk at the lake. She turned the bike and rode back up the hill on the shoulder, parked at the turnoff, and then just sat and stared.

When she'd finally looked her fill, Kelsa started downhill toward the lake. There had to be campgrounds there. In fact there were, but it took her the better part of the morning to find one that was state run, and therefore reasonably cheap.

She was sitting on a picnic table, gazing over the shimmering water and eating a slightly stale sandwich, when she heard Raven walk up behind her.

She didn't turn around.

"You're later than I expected." The cretinous bastard had the gall to sound miffed. "Did something delay you?"

"You might say that," Kelsa told him coldly. "You see, I was following the Salmon River. Like my partner told me to. Until it went in another direction entirely!"

Her voice rose at the end, and Raven winced. He must have gotten his clothing off her bike, for he was decently dressed. He could carry his own clothes now too!

"Sorry about that," he said. "I wanted you off the highway, and I thought following the river from its source sounded romantic."

Kelsa met his gaze and held it. "Why did you want me off the highway? And if you spin me some carpo answer, I'm walking away from this right now."

She could happily spend the next week here and make her way home with no one the wiser. At least until her mother and Aunt Sarabeth compared notes, and with any luck that wouldn't happen for a long time.

She might even tell her mother the truth when she got home—well, part of the truth. She probably shouldn't be too self-righteous about lying. But she wasn't about to admit that to the slippery bastard in front of her. Not when she finally had him on the hook.

He must have read the determination on her face, for his shoulders sagged.

"All right. You deserve the truth. I was trying to put it off until you were really committed, because I was afraid it might . . . ah, discourage you."

"What truth?" Kelsa demanded.

Raven grimaced. "The truth is, not everyone approves of what I'm, we're, doing. I have enemies among my . . . fellow spirits, I guess you'd call them. They—"

"Let me guess," Kelsa cut in. "They're trying to stop the quest! How terrible. How romantic. I bet that'll suck her in. How stupid do you think I am?"

"I think you're quite bright, for a human," Raven said cautiously. "That's one of the reasons I picked you. And I really haven't lied—"

"What about—"

"I just haven't told you the whole truth," he went on. "Once you blew open that nexus at TuTimbaba my enemies knew I'd found someone. They'll have assumed we'd go on to Glacier National Park and do an ice calling there, but there are plenty of glaciers down the ley, and I thought—"

"So this isn't even the next nexus? You lied about that too?"

"I thought that if they wasted their time setting up a trap for you in Glacier, maybe we could get far enough to keep ahead of them for a while. In this world they have to use their physical forms, as I do, and only a few of them can fly."

He sounded so serious that doubts began to rise in Kelsa. If he wasn't lying . . .

"Setting a trap for me? What does that mean?"

"Nothing fatal," he said hastily. "At least, not yet. The same rules that bind me also bind them. Just as I can only guide and coach you, they aren't allowed to simply kill you or attack you and take the pouch away. And all of us are forbidden to work magic that violates the physical laws of this world. If nothing else it would weaken the leys too much, and they're weak enough already."

"Go back to the part where your enemies are setting a trap for me," Kelsa told him. "Why would they want to stop me? And if they can't kill or attack me, why should I worry about them?"

"I said *they* couldn't attack you. Themselves. There are plenty of ways they can interfere with the quest. And with any luck they're still lurking around the glaciers setting them up, and just beginning to wonder why we haven't arrived there yet."

"But if that's where the nexus is . . ."

Raven made a helpless, groping gesture. "A nexus isn't a fixed point, it's a process. A place in the ley where power is pushed forward and amplified. Some places lend themselves to power more willingly than others—we're on the outskirts of the ley here, not in the center. But almost any point the ley touches is, or can become, a nexus. It depends a lot on you. I was thinking we could go past Glacier and then veer back to the deeper parts of the ley, maybe ride up to Crowsnest Pass. If you can pull the power from there, drag it past any lag points by calling it to you, that will work fine. And it will catch the doubters flat-footed, because they'd never believe you could pull power that far! I wouldn't have believed it till I felt what you did in that cave. Before that"—he offered her a tentative version of the charming smile—"we were all underestimating you. Now they're not, and that makes them far more dangerous. Whatever else you think I'm lying about, you'd better believe that. Do you?"

"I'll think about it."

Kelsa picked up the remains of her lunch and walked away. For once, he had enough sense not to follow her.

o   o   o

Kelsa spent the rest of the day thinking about what Raven had said, and what she concluded was . . . she didn't need him.

Oh, if she chose to go on she'd need him to tell her where the ley was. She wasn't even sure those convenient enemies existed. When she'd asked Raven why anyone would want to keep her from healing the leys, he hadn't answered. And even if these so-called enemies did exist, he'd admitted that they couldn't attack her.

Any point the ley touches can become a nexus. If she performed the healing magic here, using this glorious lake, and it worked . . . If she felt the same thing she had in the cave, or a tidal wave swept over the town she'd passed through at the lake head the moment she spoke, then she'd know he was telling the truth about her working some sort of magic.

She had only his word for what it did. For all she knew, she could be summoning the tree plague instead of immunizing these forests against it.

Yet . . . In most of those old myths, despite his lies and trickery, Raven had been one of the sprits that helped humanity. Though not necessarily the individual human he was dealing with.

Of course, she also had only his word for his identity in the first place.

When Kelsa went to bed that night, lake incantations seeped into her dreams.

° ° °

Kelsa was camped in the lakeshore forest, so the sun didn't hit her tent to wake her at dawn. It was past eight when she emerged, but that worked in her favor. The fishermen had all gone out, and the campground was quiet.

The stretchie she slept in was long enough for decency without her jeans on, and she topped it with not only her therma knit, but a jacket as well. She'd splashed in enough mountain lakes to know what the temperature of the water would be.

She ran through possible incantations in her head while she dressed. None of the lines that had come to her while she was riding beside the river worked now, which made her angry with Raven all over again.

Kelsa hadn't brought water shoes, since they weren't part of her camping or biking gear, so she'd either have to go barefoot or get her shoes wet. It would depend on what the lake bottom looked like.

By the time she'd walked down to the shore, the chill morning air was nipping her bare legs. If her torso hadn't been warm she'd have been shivering.

The water was clear as glass; the rippling waves distorted her view of the bottom without concealing it: jagged rocks with a coating of silt. Slippery silt, no doubt. Better to cope with wet shoes for a day than to break a toe if she slipped, or cut her foot on some sharp-edged, hidden bit of trash.

Kelsa looked around. No late-rising fishermen. No dark-haired boys watching from a distance. No giant black bird perched in the nearby trees.

She'd seen a number of real ravens, or maybe crows, on the road over the last few days, but none of them was half Raven's size.

Unless he could make himself even smaller?

The hell with him. She had a test to run.

After a moment's hesitation—the mind was willing, but her feet still shrank from it—Kelsa took her first step into the icy water. Because she was braced for it, she didn't yelp, but she had to grit her teeth against the sound as freezing meltwater poured into her shoes.

What part of "glacial lake" didn't you understand? She'd been seven or eight when her father had spoken those words, attempting to go for a swim after a long hot ride. How he'd laughed . . .

Kelsa stopped, the icy water momentarily forgotten. This was the first memory of her father, untainted by his illness, that had come to her in . . . she could barely remember back that far. Was she beginning to heal, the way everyone said she would?

But for now, she had another act of healing to perform.

As always, the first step had been the hardest. With only a few gasps for the temperature, Kelsa waded out till the rippling water almost reached the bottom of her stretchie. She looked back at the shore, thirty or forty feet away. If she wasn't "surrounded" by the lake now, she'd have to be scuba diving to make it work.

She tried to put the cold out of her mind as she reached out to the lake with her senses, but the cold was part of it, the heart of its icy crystal depths. Sunlight danced on the surface and the small waves rocked her body. It seemed precarious on the slippery stones.

It was freezing and perfect and beautiful; she felt so alive she could hardly bear the joy of it. Kelsa untied the medicine bag. The words came to her, simpler than she'd expected. Powerful only in their truth.

"Water, mother of life, cold and clear. Run clear and strong, healing all you touch."

She cast a pinch of sand into the waves, and a sudden gust of wind sent waves slapping against the shore.

"Forgive us, please, and heal. Heal and be strong!"

This time she was braced for it. This time she felt the power run through the lake, through her own body, in a great shimmering wave.

She was laughing in delight when the sudden swell knocked her off her feet, and shrieking from the cold when she splashed back to the surface. She'd barely managed to keep her grip on the medicine bag.

She waded back to the shore, dripping and swearing. She was soaked. The medicine bag was soaked.

She'd done it.

Raven stood on the shore, waiting for her, a disapproving frown on his face. "I didn't know you were going to do that. You should have consulted me."

"Th-that's what makes it a valid test." Kelsa's teeth had begun to chatter.

"I intended for you to call on water somewhere in Canada. There are plenty of lakes there."

"Not like th-th-this one," Kelsa told him. The morning air on her cold wet skin was warmer than the lake, though not by much. She squeezed some of the water out of her dripping hair and glared back at him.

The scowl vanished, and a searching look took its place. "For you, was this the lake that holds the spirit of all lakes? The perfect, ideal lake?"

"I guess." But it was. She'd known that from the moment she saw it, even if she wouldn't have put it in quite those words.

"Then that's why you could . . . Do you have any idea what you've done?"

"If I don't, it's because you never tell me anything. I came to heal the ley. Did I heal it?"

"Heal . . . You did more than just heal it. You dragged the main current of the ley into a new channel! You opened a brand-new nexus where none had ever existed! Every shifter on the planet will have felt that, and my enemies—"

"Your so-called enemies," Kelsa scoffed.

"—will be on our trail like a wolf pack. You were in danger before, but now—"

"Now they'll know that humans can heal your precious leys, so they'll have no reason to stop me!"

"Ahh!" Raven buried both hands in his thick black hair and pulled. Kelsa had heard of people tearing at their hair in exasperation, but she'd never seen anyone do it. Another habit from the time when people said "tarnation"?

"If you don't believe anything I tell you," Raven said, "then why have you come this far? Why are you doing this? And if you do believe me about the leys, then why—"

"I didn't come because of you," Kelsa told him. "I came because of my father. Because we didn't try everything."

For the first time since their argument began, Raven actually looked at her. "What do you mean, you didn't try everything?"

Kelsa's eyes burned. It wasn't any of his business, but the words spilled over anyway. "My mother wanted my father to go to a retreat. To try faith healing. That's where—"

"I know what faith healing is," Raven said.

"Dad didn't believe in it. He wanted to stay home. To spend whatever time he had left with us." The tears were falling again. Kelsa didn't care. "I sided with him. But now . . . All this . . ." She gestured to the sun-drenched lake, the magic it implied. "Would it have worked?" she whispered. "Could that kind of magic have cured him?"

She hoped Raven would deny it. Instead he frowned thoughtfully. "Where was this retreat?"

"In Minnesota. Not far from Minneapolis."

"Then no," said Raven. "It wouldn't have worked."

"How can you be sure?" Kelsa demanded. Was he lying to her again?

"Because Minnesota is too far from a major ley for any human to tap it," Raven said. "That's what your faith healing is. Humans, however clumsily, tapping into the power of a major ley. Even if the leys weren't so damaged . . . No. Going to this faith retreat in Minnesota wouldn't have saved him. I'm certain of that."

The rush of relief was so great, Kelsa's knees weakened. She'd been right. Her father had been right. She hadn't prevented him from trying something that might have worked.

She scrubbed a hand across her cheeks, though the water dripping from her hair was enough to conceal her tears. "Anyway, that's why I'm going on. I couldn't save him. So I have to save what I can."

"I suppose that'll do."

Raven stepped forward and laid a hand on Kelsa's head. She was about to pull away when she felt the water retreat from his touch, as if repelled by some antiwater magnetic charge. Drops fell faster from the hem of her shirt as dryness crept down from the top of her head. At last it poured out of her shoes, leaving her with puddles around her feet and completely dry clothing, though the flesh beneath it was still chilled.

"Thanks." It was the only word her stunned brain could produce.

"It's nothing. Or at least, it didn't take much. We'd better get on the road. Our enemies certainly know where we are, and the road from Glacier connects with ours up ahead. I'll ride with you today."

"All right." If they rode together, maybe she could get him to answer some questions. Like why the shapeshifters hadn't—

"Wait a minute. If humans can use the leys for healing, why didn't you tell us about this? Centuries ago? My father could have been cured!"

CHAPTER 6

KELSA TOOK THE ROAD NORTH by herself, fuming.

How dare they keep the power of the leys a secret when it could have saved not only her father, but hundreds, thousands, millions of human lives?

Raven had finally snapped that if his people had told humans about the leys, they would probably have treated them like the rest of this world's resources, and the leys would have been damaged beyond repair long since!

That was when Kelsa had mounted her bike and sped off without him. She was too angry to bother with breakfast. When she saw the sign for the Woodland Café, it was past lunchtime and she was starving. The café was one of those rambling log-built structures that were still common in the mountains, despite the energy efficiency of plasticrete.

The dining room held the usual booths and an old-fashioned counter for people who didn't mind eating in front of the waitress. Kelsa took the Seat Yourself sign at its word and claimed a booth next to one of the windows. It wasn't as if the place was full. The only other customers were a pair of senior citizens, who'd doubtless come from the motor home Kelsa had parked next to, and a burly man at the counter who probably drove one of the trucks that were parked on the shoulder of the road.

She would go on healing the ley, Kelsa decided. But she was doing it to stop the tree plague and save her own planet. To hell with the shapeshifters!

One of the two waitresses offered Kelsa a bright smile and a menu, and she recovered her temper enough to smile back. She might be planning how to use that Raven creep for her own purposes—even more than he was using her!—but she still had to eat.

She was weighing the merits of a superburrito against a double-lean cheeseburger and salad when the bikers pulled up and parked outside.

There were five of them, all dressed in the dark, fiber-reinforced jackets and pants that serious bikers wore. Much the same pants Kelsa was wearing, though she'd left her jacket strapped on the back of the bike.

Some college kids, out for a summer adventure, assumed the same dark clothes and ragged-cut hair as the legally home-less biker gangs. They hoped to be mistaken for kids who were tough and lawless, though they didn't do tough, lawless things like fight for routes with rival gangs and buy and distribute illegal drugs.

The elderly couple with the motor home might well be le-gally homeless too. It was a class of citizens that lumped to-gether everyone who didn't pay taxes from a fixed place of residence. The majority of the legally homeless were either re-tired travelers or college-age kids taking a year or two off to have fun before settling into a job.

But something about the young men who strode into the café made the back of Kelsa's neck prickle in primitive warning.

One of them, a boy with reddish brown hair and freckles who was probably only a few years older than she was, met her eyes. Kelsa looked down and away.

She'd just eat lunch and ignore them. It wasn't necessary to suddenly regret that Raven wasn't with her—though if he had been, she could have told him what she thought of people who held back vital information! Information that could save . . .

The bikers seated themselves at another booth, between Kelsa and the door. The waitress brought them menus and water before coming to take Kelsa's order.

She wasn't as hungry now, but that was foolish. She was in a restaurant full of people. She ordered the burger.

The bikers placed their order shortly before she was served. Since Kelsa was facing them, she could see that they cast several glances in her direction, distracting her from her angry thoughts. Another retired couple parked a motor home and came in. After a single glance at the four bikers, they took a table on the other side of the room. The first couple ordered dessert.

Kelsa finished her burger, took two bites of the salad, and decided she was ready to move on. The bikers had been served only a few minutes ago. She had to pass them on her way to the register.

"That your bike?" the redhead asked as she went by.

"Yes." Kelsa kept walking. She could feel the bikers' eyes on her back.

The redhead stood and followed her.

Her heart beat faster. She wouldn't have minded seeing Raven walk through the café door. Anytime now.

"It's a nice little bike," the young man told her. "We were thinking you might want to ride with us for a while."

Kelsa's hands were cold, her shoulders knotted with tension. "I can't. I'm meeting up with my father and some of his friends. They should be here any minute."

She approached the register and handed her receipt to the waitress.

"You should come a ways with us, anyway," the biker said. "We'd give you one hell of a ride." His eyes moved over her like hands.

Two of the others had risen as well, moving behind him to stand in the doorway. Raven wasn't coming.

"I'd like to speak to the manager, please," Kelsa told the waitress.

"Was everything all right with your meal?" the woman asked.

Couldn't she see how this creep was pushing Kelsa? The woman's expression held only professional concern.

"No." Kelsa was too frightened to care about looking like an idiot. "I want to speak to the manager. Now."

"Excellent," said the waitress. "That'll be eleven eighty-five." She pushed the scanner forward.

"I want the manager."

The waitress smiled politely, waiting for Kelsa to swipe her account card.

Kelsa looked around. The two retired couples chatted with each other, oblivious. One of the bikers was still eating, but he was watching her. The other two had staked out the door.

The second waitress set a plate in front of the trucker—though he'd been there when Kelsa came in. He picked up a small carafe of syrup, unscrewed the lid, and dumped the entire contents over his pancakes.

Then he looked up at Kelsa. His eyes were deep brown and had no whites around them. The eyes of an animal.

He was one of them.

Adrenaline slammed through her. This was the trap Raven had warned her about. But how? *Never mind. Try!*

Kelsa drew in a breath and screamed at the top of her lungs.

The biker behind her fell back several steps, but the woman in front of her didn't even blink. The elderly couples continued their conversations without missing a beat. The other waitress glanced out the window for a moment, before going to clear Kelsa's table.

The trucker stared at her with indifferent eyes and shoveled a forkful of pancakes into his mouth.

The red-haired biker had been looking around too and seen the same thing she had. Now he looked back at Kelsa and grinned.

She leaped past the register, past the oblivious waitress, and dashed through the open doorway into the steamy, onion-smelling kitchen.

The redheaded biker strode after her.

Kelsa looked for a weapon. Not a knife. There were too many enemies, all stronger than she was. She headed for the stove, past a pudgy, white-clad chef who didn't even look at her, snatched up the nearest pan and cast the contents into the biker's face.

It was in the air before the deadly reality of hot grease and frying onion registered on either of them.

The biker flung up a hand, his leather sleeve intercepting most of the grease, but not all of it. He cried out when it splattered his skin, then screamed in earnest as the pain bit.

The two who'd blocked the door had followed more slowly; now they rushed down the narrow kitchen.

Kelsa had a second to choose her next weapon, a big pot of steaming chowder that drenched them both. They shrieked and swiped at their faces.

The red-haired biker staggered toward the sink, emitting groaning pants of pain.

Kelsa whirled and ran for the back door. There was a back door, thank God. She raced outside and looked frantically for help, for a place to hide.

Her bike came skidding around the corner, with Raven riding it, though he took the turn so clumsily he almost tipped over.

"On the back. Get back," Kelsa cried, running toward him.

He stopped the bike, spreading his feet to keep it upright as he slid back on the saddle.

Then she was there, mounting, the handle grips firm and comforting under her palms. Her right hand stung with a burn she'd picked up without realizing it, but she paid it no heed, spinning gravel from under the tires as she slammed down the accelerator.

She raced down the road as fast as the dirt bike would run—the big hogs the bikers rode would be much faster.

She was hoping to trip a speed sensor—she wanted the police!

Although . . . What had happened to those people? It was as if she was invisible. Except for the trucker, or whatever he really was.

She shuddered at the memory of the indifference in those round, animal eyes.

o o o

She passed four side roads before turning onto the fifth, and she rode down it for several miles before pulling off into a thick glade where she should be safe—if the bikers were all she had to fear.

"You said they couldn't attack me!"

Raven's grip on her waist changed to a comforting embrace as the bike slowed to a stop, but Kelsa was too tense, too terrified for comfort. She knocked down the stand and leaped off the bike, out of his arms. She took off her helmet and threw it at him.

"Where the hell were you? You said they couldn't attack me. And why . . . What in the . . ."

She was crying. She'd been crying for some time. She pulled out a tissue and wiped away the snot and tears.

"I'm sorry," Raven said. "I didn't think they could get here, and get anything set up so quickly. But that's no excuse."

His shirt was fastened with two buttons, and he hadn't taken the time to put on his shoes. He hadn't *had* time to put on his shoes.

A wave of shivering swept over her, and her stomach began to churn. Kelsa wrapped her arms around herself.

"One of them was a shapeshifter. At least one. Were they all your enemies, in that restaurant?"

"No," Raven told her. "The bikers who went after you had to be human, according to the rules, and I'd bet most of the others were human as well. Describe the shapeshifter you saw."

"He was big." She could see him clearly in her memory, see more details than she'd noticed at the time. "Big, with shaggy brown hair, and hair on his arms and hands. His eyes were all dark, like a pig's or a dog's. Like brown marbles. He . . . he poured a whole pot of syrup over his pancakes."

It sounded silly, but somehow that seemed more alien than all the rest. She shivered again and began to pace.

"That was Bear," Raven said. "He's not an enemy, he's one of the neutrals. He was probably there to observe, to make sure no one on either side broke the rules."

"Killing me isn't against the rules?" Or had they intended to rape her? Or both? Kelsa shuddered.

"No." Raven's voice was gentle. "Not if they use the tools of this world to do it."

The need to think, to understand what he was saying, slowed her racing heart. Her furious pacing slowed too.

"So the bikers, they were human?"

"Yes."

"And the rest of those people . . . What was the matter with them? It was like I wasn't even there!"

That had been one of the most terrifying parts of it. Not the most terrifying.

Raven sighed. "It takes power. It takes power, concentration, and skill, but it's not impossible to cloud human minds. To make them see what they expect to see. Hear what they expect to hear." He snorted. "You sometimes do that without any help from us."

"And those bikers? They were just doing something expected?"

"Ah, that's a bit different. With them the . . . molder, call it, found a spark of desire to act that way and fanned it. Suppressed their inhibitions, the fear of the consequences that would ordinarily have stopped them."

"So anyone I meet could suddenly attack me?"

"Not really. Not unless it's something they might do anyway. It's all but impossible to force something to go against its nature, against its own will. It's only if the will to act is already there that you can use it."

The thought that dawned then was so horrible it froze Kelsa in her tracks.

"Have you been manipulating me that way?"

"No," Raven told her. "I haven't. Even if I could, it would be against the rules. And the healing of the ley wouldn't work without your uncorrupted will behind it. Of course, you only have my word that those things are true."

He said nothing more, watching her with wary dark eyes. Human-looking eyes. He had lied to her, by omission at least, many times. And she'd certainly been acting strangely this last week! But the decisions she'd made felt like her decisions. He *was* using her for his own ends. But he'd never made any pretense of anything else, not from the start.

And she had her own world to save.

Kelsa took a deep breath and let it out. "OK. So how do I protect myself between here and Alaska?"

CHAPTER 7

"That depends," said Raven slowly, "on what those bikers are capable of."

"Anything." Kelsa tried to suppress a shudder and failed.

"No, I mean . . . There aren't many humans like them, which is good! If all humans were like that I'd be working with my enemies. Would it be possible for the others to convince those bikers to chase you? Or would that be unthinkable, something they'd never do?"

"Not unthinkable. The biker gangs . . . When security in the cities became intense, when the camera net was finally connected, it became pretty much impossible to deal in illegal drugs anywhere on the grid. And in cities and towns, that's everywhere. So the gangs who made their living that way moved into the countryside. They have regular routes, and fight with rival gangs when someone tries to cut into their trade. And they're big on both revenge and pride. I don't think it would be hard to convince them that I'd dissed them and they have to punish me."

Terror rose again at the thought. She'd have welcomed his embrace now, but he merely nodded. "If the bikers are that apt for their purpose, the others aren't likely to abandon them.

But that means they'll have to work through those bikers. They'll be limited by what the bikers themselves can do, in this world, when it comes to tracking you. I think some scouting is in order."

He stood and began unbuttoning his shirt.

"You're going to leave me here? Alone?"

"If they're anywhere near, I'll come back at once. But we need to know what they're doing if we're going to elude them."

"What happens if they find me before you get back?" At this point, she didn't have much faith in his airy assurances. "Wait a minute. If your enemies can control people, can they control animals too?"

This was bear country.

"No. Well, to a limited extent. You can sometimes convince an animal that you're not a threat to it, for a short time. Some other things like that. But it's harder to confuse a simple mind than a complex one. Animals have no expectations, so they see what's really there. And if they're under any stress instinct takes over, and they do what they'd usually do. Which is run, for the most part."

"But couldn't they . . . I don't know, use birds to spy on me or something?"

Raven snorted. "Birds, the smaller ones, can't tell one human from another. And their attention span is about two minutes. The larger ones are a bit brighter, but you don't have to worry about that. Really."

She averted her eyes as he shucked off his pants, and kept them firmly averted till the sound of flapping wings told her it was safe to look as he back-winged out of the trees and swooped away.

Leaving his partner to have hysterics, all by herself. Kelsa had noticed before that he didn't pay much attention to human emotions, but still!

On the other hand, if his enemies could only work through their human accomplices she should be safe here.

That knowledge did nothing to stop the spurt of tears.

∘   ∘   ∘

Raven was gone long enough that she'd gotten past the crying jag and reached a state of near calm—though the thought of ever setting eyes on those bikers again made her heart pound.

It was hard even to remember being angry with Raven that morning. Being rescued from death, or other horrible fates, made the fact that he'd told a few lies look amazingly trivial. And it seemed he'd been telling the truth about his enemies.

Her enemies, now.

Kelsa shuddered. It didn't matter if he'd lied or not. If she was going to go on, to try to heal the rest of the leys, she needed his protection as well as his guidance.

When Raven finally returned, Kelsa watched him land on the bike's handlebars with undeniable fascination. His wingspan had to be over four feet; the wind from his landing fanned her face, even though she was seated on a rock several yards away. What other shapes could he assume? Could he become even larger? Turn into a mouse? Surely the laws of physics had to apply somehow.

She tried to watch him change, but her nerves were still unsteady and her gaze slid aside.

"If you went across the border into Canada without anyone knowing, with no official record of it, would the bikers know that too? And keep looking for you here?"

"I'm not sure," Kelsa admitted. "Most of what I know about biker gangs comes from the news. And d-vid. But I've heard that they can tap into police and security nets. The parts that aren't supersecret, anyway. Of course, the government denies that. But I can't get into Canada, with or without a report. I don't have permission to cross the border. And I don't dare get out on the highway, where they could find me."

Her stomach curdled at the thought.

"You don't need to worry about that. Not for a while, anyway. They're heading back to the clinic at Whitefish to get their burns treated. And the red-haired one is riding behind one of the others with a cold compress over his face."

Raven was smiling, fiercely, but Kelsa shuddered.

"Lord, they'll be *eager* to track me down and kill me. Your friends won't have to do a thing to encourage them."

"So if you sneaked over the border with no one knowing, they'd probably waste a lot of time looking for you around here." Raven sounded disgustingly cheerful. "That's what took me so long. I've found a way to get you across."

o   o   o

The arena was about ten miles down the highway. According to the running sign, which no one had bothered to reprogram, the horse show had ended June ninth. Yesterday.

"It's over," said Kelsa, stopping her bike. "What's so exciting about that? Everyone will be gone."

"Not everyone." She couldn't see Raven's face, with him perched behind her, but his voice sounded smug. "There are a dozen horse trailers still there, though most of them are packing up now. And three of them have Canadian labels!"

"Lab— Do you mean license plates?"

"Whatever it is, it means they live in Canada, right?"

"Yes, but—"

"So once they've loaded their horses they'll drive right over the border. If you were hidden in one of those trailers, no one would know you were there!"

"Except for the inspectors," said Kelsa, "who look into the back of trucks and horse trailers to prevent that kind of thing."

"I've watched them do that," Raven said. "They look, but they don't look hard. If you were tucked behind something I don't think they'd find you."

Kelsa had watched the inspectors too, waiting in line at border stations. If the driver didn't act nervous, they didn't look hard.

Of course, they didn't have to.

"The scanner would spot me," she said. "It's mostly set to look for chemicals and chemical weapons. Drugs, nuclear reactives, all sorts of things. But it would pick up a human's biomass and heat source with no trouble. So that won't work."

She was torn between relief—she didn't really want to run the border—and worry. Would the next idea he came up with be even worse?

"I thought about that too," Raven told her. "Would it pick up your presence, your biomass, as you call it, if you were lying on top of a horse?"

o   o   o

He switched back into Raven form to scout ahead, while Kelsa waited in a thicket of trees watching people move casually around the distant trailers.

Several people loaded their horses and left. One of the departing trailers had Canadian plates, which made Kelsa wonder what Raven was waiting for. But soon after that he flapped onto his favorite perch, let out a croak, then swooped away toward the trailers.

There was no one visible now.

Kelsa punched in the start code, deeply grateful for the electric motor's quiet hum. The tires rolling over the asphalt made more noise than the motor did.

The trailer on which Raven had perched had a horse in one of the two stalls, with nothing but a net across the back to hold it in. Kelsa rode her bike into the other stall, bumping gently over the low sill. If someone was watching the yard's security cameras and came dashing out to stop her, Kelsa would probably have time to back out and ride away. Her helmet would conceal her face, and the tape still disguised the real number on her license plate.

One of the disadvantages of computer security was that only the places they really needed to keep secure had human guards, who actually watched the monitors. Arenas like this hosted all sorts of events; their security computers were almost certainly programmed to accept a bike being loaded into a trailer as a normal event.

"But the driver will have to close up the back before he leaves," Kelsa told the huge bird as it hopped awkwardly inside. "He'll see the bike."

She looked over at the horse, a big bay who didn't seem to be disturbed by her presence or the bike. It pranced and rolled its eyes when Raven began to shift, but that was all.

"Suppose he has another horse to put in here?" Kelsa added. "And that's why they haven't left yet."

Several long moments passed. Kelsa was beginning to get impatient when Raven finally said, "See those hay bales? Whoever owns this trailer only uses this side for storage."

When she looked at the end of the compartment, it was clear that Raven was right. The stall next door, where the horse now stood quietly, had smooth wooden walls. The walls on this side of the central divider were studded with hooks and nails, from which hung all the mysterious paraphernalia Kelsa assumed was necessary for horses. The only hay in the horse's stall was a few wisps in the raised manger, and under that manger was an enclosed space that might be big enough to conceal her bike.

Kelsa and Raven hauled out a half-full sack of grain and several chests and bags containing who-knows-what, but they managed to make enough space for her bike and wheeled it in.

They were tucking a plastic tarp over the protruding curve of the back wheel when Raven froze, listening. Once the plastic stopped rustling Kelsa heard it too: footsteps on the asphalt, coming nearer.

Raven pushed her down into the narrow space behind the bales, then struggled in beside her.

"What about the chests?" Kelsa whispered urgently. "Won't he see—"

She felt the tension in the warm muscular body lying so close to hers. Could Raven control the mind of whoever owned this trailer? Make him see what he expected to see?

Raven had said it took concentration as well as power, so Kelsa kept quiet and still.

The footsteps stopped, very near. A long rattle vibrated through the floor beneath her and the light dimmed. A couple of clanks latched the back of the trailer closed, but Kelsa didn't let herself relax till the trailer levitated off the pavement.

She struggled away from the prickly hay bale, and then crawled up to sit on it. "Did you make that man see what he expected to?"

She wasn't sure if the thought of Raven controlling human minds was reassuring or creepy.

"It was a woman." Raven rose to his knees, then sat on another bale, facing her. "And I didn't have time. I told you humans often see what they expect without any help at all."

Kelsa could tell by the sudden feeling of stability when the trailer stopped hovering and moved forward, but it felt odd to travel without looking out the window. Of course, if she couldn't see out the bikers couldn't see in. Thank goodness she didn't get glide sick.

"We're about fifty miles from the border," Kelsa said. "Tell me about these enemies of yours. Why don't they want the leys to be healed?"

Light from the narrow windows above lit Raven's grimace. "I knew you were going to ask that. We'll have less than an hour before we face the inspectors. Shouldn't we make plans?"

"We'll hide behind the hay when the inspectors look in. Then I'll scramble up on the horse—and I really hope he doesn't mind—and blend my body mass with his. It might even work."

In fact, she was pretty sure it would fool the scanners. She'd seen pictures, on d-vid broadcasts, of the fuzzy red blobs and string of chemical readings that were a scanner's interpretation of a human body. A horse would be a really big red blob, with very similar readings. Hiding from the visual inspection would either work or it wouldn't.

Kelsa preferred not to wonder what the legal penalty for trying to run an international border was.

"Why don't your enemies want to heal the ley?" she repeated firmly. "Are they . . . are they some kind of bioterrorists too?"

Raven snorted, but then his expression grew thoughtful. "You know, I think they are. On a big scale. The thing is . . . I wasn't supposed to tell you this, but since any human you told would think you were crazy, I guess it doesn't matter. The reason everyone cares so much about the leys is that they exist in both your world and mine."

Kelsa stared. "Your world?"

His smile held some of the old cockiness. "You think shapeshifters belong here? Though *world* isn't quite the word. Your scientists' theories about dimensions are actually pretty close. But *world* sounds better. Anyway, the leys not only exist in both worlds, they make a big difference in the health, the stability of ours. I don't know if I can explain that to you, but clean powerful leys are as important to our survival as clean abundant water and air are to yours."

The chill that ran over Kelsa's skin had nothing to do with the cool breeze coming through the window slits.

"And what we did, ERB-1, things like that, it weakened the leys."

His changeable face was now very serious. "The tree plague was the final straw. We'd been arguing for years, for decades, what to do about the damage you were causing. When the tree plague came . . . The others didn't understand! They hadn't looked in on you for so long, they couldn't see that you were finally beginning to turn it around. To become the stewards to this planet that you could be."

"You stood up for us?" Gratitude bloomed in her heart.

"Not really. What you'd done was pretty indefensible. Your world and mine aren't the only ones affected by the leys, either."

A wondrous vision of dozens of dimensions, with a great river of healing power flowing through all of them, lurked in the back of Kelsa's mind. But more important . . .

"If you'd only told us about the leys, taught us to use them, maybe *we* could have reversed the damage a long time ago."

"Maybe. But more likely you'd have drained them to the dregs, like you did with your oil. And your climate. And—"

"That's no excuse." But it almost was. "That's still no excuse for letting us all die. Which we could, if the tree plague spreads everywhere. Nothing could excuse that."

"Not even the fact that if you don't start doing better you could threaten our survival? That's what the others were saying. That this is our chance to be rid of you, once and for all. But if we did let the plague wipe you out, as I had to admit you've deserved, it would do significant damage to our world. Others as well. Cutting off your nose to spite your face, in the old phrase. I didn't care if you survived. I mean, of course I wanted humans to survive," he added hastily, catching sight of her expression. "But the others, most of them, they said you'd brought it on yourselves. That in the long run, it would be worth putting up with the damage the ravaging of your planetary environment would do to the leys just to be rid of you. That we could heal the leys ourselves once you were gone. And we weren't the ones who started the tree plague, after all."

They weren't. Humans had done that all by themselves. "Your enemies. The bikers they control. They'd really be willing to kill me?"

"In a heartbeat, most of them. Though there are a few others who've seen that you're changing, doing better. And it's stupid to accept a massive catastrophe if you don't have to! There are a lot more, the neutrals, who aren't convinced you're changing, but who do want to heal the leys if that's possible. So"—he drew a deep breath—"they told me that if I could persuade the humans to heal the damage they'd done, they'd accept that I was right and leave you alone. But it has to be humans, working their own magic to do the healing. All of it."

"And that's where all those rules come from. They're not some sort of natural-magical laws. They're . . . political."

This new fear wasn't as immediate, as visceral, as the fear the bikers had evoked. This was a slow, icy dread that encompassed the whole world. Now, Kelsa thought, she knew how her ancestors had felt during the mad, brief period of the nuclear arms race.

"That's right," Raven said. "And those rules cut both ways. Just as I can only use the tools of this world to heal the leys, they can only use the tools of this world to stop us. If those bikers can be delayed looking for you on this side of the border, it will give us more time to reach the next nexus."

Was she just a tool? Or part of "us"?

Kelsa decided not to ask. He might be stupid enough to tell her the truth, and she wasn't sure she could deal with it.

"So, can you control the minds of the border inspectors?"

∘ ∘ ∘

It seemed he couldn't, unless he had at least ten minutes to study them and slowly insert his will into their thoughts.

Raven and Kelsa spent the rest of the ride to the border arranging better concealment. Even Kelsa had to admit that the pile of chests, buckets, and folded saddle blankets behind the hay bales shouldn't look like two people were hiding beneath them.

On Raven's instructions, she passed through the narrow slot that gave access between the stalls and made friends with the horse, feeding him a handful of oats. He was intimidatingly big, but his muzzle was soft and he lipped the grain out of her palm quite delicately.

When the trailer began to slow, Kelsa looked out the window slit and saw they'd reached their destination.

The long row of scanner tunnels proclaimed an international border, something she'd never crossed before. Were these scanners different, better, stronger than the ones on state borders? The lines of traffic in front of them looked the same.

"It'll take them a while to get to us." Raven stood beside her, peering out. "But we should probably hide now, just to be sure."

They had plenty of time for Kelsa to lie down behind the bales and for Raven to make sure she was well concealed before he disarranged everything by joining her.

The warm strong body lying so close to her still felt human, but Kelsa would sooner have been turned on by a crocodile. The being inside that body wasn't human. His careless comments about wiping out her species had proved that. Still, he was on humanity's side, and he had rescued her from the bikers. And if he was using her only to save his own world, then she would use him, his knowledge of the leys and their workings, to save hers.

The cut hay stalks were sharp against her bare arms. They smelled dusty. Kelsa resigned herself to a long wait, and she wasn't disappointed. She didn't know exactly how much time passed, but her hip was numb where it rested on the wooden floor. More important, Raven kept shifting his position. The stack of buckets that concealed their feet was rocking from his last movement when the latch that closed the trailer door clanked.

Kelsa's instinct was to freeze, but those wobbling buckets would give them away. Trying not to move the folded blankets, she shot one hand down to steady the buckets then froze, not even breathing, as someone entered the trailer . . . paused for a moment . . . and then left.

The trailer's back panel rattled down, and the latch clicked closed.

Raven was moving before she dared, struggling out from under the blankets and boxes. The buckets would have fallen if Kelsa hadn't been holding them.

"What were you doing with all that wiggling?" she whispered. "You almost got us caught."

Raven crawled over her onto the bales, planting an elbow in her ribs on the way.

"Tarnation, this form can be uncomfortable! Every muscle I've got is cramping."

Kelsa's own body was stiff as she levered herself out of the narrow slot and onto the bales beside him. "I'm cramping too, but I didn't twitch like a—"

The trailer slid into motion, silencing both of them. Kelsa shot to her feet.

"We're heading for the scanners. Now! You've got to shift into something small, and I've got to get on that horse!"

"We'll both join the horse," Raven said. "I've shifted half a dozen times today. I can't change quickly. And if I'm still shifting when we go through, those scanners might pick up the energy."

Now that Kelsa thought about it, his last few changes had seemed to take longer. But she had no time to pursue the subject.

Raven slipped into the horse's side of the trailer, pausing to murmur and stroke his neck. Then he grasped a handful of mane and swung onto the horse's back in a fluid leap that Kelsa had thought only stuntmen on d-vid could do.

He reached down a hand to help her. "Come on. We don't have much time."

The horse looked much bigger than he had a few minutes ago. Kelsa took the offered hand and tried to duplicate Raven's leap. With perfect comedic timing, the horse stepped aside, and Kelsa slid down his body and back to the floor despite Raven's strong grip. No one had ever warned her that horses are slippery, and there are no handholds.

"Oh, for Pete's sake! We're almost at the scanner!" Raven slid neatly off the horse, grasped her hips, and boosted her upward. "Throw your leg over. That's right. Good!"

Kelsa straddled the horse. It felt a lot more precarious than it looked on d-vid. She grabbed a big handful of mane, and the horse didn't seem to mind. She was only vaguely aware of the dimming light as they pulled into the scanner tunnel, most of her attention taken up by the large animal she was sitting on.

Raven swung up behind her, pushed her body down against the horse's neck, and then flattened his body on top of hers.

Kelsa didn't think the scanner was set to detect sound, but neither of them spoke as the trailer moved slowly through the tunnel. The body beneath her was certainly warm enough to mask her heat signature, and probably Raven's too. Horses came in different sizes, didn't they? Some were even bigger than this one. Surely the security data wasn't so detailed that the computer would flag the fact that this horse massed about three hundred pounds more than it had when it crossed the border before. Surely—

The light through the window slits brightened.

Raven sat up cautiously. The truck that pulled the trailer stopped for a few seconds at the final barrier, then when it lifted, the truck accelerated into Canada.

Raven dismounted, and Kelsa managed to slide down the big body without embarrassing herself.

"Thank you." She stroked the horse's neck as she'd seen Raven do. The horse heaved a sigh and sniffed his empty manger.

"We're through!" Raven's voice held the same incredulous relief Kelsa felt.

"You sound surprised. Weren't you the one who came up with this plan?"

"That doesn't mean I liked the idea of breaking you out of a Canadian jail. This is *much* better. I promise you."

"Until someone runs my PID card, and some security computer flags the fact that I appear to be in Canada without ever having entered Canada."

"We'll worry about that later," Raven told her. "For now, I'm more concerned about getting you out of this box without the owner seeing you."

After some debate, they couldn't come up with any better idea than to wing it—literally. Raven shifted into his feathered form once more. It took a lot longer than usual, but as Raven flippantly observed, every jailbreak needs someone on the outside. He squirmed through one of the narrow windows when the trailer stopped at a traffic light in the first town they passed after crossing the border.

Then the trailer ran over curving mountain roads and down winding river valleys for several hours, while Kelsa wondered helplessly if he'd be able to keep up. Finally, it pulled into a charge station.

Standing out of reach of the lowering light that came through the small slit, Kelsa watched the driver—it was a woman with short curly hair—climb out and stretch. She connected the charge plug and headed off to the flash station, no doubt to use the facilities. Kelsa would have liked to do that herself. And then eat. It felt as if a lifetime had passed since lunch, and despite all the trauma, she was hungry.

Would the woman check on her horse when she returned? What if—

The clang of the latch sent her spinning around as the door rattled up to reveal Raven, nude.

He scrambled into the trailer and grabbed his pants. "Get your bike out. It's nothing short of a miracle no one saw me, and we may not have much time."

Kelsa was already rolling her bike out from under the manger. Raven dressed and tossed the gear they'd removed back into the compartment, willy-nilly, while Kelsa backed the bike out of the trailer. He was out and pulling down the gate by the time she'd looped back for him. As soon as the latch closed, he turned and flung himself onto the bike behind her. They whipped out of the charge station and onto the road.

Kelsa's heart was pounding, but no outraged shouts followed them. No sirens. No flashing lights. She checked her speed to be certain she wouldn't trip any sensors and rode on into Canada, free and clear, with Raven's arms around her.

This time his shirt was completely unbuttoned, and he had no shoes on.

Rain began to patter down.

CHAPTER 8

RAVEN SHARED HER TENT THAT night. By the time Kelsa found an open meadow near the river, where several blackened stone rings told her camping was permitted, and then inflated her tent and rolled out her bedding, Raven's teeth were chattering so hard he could barely speak.

Her thermal pants and jacket were too small for him, but she bullied him into them anyway and set the controls on high.

The air foam pad was big enough for two. After a while he peeled off the jacket and gave it back to her, so they both slept warm, even though she gave him only one of the blankets and kept the other for herself.

He fell asleep as soon as he stopped shivering. The drizzle was beginning to let up, and even at nine thirty on a cloudy night enough light came through the canvas for Kelsa to see the dark circles under his eyes.

How many times had he changed shape on this long crazy day? She'd lost count, but clearly it was too many. She had no fear of the bikers' finding her tonight. Those horrible moments in the Woodland Café seemed as if they'd happened days ago, instead of just this morning.

She was in Canada now, and safe, for a while at least.

Still, Kelsa stared out into the dripping twilight of the northern night for a long time before she slept.

o   o   o

Raven was gone when she awoke, and an uneasiness that was almost fear swept over her before she heard the crackle of the fire.

Kelsa dressed and visited the bushes before joining him beside the dancing blaze. She wondered where he'd found dry wood. Or had he dried it with magic, as he'd dried her clothing back at Flathead Lake?

He'd figured out how to work the self-heating can, but he still held it tentatively, as if he expected it to explode in his hand.

Kelsa was about to tell him that it wouldn't, and that all its components were biodegradable within five years, but Raven spoke first.

"You said the bikers carry illegal drugs with them. How can they get past those scanners? Isn't the border station there to stop people like that?"

"It's mostly to stop the kind of people who started the tree plague," Kelsa told him. "But the scanners detect illegal drugs too. What the drug gangs do, according to the newscasts, is ride a couple of days off-road, into the wild country along the border. That's why their bikes have tires like mine. They'll hide the drugs, mark their coordinates, then go through the border station carrying nothing that's illegal. Once they're in the country legally, all they have to do is ride back and collect their stash from the other side."

Raven looked puzzled. "If it's that easy to get around them, why didn't you just ride your bike across the border?"

"There are patrols," Kelsa told him. "And cameras at most of the easy crossing points, and the patrols move other cameras around. That's the main reason biker gangs make the effort to tap into the security nets, so they can know which areas are being monitored."

"Then why do you have these border stations at all?"

"They were built to prevent terrorists from smuggling bombs and bioweapons into the country," Kelsa said. "And across state lines. Catching drug smugglers is a side benefit."

"Don't terrorists just go around it, the same way smugglers do?"

"No. The border stations caught a few of them at first, but now terrorists just go to the place they want to destroy and construct their weapon there. But it's easier to do that than it is to distribute illegal drugs without getting picked up on the camera net, which is why most crime takes place off the grid. Outside of cities and towns," she added.

"Human logic," Raven muttered, not quite under his breath. "No, don't explain. From what you say, if they want to keep their cargo safe, your bikers will take longer to cross the border than we did. And don't they need government permission too?"

Kelsa shook her head. "The people who apply for legally homeless status are travelers. They usually get permission to cross all North American borders when they apply."

Raven stared at her. "Then what good does the border station do?"

"Well, it makes it possible for security forces to track the movements of suspects, and . . . and other things."

Raven shrugged. "But it will take the bikers longer?"

"If they want to keep their drugs, it will. By several days. I think it would go against a lot of their instincts to leave those drugs behind."

"So after we heal the next nexus, we'll have some time before they could catch up with us?"

"Some," said Kelsa cautiously. "A few days at least." Assuming, of course, that the newscasts were accurate.

"Good," said Raven. "Because I really need a bath."

∘ ∘ ∘

Since a hotel would demand PID cards when they booked a room, Raven was persuaded to settle for a shower in the next campground, which would be somewhere in Banff National Park. The craggy, ice-capped peaks with glacial blue streams running below were different from the uplift mountains Kelsa was used to, and so beautiful that she kept slowing the bike to stare. Raven seemed to enjoy them too—he didn't start nagging her to speed up till clouds began to gather among the peaks.

Kelsa didn't realize they were approaching the provincial border till she saw the sign, LEAVING ALBERTA: WILD ROSE COUNTRY. Her heart rate accelerated, but she didn't stop the bike—there were cameras posted on the approach to any border station, watching for just that kind of suspicious behavior. She did slow down enough to talk to Raven.

"What are we going to do? You didn't warn me about a border station! In the middle of a national park? They'll run my PID card, and I'm here illegally, and you don't have one!"

"Don't worry about it," Raven told her. "Just keep driving."

"But there's no way they won't . . ."

The next sign said WELCOME TO BRITISH COLUMBIA: THE BEST PLACE ON EARTH. Kelsa drove several hundred more yards, then pulled off at the widened patch of asphalt where drivers could check their brakes.

She turned in the bike saddle and looked at the back of the welcome sign. It said LEAVING BRITISH COLUMBIA: THE BEST PLACE ON EARTH.

"But . . . where's the border station? Where's the scanner, the guards, the . . . the security?"

"Maybe," said Raven, "the Canadians didn't want to waste their money on something that doesn't seem to stop either terrorists or crime."

"But . . . but . . ."

Kelsa half expected the border station to appear around the next curve of the road, or the next. She'd ridden five miles, or in the Canadian system about eight kilometers, before she was forced to accept that there was no border station. It seemed even more alien than seeing "100" posted on a speed-limit sign.

The clouds were looming heavily when they reached the tourist town of Lake Louise, and Kelsa had only one set of rain gear.

"You could shapeshift and keep warm that way." But she said it reluctantly. Now that she knew what his enemies were capable of, Kelsa wanted him behind her, in human form, able to come to her defense at a moment's notice.

"I've got a better idea," Raven told her. "Why don't we get that shower and go shopping?"

Kelsa hesitated. Paying their way into the park, plus the fee for a night's camping, had almost exhausted her debit account.

On the other hand, if it was raining tomorrow, all the thermal knit she could loan him wouldn't keep him warm on the bike.

"OK. But it'll have to be *cheap* clothes. Off the sale rack."

"Yes, madam." A mischievous flash in the dark eyes negated the meek voice.

Kelsa sighed.

o   o   o

They had to shower one at a time because Raven had to borrow her account card to pay the dollar it cost to turn on the water. Kelsa didn't mind waiting. An amazingly tame herd of elk was grazing in the meadow next to the shower building, to the delight of all the passing campers in this large, crowded campground. There were even more tourists here than in Craters, but if Kelsa got off on one of the lonelier trails she could probably find a place to work her healing without an audience.

If the power of the nexus manifested itself in physical beauty, the one under this park must be incredible.

By the time they rode into the parking lot that served the cluster of shops, it was raining in earnest, and it had gotten cold enough to make Raven's point about both of them needing tempcontrol clothes.

Eyeing the glass and flowstone buildings, Kelsa had some misgivings about the state of her debit account. By her loose tally, she had about a hundred dollars left.

"The sale rack," she said, following Raven into the store. "The cheapest possible sale rack."

"Don't worry about it," he said. "I'll take care of that. Why don't you see where we can get something warm for dinner?"

What did he plan to do? Mesmerize the sales clerk into thinking he'd paid? That might work on the clerk, but it wouldn't work on the store's security cameras. Kelsa probably had enough money to pay for a cheap bike suit. Barely.

She wasn't surprised to see him go straight to one of the most expensive brands and pull a jacket off the rack.

Bike suits were designed to be worn over other clothing, so he didn't have to go to a dressing room. And the moment he approached that rack a clerk darted over to assist, so Kelsa couldn't intervene. Let him embarrass himself at the checkout counter, she thought grimly. Maybe he'd learn to listen to the person who understood how things worked in the twenty-first century.

She had to admit, the sleek black bike gear suited him.

She winced when he went over to the boots section and chose a pair to go with his outfit, but if he was going to blow it, he might as well blow it big. She was pretty sure he wasn't carrying enough to make it grand theft when he finally approached the counter—and pulled out a wad of hundred-dollar bills so thick it made the clerk blink.

Most people paid with account cards these days, but a few used cash. The clerk took the money—four bills, Kelsa was shocked to see, with still more of them in his hand—and gave him his change without comment.

Raven was out on the sidewalk headed for a nearby restaurant when Kelsa recovered her wits and caught up with him.

"Where did you get that?" She kept her voice low and chose her words carefully. A lot of people had decided to spend the rainy evening shopping.

"I made it." His dark eyes danced. "How else does one get money?"

Kelsa looked around the crowded sidewalk and didn't dare accuse him of magical counterfeiting. Not here. Not now.

Raven treated her to the most expensive meal she'd had on this trip. She couldn't help but enjoy the change from energy bars and peanut butter, despite her ethical qualms.

She waited till they'd reached the privacy of her tent, where the pattering rain assured her that no one strolling past their camp would overhear, before she confronted him.

"It's fake, isn't it? All that money you spent."

"Of course. But the change people gave me is real. I was thinking we could start spending that, and spare your debit account for a while."

Kelsa felt her face grow cold as the blood drained out of it. "I don't care how good it is, there are dozens of ways, technical ways, to detect counterfeit money—and track it back! When they catch you . . . Counterfeiters spend *years* in prison!"

Could she convince them she hadn't known the money was fake? She hadn't spent any of it herself, but . . .

"Relax." Raven was spreading his blanket. "They'd have to have the money in order to prove counterfeiting, and those bills will probably turn to dust before anyone gets around to examining them."

A wisp of memory from her research on trickster spirits sprang into Kelsa's mind. "You mean it will vanish, like . . . fairy gold?" It sounded ridiculous, but Raven nodded.

"Exactly like that, though I'm surprised that term made it to this side of the ocean."

"How does an Indian spirit know about leprechaun stories?"

He stopped making his bed to look at her. "I'd have thought you'd have figured that out. Or maybe not. This is pretty new to you."

"Figured what out?"

"The reason I'm Raven here, along this ley, is because for thousands of years the humans who lived here thought of me as Raven. So that's the shape the ley's power wants me to take, which means it requires far less power to assume and maintain. Along other leys, I'd take other forms."

"Wait. Are you telling me that if we were in Ireland you'd be a . . . a leprechaun?"

"I'd be Leprechaun," he corrected. "There is ever only one of me."

Kelsa stared at him, handsome and solid, as real as she was, in the fiber-reinforced bike gear from which he'd just removed the tags. "In a little green coat, with a pipe. Top o' the mornin' to ya."

He broke into laughter, a deep sincere laugh she'd never heard from him before. "Of course not. That's an image your advertisers created. Would you like to see the original?"

He started to change before she could find her voice to answer, and she watched as he shrank, his clothes falling away. The change from one human form to another wasn't nearly as horrifying, and she kept her eyes on him as his nose grew long and sharp, his brows thick and bushy.

When the transformation was finished he stood about three feet high, clad in something that looked like a coarse sack, snugged around his skinny body by a wide leather belt. His feet were bare and muddy, and though he was no larger than a child, his face was that of a man in middle age, lined and forbidding.

"How weird." Goose bumps were popping out on Kelsa's arms.

Raven, Leprechaun, cast her a sardonic glance and said something in a language both liquid and harsh, which she didn't recognize.

"Is that Gaelic? What does it mean?"

This other version of Raven looked . . . old. Ancient and alien. How many versions of him were there? Almost every mythos in the world had a trickster spirit in it.

"I said, 'Don't go spending fairy gold, girl, or they'll be looking for you when it vanishes.'"

Even his accent was different. Not the over-the-top brogue of the cartoon leprechaun, but something like a real Irish accent, only rougher, thicker.

He picked up his jacket and pants and pulled them on, holding them up as he changed again, expanding back into them, becoming the boy she knew.

"Hey! Why did you have clothes when you shifted just then? Leprechaun clothes."

He waited till the change finished before he answered.

"I can create clothes if I have to, but it takes a lot more power than changing my living shape, and power to maintain them. But a living form will maintain itself, just like your own body does."

He rubbed his face as if suddenly tired, pulled off his boots, and rolled into his blanket.

Kelsa was still struggling with this new information. "So you can shapeshift nonliving things, like money, but once the power that maintains it wears off, it turns back into leaves or whatever."

"That's right. Except once you've disrupted their molecular state to that extent things don't change back, they just disintegrate. In a few days nothing will be left of those bills but dust, and some bank clerk will come up short and blame it on an accounting error. They'll have no idea where the error came from, and no one will even be scolded for it—so stop worrying about counterfeiting and go to sleep. You've got a healing to do tomorrow."

He turned onto his side, away from her, and Kelsa slowly lay down beside him. "Disrupting molecular structures. You said what you did was magic."

"You say *potayto,* I say *potahto.* Get some sleep."

Easy for him to say. The leprechaun's wrinkled face had brought home to her that he really wasn't a boy—or even human—in a way that shifting into animal form hadn't. And magic might be a convenient label for what he did, but if it really was some form of alien physics . . . Aliens, enemy aliens, in her world, helping humanity destroy itself. It seemed more real to her now.

But human or not, he was her only chance to heal the leys. Humanity's only chance for survival? Remembering his flashing, untrustworthy smile, that thought made her blood run cold. But he had rescued her. He was trying to help, whatever he might be. Eventually, the sound of his even breathing lulled her into sleep.

o   o   o

It was still drizzling the next morning. They had to put the tent away wet, which might make it moldy eventually, but Raven didn't want to dry it, wasting energy he might need later. With tempcontrol bike gear to keep them warm and dry, the rain wasn't much of a hardship, though Kelsa was sorry when the low clouds obscured her view of the towering peaks.

The road that ran through Banff and into Jasper National Park was beautiful, even in the rain. For the most part it followed the chalky glacial rivers, and any break in the clouds revealed jagged mountains that took Kelsa's breath away.

Despite the distraction of a herd of bighorn sheep grazing right beside the road, they soon found themselves climbing up, mile after mile, into the peaks that held the ranger station that celebrated the Columbia Icefield.

"This is getting old," said Kelsa, looking at the crowded parking lot. "Are there any nexuses that aren't packed with tourists?"

"Don't worry," Raven told her. "There won't be nearly that many out on the ice. According to the park brochure, they only allow people to go onto the glacier from the buses the rangers run, but once we get up there we can wander off by ourselves. As long as they can't hear what you say, there's nothing for anyone to see except you dropping a pinch of dust. They won't even see that if you're careful."

"Unless the healing triggers an avalanche or something and kills us all."

But when they went into the building to sign up for the glacier bus, the clerk told them no buses were running that day. "The rain makes the ice too slippery," she said, with the firm smile of someone who'd been disappointing tourists all day. "Liability issues. You understand."

Kelsa did, but Raven was scowling. "Isn't there any way we could see the glacier up close? From a trail, or something?"

"Certainly," the clerk said. "There's a trail to the base of the glacier from this road here." She pulled out a map and showed them. "You can't go out on the ice, but you can go right up to it."

"Thanks." Raven turned to go. "That'll do."

"But it's raining," Kelsa told him. "Couldn't we do this another day? There are lots of glaciers in Alaska."

"There are," said Raven. "But we have to heal this one."

Kelsa frowned. "You said any lake would do. As long as it was the lake that was the essence of 'lake-liness' for me, any lake would work."

"But if you'll remember"—Raven was steering her toward the exit—"not just any cave would do. The Columbia Icefield carved the spine of this continent, and its meltwater flows into three oceans. This is the best glacier by far for the calling of ice. You don't have to stand on it. As long as you can drop the dust on it and touch it, reach out to it, you'll be fine."

"Three oceans? The Atlantic, the Pacific . . . ?"

"And the Arctic," said Raven. "Where we're going."

o   o   o

By the time they reached the parking lot below the glacier, *arctic* was beginning to feel like the right adjective.

They were high in the mountains now, and between the altitude, the rain, and the great ice floe above them, it was cold. Kelsa turned up her tempcontrols, then pulled out her therma knit and wrapped the sleeves around her head and ears.

"That looks ridiculous," Raven told her.

"At least I'm warm," Kelsa retorted. When he was in this form, it was almost impossible to think of him as anything but the boy he appeared to be. Surely he remained himself inside, whatever face he wore. "Maybe you could take some under-wear and wrap it—"

He pulled her out of the parking lot and up the trail without further ado. Having looked at the map in the ranger station, Kelsa was not surprised that the trail was all uphill, but its steepness and the altitude took her breath away.

The fine-ground glacial silt made for slippery mud where it coated the rocks, and the patches of hard-packed snow, with melting slush over the surface, were even more treacherous. Paths across the snowbanks had been carved by the feet of dozens of chattering tourists, who wanted to see the glacier up-close despite the persistent drizzle.

"This rain." Kelsa gestured to the ice field that filled the valley above them, its higher reaches vanishing into the mist. "Is there any chance your enemies sent it to keep us from reaching the glacier?"

Raven's brow creased in a thoughtful frown. "It's not impossible. They know as well as I do that this is a place of far-reaching power, and tinkering with weather systems just a little doesn't take much out of the ley. Making the weather do something completely unnatural, like a blizzard in the desert in July, would be different. But this kind of rain is so normal here that it's probably normal rain, and not my enemies at all. Don't be paranoid."

Kelsa sighed.

Higher and higher they went. Kelsa tried to think of words to summon up the essence of a glacier, but aside from *cold* nothing came to her. Several panting minutes later she reached the top of the slope. The glacier loomed before her, a rolling wall of white . . . with a line of orange plastic back-off tape stretched about twenty feet in front of it. A smiling female ranger was posted there to enforce order.

"Carp," she muttered. "I can't reach it after all."

"The clerk said we could go right up to it," Raven protested.

"This is right up to it, in glacier terms. If we try to cross that tape, the ranger will stop us."

It was a lower-tech barrier than Mr. Stattler's rabbit fence, but the simple presence of a human guard made it far more effective. Even if Kelsa was prepared to dart past the woman and fling the dust at the glacier, it wouldn't work. She needed to connect with the glacier before she could call it. And she wasn't in the mood for healing.

"We can't," she said. "We'll have to find some other ice field. There are plenty of glaciers in Alas—"

"What about that?" Raven gestured to their left. Several hundred yards down the glacier's front, a dip in the ground swallowed the tape for a while before it emerged on the other side. "If you were down there the ranger couldn't see you."

"Assuming it's more than three feet deep," Kelsa said. "Assuming there's not another ranger posted there."

"She's only here to keep people off the ice," Raven replied, in the confident tone that usually meant he was bluffing. "If we got up on the ice she could see that from here. I'll distract her."

He strolled toward a group of tourists, who were already distracting the ranger with questions.

Kelsa looked over the muddy debris field the glacier had left in its wake. Several other tourists were hiking along the glacier's face. They were another set of witnesses who might rat her out to the ranger, but their presence meant that people were allowed to wander in that area.

Swearing under her breath, Kelsa switched her com pod to record mode and made like a tourist, taking pictures of the glacier as she hiked over the rugged silty rocks.

Like the glacier itself, the dip was bigger than it had looked from a distance. Kelsa stared curiously, for this shallow trench was nothing like the water-cut gullies and canyons she was accustomed to, just a slightly deeper groove amid hundreds of others the glacier had carved into the mountain's stone. She couldn't see the ranger anymore, and no one else was in sight.

Heart pounding, since she was usually a law-abiding person, Kelsa scurried under the orange tape and up the glacier. Clearly others had taken advantage of this dip in the landscape, for there were words scratched in the dirty melting snow that covered the glacier's face: *Burt was here. Nicklaus and Gretta 2094.*

Kelsa could see nothing now but a wall of white curling away, for its top was far higher than her head. It didn't look very inspiring, but this dirty snowbank was just one branch of an ice field that could be seen from space, and that even now was carving away the peaks that towered around her.

Kelsa pulled out the medicine bag and untied the neck, then folded the top down to prevent it from spilling as she put it in her pocket. She stepped forward, trying to keep her feet out of the trickling stream that undercut the glacier's lip, and laid her hands in the half-melted snow that covered the ice.

She stilled her thoughts, pushing aside the embarrassment discovery would bring. Slowly her awareness stretched beyond the icy wall, into the immense depth and weight that lay behind this lacy outlier. The words welled sluggishly out of her subconscious.

"Carver of mountains. Source of rivers. Ice that carries the memories of our planet, carry this healing from the peaks you cut to the seas—be strong!"

Keeping one cold hand pressed against the ice, she pulled the bag from her pocket and dashed a wisp of sand onto the glacier.

The hard wall beneath her palm was still, but Kelsa felt the slow grinding power roll through her and shuddered with terror and joy.

Boom. Boom. Boom. The deep hollow voice of the cracking glacier echoed off granite peaks like cannon fire. *Boom. Boom.* More cracking, fainter, and then more, finally fading into the distance.

Kelsa pulled her hand away, smiling at the sight of the prints she'd left, at the knowledge that her mark on the glacier's face would do more good than Burt's had.

In moments she was back under the tape, clambering up the muddy rise till the ranger and the others came into view.

The tourists were exclaiming and waving their arms, much as they had in Craters. The ranger was explaining that it wasn't uncommon for glaciers to crack on a warm, rainy day, even multiple fracturing when the atmospheric conditions were right.

Raven stood at the edge of the crowd, grinning with the same delight Kelsa felt. In that moment, she could almost forgive him for the lies, for all the information his people had withheld.

Whatever the danger, surely this was worth it.

⚬ ⚬ ⚬

They'd been on the road that led down toward Jasper for only a few minutes when a traffic jam, caused by drivers on both sides of the road stopping to take pictures of a mother bear and her cub, brought the bike to a halt.

"The rangers say you shouldn't stop like that," Kelsa told Raven, watching the furry brown lumps. "The bears become accustomed to people and cars, and that endangers both them and the people."

In her heart she found it hard to blame the drivers. If she'd been closer, she'd be taking pictures too.

"You did well back there," Raven said. "I didn't think a human could have that kind of aptitude for calling."

Kelsa's tentative forgiveness vanished in a wave of annoyance. "Do you have any idea how condescending that sounds? Maybe humans have more going for them than you think they do."

His species might have some abilities hers didn't, but they weren't better *people*. In some ways they were worse!

"I don't think so," Raven said. "There have always been a handful of humans who could work the leys, but never more than a few. It took me forever to find you. You're quite astonishing, for a human."

Was this his way of trying to be nice? Kelsa sighed.

"It was harder with the glacier," she admitted. "I know it's bigger than the part I could see, but it didn't look very inspiring. I mean, it's really just a big chunk of ice."

Raven snorted. "Look back."

Kelsa turned to look at the mountains behind her, and her breath caught. Three gleaming rivers of ice poured down the rugged slope. Kelsa knew glaciers were one of the heaviest forces on the planet, but they seemed to float above the roughness of the earth, white and ethereal.

She didn't turn away till the cars behind her began to honk, because now she was the one blocking traffic. She stopped smiling, for the fragile, ephemeral beauty of something so solid that it ground mountains to dust had sobered her.

Humans had almost destroyed the great glaciers, though they were growing again, and the sea level was coming back down. Raven's contempt for humanity might not be so misplaced. And right or wrong, his enemies now knew exactly where Kelsa had been.

It was time to move on. Her hands were cold again as she put the bike in motion.

CHAPTER 9

THERE WAS A TRAIN IN Jasper. It was a bigger town than Lake Louise, and even more beautiful, but once a late lunch had satisfied his teen-boy appetite, Raven was interested only in leaving.

"It's perfect," he told Kelsa. "We can take the train all the way to"—he peered at the schedule board—"Prince Rupert. It's the last thing they'd expect us to do because all that steel and the magnetic current will take us out of contact with both nature and the ley."

"We can't take the train," Kelsa said. "Even in Canada they'll check our PID cards before they sell us a ticket. A PID that, in case you haven't noticed, you don't have. And officially, I'm not even in this country!"

"I know." He sounded insufferably smug. "That's why I picked this up."

He held out a Canadian ID card belonging to Robert Winslow, who judging by the photo, was a heavyset man in his forties.

"You stole . . ." Of course he'd stolen it. And it wouldn't do any good to protest, because he wouldn't care. "But you don't look . . ." And that didn't matter either. He'd look just like

Robert Winslow when he bought the ticket. "What will you do when Robert reports his card stolen? The police can stop this train, and there you'll be, stuck."

He could abandon her and fly, but she'd prefer not to be abandoned now that his enemies knew where she was. The bikers might not be able to get here for several days, but who knew what other human tools they could use.

"He won't report it stolen until it disappears," Raven said. "If he tried to use it, the scanner strip wouldn't work. It only looks like it should, which is why I kept the real card. But Robert Winslow lives here, so he won't have to use it. We've got three or four days before it vanishes, and by that time—"

"We'll be in Prince Rupert. But what about me?"

"Robert can buy a ticket for his niece, as well."

Kelsa scowled. In the U.S. that wouldn't work, but Canadians were so casual about security that here it might.

"I can't afford it," Kelsa told him. "No matter what the tickets cost. Not to mention shipping my bike along with us."

"I can." Raven pulled out his wad of bills. "This will last a few more days, and when it goes I'll make more."

"But that's . . ." Kelsa didn't want to use the counterfeit money herself. Even if it only hurt some bank that could easily take the loss, it was stealing.

But her debit account was almost empty. If she was going to reach Alaska, she had to use Raven's money. Surely healing the planet, preventing the tree plague's destruction of the northern forests, was more important?

Her father had hated that kind of argument. He'd said that worse evils were committed by people who believed that the end justified the means than by people who were flat-out evil.

Kelsa's father was dead. Dead of a growing cancer epidemic that the doctors couldn't explain. If healing the leys kept that from happening again, to anyone, then she didn't give a damn about some bank's balance sheet.

She let Raven purchase her ticket and shipping for her bike in silence.

While he ducked into a men's room to change back into himself, Kelsa stowed her bike in the baggage compartment, strapping it to the rack the porter showed her. Then she went to find their seats, claiming the window before Raven returned. The seats in this car were intended for overnight occupation— wide, comfortable, and fully reclining. Looking at her ticket Kelsa saw that they would reach Prince Rupert at midafternoon tomorrow.

"You should have told me we'd be on the train all night. I'd have gotten my toothbrush off the bike, and some other things too."

"You'll survive," Raven said. The train car shuddered and began to move. "And this will throw anyone trying to trace us by magic completely off our trail. By human means as well," he added. "Though it should take some time before your bikers can catch up with us."

Kelsa glanced around. There weren't many other passengers, and no one was sitting near them. Still . . .

"You might not want to use that *m*-word quite so freely. And they're not my bikers. I can't believe the clerk didn't insist on seeing my PID at the ticket center. Or at the province border, or even when—"

Her com pod chirped. Kelsa jumped and pulled it out of her shirt, along with the medicine bag.

Her home com address. Her mother. Kelsa hadn't checked in for . . . how long now? Thank goodness her mother hadn't called Aunt Sarabeth's apartment! She might yet if Kelsa didn't pick up.

She cast a furious glance behind her. A train was a train, and her aunt was always talking about taking Chicago's famous L. Kelsa narrowed the focus so her mother wouldn't be able to see much except her face and opened on the fifth chirp.

"Hi, Mom."

"Kelsa!" Her mother's face appeared on the small screen. She looked tidy and relaxed, better than she had when Kelsa had seen her last. Her life probably was easier, since she didn't have to fight with her daughter all the time.

"How are you doing with Sarabeth?" her mother asked. "Are you having a good time?"

"I'm doing better than I expected," Kelsa said truthfully— sort of. "It's been interesting."

Her mother squinted. "Are you on a bus? It doesn't—"

"The L," Kelsa said, abandoning the truth. "I'm going downtown to meet Aunt Sarabeth, and she's going to take me around some museums. Art and . . . and stuff."

She knew Chicago had an art museum. It was another of the things her aunt had talked about.

"That doesn't sound like something you'd care for," her mother said curiously. "But you look good. Better than when you left."

"I'm checking out the city lifestyle," Kelsa said uncomfortably. "It's different, but interesting. Museums are part of it. Or at least, that's what Aunt S. says."

Her mother was squinting again. "What's that around your neck? It doesn't look like something Sarabeth would buy you."

Kelsa's hand rose guiltily toward the medicine pouch, and she forced it down. "There was a folk art show when we first got here. I . . . uh, my stop's coming up. I'll call you in a week or so. I'd like to stay here longer, if that's OK?"

"Of course. I'm glad you're enjoying yourself."

Was that relief flashing over her mother's face?

"I am," Kelsa told her. "I'll call you again in a few days. Say hi to Joby for me. Bye."

Her mother barely had time to say "Bye" before Kelsa cut the connection. Her stomach was quaking. Her heart ached too. Someday, she and her mother would have to get past this . . . this wall between them. Because even now, lying to her mother made her feel worse than defrauding the bank.

"Excellent," said Raven, who'd had the sense to keep silent. "You'll need at least another two weeks to finish the healing."

"Yeah," said Kelsa grimly. "I'm doing great. I'm lying to my family. I'm in Canada . . ." There had to be some security in the train cars, even in Canada, and *illegally* was the kind of word security computers screened for. "And a bunch of angry people are chasing me. I'm fabulous."

"You're also helping to save your planet, making up for centuries of human folly. Doesn't that matter more?"

"Yes." But her heart still ached.

The train had left the town behind while she talked to her mother, and Kelsa gazed out the window as a curving mountain canyon gave way to a long straight river canyon, and eventually to rolling hills.

The new forests, replacing those that had been destroyed in the beetle epidemics at the beginning of the century, teemed with life. Kelsa spotted five bears grazing on the grasses and roots that grew beside the tracks, and deer, and a pair of geese trailed by half a dozen fluffy goslings.

Lakes, no longer full of glacial silt, glowed royal blue. The flatter land between the hills was covered with meadows and hay fields.

"This is the area where I'd intended for you to call on water," Raven told her. "As you see, there are plenty of lakes."

Had he been here before? His expression, as he gazed at the sunset glow reflected on the shimmering waves, showed only appreciation for its beauty. No nostalgia. No regret.

"What was the Native name for this area?" Kelsa asked.

"In which language? There were a dozen names, though several of them translated to something like Land of Waters. Not very imaginative. What do they call it now?"

Kelsa pulled out her com pod and brought up a map. "The Lake District."

Raven laughed.

It never got completely dark. Unaccustomed to sleeping on a train, Kelsa kept waking to look out the window. Even at 2 a.m. a dim gray light suffused the landscape.

The sun rose as early as it had set late, and she woke with it, rumpled, stiff, and even more annoyed that she hadn't been warned to get her toothbrush out of her pack.

"Excellent," said Raven, as she moved her seatback upright and glared at him. "We're almost there."

Kelsa looked out the window. Snowcapped peaks reared up to the west and north. It didn't look like they were approaching the sea. Besides . . . "The ticket says we're not supposed to reach Prince Rupert till two thirty in the afternoon. It's only—"

"It's Smithers," said Raven. "We're getting off here."

○ ○ ○

Kelsa was still furious when they got the bike out of the luggage compartment. "I understand that you bought tickets for Prince Rupert to confuse anyone who tries to check up on us, but you should have told *me*."

The compartment reeked of cheap perfume, as if someone had recently broken a full bottle. The strong scent made Kelsa sneeze, and Raven broke into a coughing fit and backed out of the car, leaving her to remove the bike on her own. Typical.

"I realize that the truth means nothing to you," Kelsa went on grimly. "But I *need* to know where we're going. In case we get separated, if nothing else. Not to mention trust, or honesty, or respec—"

"Can I drive?" Raven was breathing deeply in the fresh air. A single towering peak loomed over Smithers, and the sun gleamed on his dark hair.

In his black biker gear, he could have posed for the cover of a teen-girl flimsy, and despite all she knew about him Kelsa's will began to soften. "Do your powers give you the ability to do something without having to learn how?"

He cocked one eyebrow. "Powers?"

"You know what I mean. Do you have some magical way to know how to do something without learning to do it?"

"I like that. Powers."

Kelsa waited.

"No," he admitted. "But I'm tired of—"

"Under no circumstances are you driving."

o   o   o

The road north from Smithers took them up the deep-carved granite of the Buckley River Gorge. The place where Kelsa pulled over so they could eat breakfast perched above a spot where several fallen boulders compressed the river into a rushing cataract.

She brought out the peanut butter. "Next time we're going to remember to stop in town, and spend some of your counterfeit money on rolls and a sausage."

Raven gazed down at the rocky platform with an odd, remembering expression.

"The people who once lived here, they fished for salmon off those rocks. It was a huge gathering, drawing tribes, families, from miles around. They'd work like mad all day, catching, gutting, and curing fish, then feast and party around the fires."

Kelsa looked down at the tumble of boulders. She could almost see a crowd of dark-haired people working there. People her cultural ancestors had wiped out.

A pang of collective guilt struck her, and she sighed. "They were better guardians of the planet than we were."

"Not really," said Raven. "They just didn't have enough technology to do serious damage. Humans are all—"

He stopped, but it was too late.

"Children? Idiots? I'm getting tired of this attitude of yours. I'll concede that we didn't do a great job taking care of things, but we had no way to know the leys existed! And your people did nothing to help. Instead of frolicking around, pretending to be spirits and saints and things, you should have—"

"It's not our job to take care of *your* world." His face darkened with real anger—and maybe a hint of the same kind of guilt Kelsa had just been feeling? "You're the ones who had to half destroy this world's climate before you woke up and realized you could die too!"

"And you," Kelsa shot back, "treated this world as your . . . I was going to say playground, but playpen is more like it! You'd come here and get drunk, and get worshiped—Yes, I figured out that you've been gods as well. And that any legendary artifact that mysteriously vanished was probably your doing. So you got worshiped, and got laid, and played with us like toys, and never bothered to tell us about things that you could see and we couldn't! So don't give me any carpo about how inferior humans are, you irresponsible jerk!"

They quarreled about responsibility and lies all through breakfast, and the rain that started falling as they neared the beginning of the Cassiar Highway put the cap on Kelsa's bad mood.

She turned off at the junction, then stopped to read the running neon script of the road sign: "Cassiar Hwy. repaving for magneto-electric drive. Off-road vehicles only, between Iskut and Good Hope Lake."

"Wonderful," Kelsa muttered.

"We're driving, no, *you're* driving an off-road vehicle," said Raven coldly. "What's the problem?"

He had been crazy enough to compare his people's failure to teach humanity about the leys to her trivial—and justified!—refusal to teach him to drive the bike. And he evidently wasn't prepared to let it go. Which was fine with Kelsa.

"You've never been on a road they're repaving, have you? It'll be a mess."

Raven shrugged. "This is the only road that runs anywhere near the ley." He sounded as if he blamed her for that too.

"All right." Kelsa sighed. "But don't say I didn't warn you."

∘ ∘ ∘

The first section of the Cassiar Highway was newly paved, and it would have been gorgeous if the rain had lifted enough for them to see the mountains that surrounded them.

"Are you sure this rain wasn't sent by your enemies?" Kelsa slowed for a curve that gleamed with water, even in the dim light.

"Look at the vegetation." The words *you idiot* hung in the air between them. "It rains here most of the time."

It was probably true. The lush forest around her was full of moss and ferns, more like the coastal rain forests of Washington and Oregon than the dry woods of the Rockies.

They rode on and on, stopping for lunch at a pullout overlooking a lake whose water was the limpid blue of a tropical lagoon, even under cloudy skies.

Soon after they passed Iskut and started up to Gnat Pass, the drizzle began to let up, the forest grew drier . . . and the road disintegrated. The smooth surface of magneto-repellant asphalt gave way to a patchwork of repaved and unpaved potholes—and even that was better than the places where the road had been taken up to lay the charge bars that would keep the surface live once they were installed. Now, stretches of rock-strewn dirt appeared every few hundred yards—usually right after a blind curve, so Kelsa didn't have time to slow down for them.

She reduced her speed to a crawl, but the bike still kicked and lurched beneath her, and Raven's arms were tight around her waist. At least he'd stopped asking to drive.

Gnat Pass, 1,241 feet according to the sign, felt like timberline back home. The scattered pines were stunted and twisted.

Kelsa slowed to look at them, and when the road needed all her attention, brought the bike to a stop. There wasn't enough traffic to worry about.

"The tree plague hasn't made it this far north, has it?"

Some things were more important than offended pride.

"No." Raven's voice was calmer too. "A thousand feet is pretty high, this far north."

Kelsa remembered the map she'd looked at on the train. Gnat Pass . . . "We're almost to the Yukon." Her voice was hushed with awe. She'd never expected to get that far, not really. She set the bike in motion once more.

"You sound surprised," Raven said critically. "You've driven almost every foot of—"

Perhaps it was fortunate that at that moment the bike heaved up like a bucking bull. Kelsa's teeth slammed together, but she managed to stay on her seat and keep the bike upright as they rolled to a stop. She kicked down the stand and looked.

"Carp." She could see where the tire had ruptured, a long split in the groove of the tread. "There's no way to patch that. We need a new tire."

They had to walk the bike for over an hour before an old-fashioned pickup truck pulled up behind them, though on closer inspection, it wasn't so much old-fashioned as simply old. The driver's broad, high-cheekboned face looked like a mature version of Raven's, but when Raven spoke to the driver in some rippling tongue, the man looked blank and answered in English.

He was very kind, not only offering them a ride but helping them drag the bike up onto his truck, a process that left Kelsa exhausted and all of them smeared with mud. The driver not only took them all the way to Deese Lake, but also dropped them off at Charlie's Garage and Salvage Yard, and called Charlie on his own com pod to bring him out to make the repairs—even though the garage had closed over an hour ago.

"I don't mind coming in." Charlie was a hard-muscled man in his fifties, with pale eyes and the weathered skin of a man who mostly worked outdoors. "I was just watching d-vid, and I can always use the business."

To Kelsa it looked like everyone in Deese Lake needed business. The town advertised itself as a resort for off-roaders, but it appeared to be a bit too far off the road. Almost a quarter of the buildings along the main street were closed, and those that were open had the rough, untidy look of a town on the edge. At least a town that could be reached only by off-road vehicles had a wide selection of tires.

Charlie plugged her bike into a flash charger while he replaced the shattered tire with a new one, and he was balancing it when the charge finished. When the bike was back on the ground, good as new, he wiped his hands and said, "That comes to $217.58, with tax."

Raven had already reached into his pocket, and Kelsa saw the blank expression sweep over his face. He controlled it before it turned to panic, but she knew what had happened. His counterfeit money had poofed, just like he'd said it would.

Kelsa's heart began to pound, but her mind was clear. She was already reaching for her charge card, but she had less than a hundred dollars left in her account. Raven had some real money, but it wouldn't be nearly enough. Charlie might be willing to leave his d-vid to help them, but he wouldn't let them abandon a bill that large half paid.

He would call the police.

Kelsa met Raven's eyes. She pulled her hand out of her pocket, empty, and he nodded. Charlie would call the police, and Raven had another man's ID in his pocket and no way to shapeshift to match that card. Kelsa was in this country illegally, a fact the police would certainly check, no matter how slack Canadian security seemed to her.

"I'll have to charge it." Raven's smile, the charming one, flashed at Charlie. "Where's your reader?"

Kelsa knew what she had to do, but regret pulsed through her as Raven pulled Charlie toward the back of the shop, and she quietly straddled the bike and rolled it out of the repair bay.

It was a rotten way to repay Charlie for helping them, and guilt clutched at her as she keyed the motor to life. Charlie's startled shout rang in her ears as the bike sped off into the northern dusk.

She would pay him back, eventually. She'd borrow the cash from her mother and spend the rest of her life working it off if she had to. With interest.

A shapeshifter could always get out of jail, and Kelsa couldn't.

If she was arrested, the healing would end. Even if Raven could find someone else to help him, the police would confiscate something as unusual as her medicine bag, and probably destroy its contents making sure it really was dirt, and not some new illegal drug.

Kelsa was doing the right thing. It only felt like theft, and abandoning a partner in trouble.

Sometimes towns like Deese Lake weren't even part of the security grid, but Kelsa got well outside it before she pulled off the road into a picnic area, and then into a deep grove where no one could see her from either the road or the air.

Raven could find her; she had no doubt about that. He would sense the magic of the medicine bag or her presence through the ley, or find her the same way ravens located their prey. Then they'd cut across country to avoid the roadblocks the police would set up ahead of them.

All Kelsa had to do was wait. She didn't expect him to show up before morning, at the earliest. But only a few hours later the bushes rustled, and a large otter waddled into the glade and began to change, broadening, thickening, till a naked elderly woman raised her graying head and regarded Kelsa with dancing brown eyes.

This wasn't Raven. Kelsa was reaching for a rock when the woman's laugh pealed out, warm and merry.

"I shouldn't laugh. You're right to be wary, my girl. But I'm the one who's going to help you heal the ley between here and the Alaska border. Because it's going to be hard for that reckless boy to travel in Canada for a while, now isn't it?"

CHAPTER 10

LAUGH LINES CRINKLED AROUND THE old woman's eyes, though she rose to her feet with an ease that belied the sagging breasts and wrinkled skin. The warmth in her expression reminded Kelsa of her grandmother, who now lived in D.C., but who'd made cookies with her, played d-games, and still sent exactly the right presents at Christmas.

The old woman clearly had Raven pegged. Kelsa let go of the rock.

"Raven sent you?"

"Of course. He had to give me the sense of that medicine pouch, or I wouldn't have been able to locate you. And heedless as he may sometimes be, he knows it's not safe for you to travel alone."

Relief flooded in. Kelsa hadn't wanted to admit how frightened she'd been. "He said he had allies, but he never told me who they were. Will he be able to get away from the police?"

"If that isn't like him." The old woman shook her head. "Raven's heart's in the right place, most of the time, but I wonder about his head! Suppose you got separated, like now? Suppose you needed help? You need to know who his allies are."

Kelsa couldn't have agreed more.

"Eagle and I are foremost among them," the old woman went on. "And Fox, Salamander, and Wolverine. I'm Otter Woman, though you've probably guessed that already."

The woman seemed completely unconscious of her nudity, but the wrinkled skin was beginning to show goose bumps. She looked to be about Kelsa's size, and while therma knit and rainwear weren't as good as tempcontrol bike gear, they were much better than nothing.

"Raven's way too arrogant." Kelsa dug into the bike's pack. "I kept telling him I could work better if I had information. But he will be able to get away, right?"

"Of course," the old woman assured her. "But it might take a while. He could shapeshift through those bars anytime, but before he does that he'll have to dominate one of those policemen into turning off the security cameras—and that's not something they'd ordinarily do. I expect he'll catch up with us sometime after we cross into Alaska. But you still have the catalyst, don't you?"

"Of course." Kelsa handed Otter Woman a stack of clothing, then pulled out the medicine pouch to show her.

After a blink of surprise the old woman began to put on the shirt. "Well, I'm glad Raven wasn't carrying it! That would stop us right here. Would you like me to keep it safe for you? If we lost that little bag . . ."

Catastrophe. But Kelsa had been carrying the pouch for so long, she was reluctant to give it up. The control-freak side of her, but still . . .

"Raven said carrying it would make it easier for me to use," she said. "And after all, he's the one who ended up in jail! But

I'm glad he won't be there long. I wouldn't like to leave him in trouble, even if he is an arrogant jerk."

The old woman's warm laugh rang out once more. "I'd have said 'arrogant young fool.' But as for leaving him, he's the one who sent me to guide you until he can rejoin us. So don't feel badly about leaving him behind. You look exhausted, poor girl. The police have set their trap on the road ahead—they're not looking for you until just before Hope Lake. We can camp right here tonight."

∘ ∘ ∘

Not having lived on it for over a week, Otter Woman dug into peanut butter and crackers with relish. "This nut stuff is very nourishing. I've never eaten it before. And you'll need the energy, my girl. We've got to go a long way back for the tree calling."

"Back?" Kelsa, who'd been folding up the tent, turned to stare. "I can't go back through Deese Lake; the police may be looking for me. Why should we go back?"

"I can take you around the town," the old woman told her. "But we've got to go back. The best place to call on trees, and all the living green of this world, lies on the other side of that . . . what is it called, Bug Pass? There are other places along the ley where you could call on trees, but the ancient grove is . . . well, it's special. I can't think why Raven took you past it."

"We were arguing." Kelsa fought down a pang of guilt. "He may have thought I couldn't focus, or something."

"Perhaps that's it." The old woman nodded wisely. "But it's still the best place for the calling of trees, so back we go. Don't worry about the police. As I said, they're not looking on the road yet."

Kelsa wondered how she knew. Perhaps this Eagle was scouting for her, or some other ally. Unlike Raven, Otter Woman would be smart enough to accept help. Still . . .

"I'd rather keep moving north," Kelsa said. "If we go back, it will give those bikers more time to catch up."

Her skin crawled at the thought. The old woman might be smarter than Raven, but fighting against a biker gang, Kelsa would rather have a strong young man on her side. Of course, Otter Woman might be able to be a strong young man if she chose to.

"The bikers? Oh." Angry contempt swept over the wrinkled face. "Don't concern yourself with those useless creatures. They're probably still groaning over their hurts and hiding their precious drugs on the other side of the border. They're no match for me."

Raven wasn't the only one with an arrogant streak, but in this case Kelsa found it reassuring. "Well, if the best nexus is behind us . . . All right. How are we going to get around Deese Lake?"

o   o   o

It turned out to be easier than Kelsa expected, though it took a long time. The old woman guided her for almost a mile through the brush-choked tangling woods to a fishing trail that followed the Cottonwood River, and then ran along the far shore of Deese Lake itself. It was even slower going than the potholed road, but Kelsa was accustomed to wrestling her bike over mountain trails. She was almost sorry when, in the late afternoon, the old woman instructed her to turn onto one of the paths that led back to the Cassiar Highway.

Kelsa rode back up the other side of Gnat Pass, taking the stretch where she'd blown out her tire at a cautious crawl.

It felt wonderful to reach the place where the new paving began, to increase speed till the wind tugged at her clothes, and to sweep around the curves. For once, the road was dry.

It was just past dinnertime when the old woman tapped her shoulder.

"Slow down!" Her voice was as thin as a bird's, and she shouted over the wind. "We're almost there."

Kelsa slowed obediently. There was still no traffic to speak of.

The small white sign, Ancient Forest Trail, was so unobtrusive Kelsa wasn't surprised she'd missed it before.

There wasn't even a paved parking area beyond the shoulder, but a swath of rocky earth had been graded out of the base of the hill, and Kelsa pulled the bike over and stopped.

It wasn't raining, but when she took her helmet off the air was soft with moisture, caressing her skin like Joby's baby fingers. Her hair would frizz up like a clown's in this much humidity. Stupid as it seemed, she was glad Raven wouldn't be there to see it.

The old woman dismounted the bike with the same surprising grace with which she'd ridden all day. She hadn't demanded to drive, either.

"This small forest has never been cut." Otter Woman gestured to a rugged-looking trail that ran up the slope. "It's not large, just a cleft in the hillside. I suppose it was too steep for them. A few years ago one of your nature tribes took control of the land and forbade anyone to cut the trees. Some of them are almost a thousand years old."

"How do you know all that?" Kelsa asked curiously.

Otter Woman looked surprised. "It's on another sign." She pointed up the trail.

Raven would have pretended some mystic source of knowledge, or at least been amused by such a literal answer, and Kelsa felt a flash of regret for his absence. Not that she missed him. And he should be back soon, anyway.

An uphill scramble from the road brought them to the top of a small rise, where a more or less flat plateau held a large sign that confirmed the old woman's information. It also displayed a trail map with three loops.

"Which one do we take?" Kelsa asked.

Otter Woman shrugged. "Whichever holds a tree that speaks to you. That's what's needed."

Kelsa turned back to the sign, waving off the mosquitoes clustering around her. Thank goodness her father had insisted on keeping her repellant shots up-to-date.

"Big Tree Loop sounds promising."

"Then Big Tree Loop it is," Otter Woman said. "You go first."

This forest had survived because its slopes were too steep to log, so it was no surprise that the trail was steep too. Steps cut out of fallen logs and wobbling rocks alternated with flat patches, where plank bridges kept Kelsa's feet out of the bog. Even though they wouldn't bite, the mosquitoes were attracted to her body heat and swarmed around whenever Kelsa stopped to catch her breath. She noticed that they didn't bother Otter Woman either, but that was no surprise.

There were more open places than Kelsa had expected. Places where some ancient giant had crashed down, letting in swaths of sunlight that glowed on the ferns and the floating, thorny beauty of devil's club.

Crude wooden signs marked forks in the trail. Almost any of the towering cedars, whose ribboned bark ran up hundreds of feet before the lacy foliage appeared, would have done as far as Kelsa was concerned.

She was beginning to tire when she spotted three huge trees standing together. Kelsa stopped, bending her neck till she could see the sunlit branches far above—all healthy, as far as she could tell. When she stepped off the trail, the damp loam of the forest floor bounced under her feet like the floor in a really good gym.

The forest wasn't silent. Water trickled through a dozen streams, mosquitoes hummed, and wind sifted through the branches above. But its soul was utterly still, with the quiet aliveness of trees.

"Here," Kelsa said. "This will do."

The old woman nodded. Kelsa untied the neck of the medicine bag, and then folded it into her pocket.

In Raven's presence, she might have felt silly performing the obeisance to trees her father had taught her. But she thought the old woman would understand, and she swept her hands up and around, ending in a deep bow.

"Greetings, your majesty."

The cedar's spirit felt different from that of the great cottonwood back home—older, more self-contained, but not unfriendly.

Kelsa laid her hands on the smooth bark. Despite a level of humidity that made her sinuses run, it felt dry under her palms.

For trees, the words came to her easily.

"Child of time, watching the ages pass. Part of the life that breathes for all the earth, breathe for us now. Heal and be strong."

She cast a generous pinch of sand over the tree, then replaced her hand against the cool trunk. The scent of cedar and wet green life filled her lungs. Kelsa's sense of the forest's spirit was as strong and deep as ever . . . and nothing changed.

No welling of power. No surge of reaction. Nothing.

Kelsa turned to the old woman, dismayed.

"Is this the wrong tree? I didn't feel anything. No ley power at all."

Astonishment swept over Otter Woman's face. "You can sense the ley? Raven didn't tell me that."

Raven, who'd been so surprised by her ability to feel the blast of power through the nexus, hadn't mentioned it to his allies? Raven, who'd taken Kelsa right past this place. Raven, who hadn't tracked them down in a full night and day in a form he could take safely even in Canada.

Cold certainty swept over Kelsa. This forest wasn't on the ley at all, and Otter Woman had brought her back here deliberately.

She wasn't Raven's ally. She was the enemy.

CHAPTER 11

Kelsa's pulse thundered in her ears. "I must have picked the wrong tree." She looked into the woods, concealing her expression as her mind raced.

"Most humans can't sense the leys at all." The old woman's voice was thoughtful, and so cold that Kelsa shivered. She couldn't just deny it, but . . .

"I was almost certain I felt something, at least once. But I have to admit, the other times it was hard to be sure, and Raven had to confirm I'd done it. Did you feel anything?"

"No." The warm brown eyes searched her face. Raven had never been good at reading human emotions. Kelsa could only pray his enemies were worse.

"Raven did say some nexuses would be quieter than others," Kelsa went on. "Maybe you could pick out the right tree?"

"Maybe I could." The old woman turned and led the way farther up the trail. She stopped five minutes later, at a tree with a sign in front of it: Big Tree.

Kelsa remembered Raven's comments about unimaginative human names, and fought down a pang of fear and loneliness.

"All right," she said with a bright smile. "This time I'll try harder."

She pressed her hands against the tree, inhaling deep breaths of the damp air, taking a minute to think. Assuming she succeeded in bluffing her way past this moment, then what? Since Otter Woman hadn't simply killed Kelsa or stolen the medicine bag while she slept, Kelsa had to conclude the rules still applied. So if the enemies wanted to keep Raven from rejoining her, they'd have to use the tools of this world to hold him, which meant he was probably still in a cell in Deese Lake. How they were keeping him there Kelsa had no idea, but she knew where to start.

And she didn't dare stall much longer.

"Child of time, watching the ages pass . . ."

Kelsa repeated the incantation like a prayer, with all her heart in it, then cast a pinch of the precious dust over the tree trunk. This time the lack of response didn't surprise her. She pasted a hopeful expression on her face and turned to Otter Woman. "Did it work? I thought I felt something that time, but I wasn't sure."

The suspicious gaze searched Kelsa's face once more, then the old woman nodded. "Yes, you got it right that time. The ley is healed and we can move on."

"Good!" Kelsa tried not to overreact, but it was hard. A human would have realized that she was lying. Otter Woman simply started down the trail toward the road.

Kelsa followed, her gaze darting around for a club-size stick or even a convenient rock, but the wet verdant forest didn't produce much in the way of weapons. Even if she found something . . . In their human form shapeshifters had human weaknesses. If Raven had been knocked out when she pushed him into the river, he'd have drowned. Kelsa's father had been careful to point out that the d-vid version of knocking someone unconscious, where they were out for a few hours and then suffered nothing worse than a headache, was pure fiction. If you hit someone hard enough to knock them out, you stood a good chance of killing them. That might be less true of a shapeshifter, but it was probably more true of someone who wore the body of an elderly woman. Kelsa might be willing to defraud a bank, but murdering an old lady—or even a being who looked like an old lady—wasn't something she could do.

Then how could she escape? Just running was out. If Otter Woman couldn't shift into something that could fly, she had friends who could. In human form they had human weaknesses. They got hungry, thirsty, tired. Would they react like a human to human drugs?

By the time they reached the bike, she had a tentative plan.

"Since we're close to Smithers," Kelsa said, "would you mind if we went back there and did some shopping? We're getting low on food, Raven will have to leave his bike gear in a jail cell, and you're going to need some for yourself before we go much farther. According to the map the next big town is Whitehorse, and that's too far."

And going south, to Smithers, would take Kelsa farther away from Alaska. At least this time they were trying to lure her off the path instead of killing her.

If they managed to separate her and Raven permanently, they'd win.

Volunteering to head south again, at least for a short time, was the right move. Otter Woman's bright gaze was less suspicious now. "That sounds sensible. As long as it won't delay us too long. You have a world to save, my girl."

That last sentence was probably the first true thing the old woman had said. Kelsa gave her truth in return.

"Don't worry about that. I finish what I start. Always."

∘ ∘ ∘

Raven had said that his enemies hadn't looked in on this world lately. Kelsa made a mental list of the things she'd need, most of which, praise God, probably hadn't existed when Otter Woman last dealt with the human race.

Kelsa received confirmation of that theory when they pulled into Smithers after sunset. The old woman stared at the blazing lights and teeming streets of the small city with astonishment, and something very like dismay.

Kelsa smiled grimly. "I hope you've got money."

Otter Woman did, and Kelsa didn't ask how she'd acquired it. For dinner she dragged her companion into a restaurant with live music. Loud live music. By the time they reached the parking lot, the megastore was open for only two more hours.

There was nothing unusual about the store by Kelsa's standards, but Otter Woman gazed in fascinated shock at the array of goods for sale. Kelsa loaded the glide cart with clothes, including a set of Otter Woman–size bike gear, before hurrying on to the grocery section.

It might be a while before she had another chance to shop, so she stocked up on camping food, including a careful selection of self-heating soups. Cosmetics were more challenging, but by now the old woman was accustomed to watching Kelsa throw things into the cart.

"Cosmetics?" She was staring at a selection of stick-on face gems. The card she was watching rotated slowly through all the colors of the spectrum. The card next to it flashed alternately silver and midnight blue. "Makeup?"

"And sunblock," said Kelsa, tossing in the darkest foundation she could find. "To keep me from getting sunburned in these long days. And soap and shampoo." And small packets of temp hair color, black, and a bottle of clear brown nail polish, because she couldn't think of a better way to alter her PID.

By the time Kelsa swept into the pharmacy section, Otter Woman was so numb she hardly bothered to ask.

"Vitamins. Also, I have some allergies."

One packet of capsules looked very much like another, after all.

Kelsa had Otter Woman put on her bike gear in the parking lot while Kelsa unpacked the shopping cart into the bike's packs. They bulged when she finished, too full for aerodynamics or passenger comfort, but that wouldn't last long.

The last thing she did before leaving Smithers was to flash charge her bike. "We can't stay in a hotel," she told Otter Woman. "Not unless you have an ID card that lets me be here legally. And one for you as well."

"If Raven was half as smart as he thinks he is, he'd have provided some," the old woman snapped. "I'm tired. We'll camp in the first open place outside this noisy city."

Kelsa didn't argue. If she was careful, she could make the trip to Deese Lake last a full day.

They both slept late in the morning. Otter Woman presumably because she was tired, and Kelsa because the longer she pretended to sleep the less time she'd have to kill.

First, she had to escape from Otter Woman. After that, her plans were more vague—and even the thought of pursuing those vague plans made her heart pound. It was one thing to lie to her mother, run away from home, even to run the border. It was another thing entirely to break someone out of jail.

The paved road gave her no excuses to slow down, though she managed longish stops for breakfast and lunch, where she demonstrated the use of the self-heating cans.

"They're convenient," Otter Woman admitted, finishing the low-sodium potato soup. "But it's not very tasty. I liked peanut butter better."

It had been the blandest thing Kelsa could find. "You can have peanut butter too." She held out the jar. "And I'll open a better can for dinner tonight."

Once she hit the unpaved road, Kelsa started to take her time.

"Didn't you go over these bumps faster yesterday?" Otter Woman complained.

"I was trying to get away from Deese Lake as fast as I could," Kelsa told her. "The last time I came up this road I blew a tire—that's what got us into trouble in the first place. I don't dare risk that again."

They ended up camping on the other side of Gnat Pass, less than ten miles from Deese Lake. It was only six in the evening, and it would still be light for almost four hours, but after two scant meals Kelsa was hungry. "And I don't want to start biking through the woods, or even over the lake trail, with only a few hours before dusk," she told the old woman firmly.

Otter Woman shrugged. "I don't mind stopping here. On a bouncy road, hanging on to that bike of yours is more tiring than riding a horse."

"I wouldn't know," Kelsa said. "I've never ridden a horse."

"Never?"

They chatted as Kelsa fixed dinner—which didn't take long with crackers and self-heating cans of spicy chili.

She had no idea how the sleeping capsules would taste, but even if the strong flavors of the chili didn't mask them, Otter Woman probably wouldn't know the difference.

Her body shielded the cans from the old woman as she popped the tops. She used one of the strong, ecoplastic lids to slice open the capsules and dumped the powdery contents into one of the cans. Two pills was a normal adult dose. Kelsa doubled it, for Otter Woman had to fall deeply asleep. If two were perfectly safe, surely four wouldn't kill her?

Kelsa was breathing faster as she stirred the chili, mixing the heated contents, mixing in the drug. She handed the old woman the drugged can and a spoon, hoping her smile didn't look as fake as it felt.

"This isn't as boring as the one you had for lunch."

She took a bite herself, watching with what could surely be taken for a hostess's concern.

The old woman took a spoonful and chewed the chili cautiously.

Kelsa had to remind herself to breathe.

"Spicy." Otter Woman took another bite. "But not bad. I'm going to start missing fresh food soon, though." Her spoon dipped into the chili once more.

Kelsa felt as if she were melting with relief. "If it's too spicy you can mix in some of the crackers. And we'll have apples for dessert."

While they ate, they discussed which fruits and vegetables traveled well. As soon as she finished eating, Kelsa yawned. "That rough road really takes it out of you! I'll set the tent up now."

Human form, human weaknesses. The old woman yawned in sympathy. And again a few minutes later.

By the time Kelsa had set up the tent and laid out the bedding, the wrinkled eyelids were drifting down.

"My, I'm sleepy. I don't remember it coming on this fast."

How long had it been since this being had worn a human form?

"It can," Kelsa told her. "Especially after a day of exercise in fresh air. I'm certainly ready for bed."

She pulled off her boots and rolled up in her blanket to prove it, and a moment later the old woman joined her. Less than ten minutes later, the woman's breathing assumed the deep slow rhythms of sleep.

Kelsa wanted to check her pulse, to make sure the old woman's heartbeat was still OK, but she didn't dare touch her. The woman's breathing showed no sign of distress. It would have to do.

Kelsa rolled out of her blanket, then crawled out of the tent as quietly as she could, taking her boots with her. Otter Woman didn't stir.

After donning her boots, Kelsa walked the bike away from the tent. The electric motor didn't make much noise, but that wasn't the same as no noise. The soft crackle of forest detritus under the tires would register on the woman's subconscious as a natural sound, but the hum of the bike's engine might not.

It cost Kelsa a pang to abandon the tent she'd shared with her father, but if that was the price of escape, so be it.

∘　∘　∘

It was almost eight p.m. when she pulled the bike into a clearing—only a few miles down the road from her camp, but she didn't dare get closer to the town until she'd made some changes.

If she was going to stop the tree plague, she had to get Raven out of jail. She wasn't sure exactly how to do that, but the first step was to get in to see him and find out what was holding him there.

Kelsa had never had to change her appearance to fool the omnipresent cameras of the grid, but she'd listened to other kids talk about how it was done. One thing they all agreed on was that changing race was easier than changing gender.

First she cut her hair. This was the dry side of the mountains, but when the long strands fell away the rest sprang into frizzy curls. Not quite like a black girl's hair, but not unlike some of the mixies she'd known.

With only her bike's rearview mirror, tipped to the side for the best possible view, Kelsa went for the modish cut her mother had been urging her to try. She shaped the curling mass into a wedge over one eye, with thin spikes darting down in front of her ears and another deep wedge on the nape of her neck. At least it felt like she'd cut a clean wedge in the back, but she was working by touch at that point and couldn't be sure.

It did make a difference—her face looked rounder, her cheekbones more prominent. She had to admit, her mother had been right about that.

Darling, you look so cute! Kelsa grimaced, and tried to push the thought of her next conversation with her mother aside. A conversation she dreaded. After this, the police would be looking for her. And the first thing they'd do was call her mother. After this, she couldn't just go home and pretend nothing had happened.

The thought of a felony on her record, of maybe even going to jail, made Kelsa shudder. Her counselor had warned her about doing things she might regret, and while a judge might accept grief for her father as an excuse for lesser crimes, Kelsa was pretty sure it wouldn't get her off for jailbreak.

But the alternative was to give up, go home, and watch her planet die. And even if Kelsa could have done that, she couldn't leave Raven in jail, at the mercy of his enemies. She owed him too much, and she liked him too much for that.

Human or not, he'd become a friend. And friends didn't leave their friends in jail.

She spread the temp color over her palms and rubbed it into her hair, disarranging the careful style. When she was certain she had completely worked in the glossy black coating, with no brown patches to give her away, Kelsa washed her hands and wiped the smudges off her face and neck.

It would take a few minutes to dry, which meant it was probably time to get Charlie out of the way. Kelsa had been off-roading with her father and some of his friends in the red-rock desert when one of them bent a wheel rim, so she knew this kind of message was sent as text—if nothing else, her father's friend had explained, it gave you some wiggle room if you happened to hit the wrong mechanic.

To: Charlie's Salvage and Repair
Your page says you do towing. I've bent a wheel rim on the jeep road up by Deadwood Lake.

Kelsa had to stop and bring up a map to get some plausible coordinates.

Can you come up and haul me in? Everyone's all right, so there's no need to report this to traffic cops or anyone. Your rates looked really reasonable. I'd be willing to pay twenty percent more—and throw in a beer—for a discreet tow tonight. We were fishing. You know how it is.

She signed it Johnny Phillipini, in case Charlie decided to check the pod's registration before he came. Her father's friend said that as long as no one was hurt, most tow drivers were willing to keep quiet about bringing you in, even if you'd had a few too many. After all, tow-truck drivers weren't legally required to report anything. It was just custom, and customs were open to compromise.

If that was true in Utah, it would certainly be true in the far less security-conscious wilds of Canada. But while a tow-truck driver might be bribed into letting some details slide, the police wouldn't.

Her hair had dried. Kelsa pulled out her comb and teased the black fuzz back into place. She was opening the foundation when her pod signaled that a text had come in.

To: Phillipini
Can do. Provided no one hurt. Charlie Rigby.

Kelsa put down the tube to type in her reply.

No one hurt. Honest. Thanks. Johnny.

The dark foundation spread smoothly over her face, neck, arms, and the back of her hands. It looked like brown putty, but Kelsa knew that a good foundation soaked in. She picked up the clear brown nail polish and carefully painted a thin coat over the picture on her PID.

Even when she tilted the card toward the descending sunlight, it didn't make any difference. There was no way the brown-haired, white-skinned girl in the picture could be taken for mixed race. The police would look at an ID card whose owner was visiting a prisoner in their jail. Particularly if they couldn't run it on the net.

Kelsa wiped off the still-wet polish, and after a moment's thought poured a small amount of polish into a cup, then squeezed a few drops of temp color out of the bottom of one of the packets and stirred. It certainly got darker.

She painted the mixture over the plastic card and held it up to the light once more. The blue backdrop had turned a sickly green, but there was no standard background color, so that didn't matter. The severely braided hair looked darker—it could have been black. The skin was darker too, not beautiful mixie gold, but muddy gray. Still, that could have been caused by bad lighting. PID photos were notoriously hideous, anyway.

Kelsa looked into the bike's mirror. The foundation had sunk into her skin, as advertised. It wasn't as dark as she'd hoped, but the color was even and looked surprisingly natural. Her mouth and nose weren't right, but she knew several mixie kids who'd drawn paler skin and Caucasian features out of the genetic lottery. She didn't look like a white girl anymore, and her PID photo looked more or less like her.

She quickly cleaned up the color packets. She wanted Charlie to get well out of town before the police tried to call him, but she had another task to perform, and she wasn't sure how long it would take.

After a final check to make sure the dark coating on her PID was dry, Kelsa biked toward town.

Her father had liked taking his bike down small, unnamed roads, so Kelsa knew what she was looking for. Eventually she spotted the double track of an off-pavement service vehicle heading into the hills. It could have been a forest service access road, or even a loggers' trail, but for once she got lucky. Only half a mile from the pavement, she crested a rise and saw the town's com tower.

Surrounded by a chainlink fence, with a locked gate.

Kelsa took off her helmet and pulled out the bike's tool kit. Her conscience might flinch, but if you were planning a jailbreak it was stupid to worry about vandalism. And at least there were no cameras. Places like this relied on seclusion for their security. Seclusion, and the fact that there was no reason for anyone to sabotage a small-town satellite link.

The wire cutters were designed for the bike's thin electrical wires, and by the time she'd finished cutting a gap in the fence her hands ached. But once she was inside the fence, the screwdriver worked just fine to pry the cover off the master board.

Kelsa had no idea what the blinking lights indicated, what the various wires and circuit boards did. It would be nice to do something clever, to make the damage look like an accident . . . if she'd been a trained electrician and had the tools she needed and all the time in the world.

If she couldn't be clever, Kelsa decided, she might as well go for maximum damage. She was committed now.

She ripped out thin plastic circuit boards, leaned them against one of the tower's metal legs, and stamped on them to break them. Then she cut every wire she could reach. By the time she finished, all the lights were dark. But there was one final test.

Kelsa pulled out her com pod and tried to access the net. No signal.

Good enough. Now she'd better get out of here before the repair crew arrived. Kelsa reached the paved road in minutes and headed into town, keeping well within the speed limit. There was no way for anyone she passed to know she was a vandal . . . and planning a jailbreak.

The police station was on the main street, marked with a sign. It was the Royal Canadian Mounted Police, even after centuries of independence and almost two centuries after the advent of the automobile.

Kelsa parked her bike in the lot and walked through the front door, like any law-abiding citizen. The police couldn't know that her heart was hammering against her ribs. There were only a couple of officers on the evening shift, a man and a woman, scowling at a deskcomp. The woman looked up when Kelsa came in.

"Can I help you?" Her soft Canadian accent was more pronounced than most, and she summoned up a smile despite her annoyance. The quivering tension in Kelsa's belly eased. Cops were human. After Otter Woman, that seemed like a very good thing.

"I'm not sure," Kelsa told her. "A friend of mine was supposed to meet me today, to do some trail biking, but he never showed up. I know it's early to report someone missing, and he's not . . . it wouldn't be the first time he missed an appointment. But he usually coms if he's going to be a whole day late, and I haven't heard anything. So I thought I'd better see if something happened to him."

"He was probably just delayed," the woman said soothingly. "And if our link wasn't down, I could check the accident reports. But I'm afraid—"

"It's probably squirrels again," the man put in. "They gnaw the wires."

"I can tell you if any of our officers dealt with him," the woman offered. "What's his name?"

"He goes by Raven." Kelsa had anticipated this question and had a story ready. She hoped it didn't contradict whatever he'd already told them, but the scenario she'd come up with should cover any discrepancies.

The woman's hands, poised above the keyboard, froze. "Is he a First Nations boy, about seventeen, five foot ten, 155 pounds?"

"Yes," said Kelsa. "At least, I guess that's what he weighs. Did something happen to him?"

The difficulty was keeping anxiety out of her expression, not letting some leak in. If Raven had somehow avoided arrest, and just not managed to find her, all of this would be for nothing.

The woman snorted. "You could say that. He's right here, in a cell in the basement. In jail," she added, to clear up any doubt.

"But . . . did he crack up his bike? He's not much of a drinker. Really."

"No, nothing like that," the clerk said. The male cop had drifted over and was listening. "He just blew a tire. But after it was fixed, his girlfriend took off on the bike leaving a two-hundred-dollar repair bill. The garage owner kept hold of him and called us."

"But why didn't he just . . ." Kelsa began artfully. "Oh. Wait. I bet he didn't have enough cash on him to pay for the repair. Right?"

"He didn't," the woman confirmed. Her voice was still friendly, but her gaze was sharp. Kelsa could see both of them comparing her with Charlie's description of the girlfriend—and not finding a match. When they'd call him to come identify her, he wouldn't be home.

"He also had no ID and no account cards," the woman continued. "And he refused to give his real name."

Kelsa sighed. "He's such a jerk. But in a way you can't blame him. If his father found out where he was, he'd be dragged home in a heartbeat. And he really, really doesn't want that. They know he hasn't been kidnapped or anything," she added. "He lets them know he's OK. But . . . Well . . ."

"So what is his name?" the woman asked. Her voice wasn't so polite now.

"I don't think I should tell you," Kelsa said apologetically. "Not if he didn't. He's going to be eighteen in eight months, and then it won't matter nearly as much, but for now . . . Well, you understand."

"No," said the woman. "I don't. What's your name, Miss? And may I see some ID, please?"

"Sure." Kelsa handed over her card. "I'm sorry he made so much trouble for you. He doesn't mean to, but there are some things he just doesn't get. He grew up with other people taking care of things like bike repairs."

The woman looked at her picture, then at her nonfunctional card reader, and sighed. "Kelsa Phillips?"

"That's right," Kelsa said. "How much did you say that bill was?"

"Over two hundred dollars," the male cop put in. "I don't suppose you're prepared to pay it?"

"I can't," Kelsa told them with real regret. "But he might be willing to let me contact someone who can. Who could take care of all of this, in fact. Can I see him?"

"You can't contact anyone till the link's back up." The woman gave her PID back to her. "But when he wouldn't tell us his name, we ran his face on a net ID program. We couldn't find him anywhere."

"Which should have told you a lot right there," said Kelsa. "Everybody's got a picture somewhere in the net. Please, I know it's late and stuff, but if I could talk to him maybe he can tell me who to get in touch with about this bill. And when they get your link fixed, we could settle it without his father getting involved. Because trust me, that's the last thing anyone wants."

She could see they weren't completely convinced. A runaway rich kid fetching up in a Deese Lake jail was pretty unlikely. On the other hand, abuse was as possible in a rich family as in any other, and a boy who'd rather sit in a cell than give his real name . . . Choosing between standing up to a powerful wealthy man and returning a teenager to an abusive situation wasn't a decision any cop wanted to make.

"Talk to him in private," Kelsa added firmly. "Mikes off." According to the lawyer vids, any visit to a prisoner would be recorded visually, but private conversations were a civil right.

At least they were in the U.S., and surely Canada wasn't too different.

The two cops looked at each other.

"I don't see any problem with letting them talk," the man said at last. "If it gets settled, good. If nothing comes of it, there's no harm done."

"Mikes off," Kelsa insisted.

"Of course, Miss Phillips. That's standard for prisoner conversations unless we've got a warrant."

"Oh. I didn't know that. Please, call me Kelsa."

She'd expected an interview room, but the male cop took her down a flight of linoleum-covered steps to a linoleum-floored corridor with many doors off it. Two of the doors consisted of steel bars.

Raven lay on a narrow cot, frowning up at the ceiling. He must have been foolish enough to resist, somewhere along the line, because he had a black eye. The fact that he still bore those bruises told Kelsa something was seriously wrong. And if Charlie had done that, she no longer felt bad about sending him into the back country on a call that wasn't there.

"What are you doing here?" Raven demanded before she could speak. "You haven't . . . ah . . ." He cast the cop who accompanied her a fierce glare.

"No, I haven't told them who you are," said Kelsa. "Or who your father is. Though you were an idiot not to carry enough cash to pay your bills!"

Raven opened his mouth and closed it without saying anything.

The cop suppressed a smile. "You can use this." He pulled a folding chair out of a closet, opening it in front of Raven's cell door. "And the mikes are off, but I'm obliged to tell you that you're being visually monitored at all times." He gestured to the cams at either end of the corridor, and Raven glared up at one corner of his cell. It must be monitored too, but as long as the mikes were off that didn't matter. Clearly something else prevented him from shapeshifting, or his bruises would be long gone.

Kelsa sat down in front of the barred door. The cop cast a final glace around and went back down the hall.

"Are you all right?" Even if the cop overheard, that question would sound perfectly normal.

"No." Raven rose from his cot and came to sit, cross-legged, on the other side of the bars. He peered through to make sure the cop was out of earshot before going on in a much lower voice. "All my abilities have been suppressed. Fenesic. It's one of the few things in this world that can affect us. But if my enemies managed to poison me, they must know exactly where we are! You've got to—"

"I've got to get you out of here," Kelsa told him. "Preferably before morning, because that's the soonest the drug is likely to wear off. It might last longer, but we can't count on that. What's this Fenesic stuff, and how could they poison you? We've been eating the same food, mostly from sealed packages, and drinking out of the public water supply."

"Who did you drug? And if they had you, how did you escape?"

"It was Otter Woman," Kelsa said. "And I was able to escape because, like you, she's not as smart as she thinks she is. I'll tell you about it later, but right now we need to get you out of jail! How did you get poisoned?"

"I think it was the perfume," said Raven. "Remember in that baggage car when we were getting the bike out? Fenesic is one of the best poisons to use on someone in this world, because it's not only inhaled, it acts slowly and subtly. It won't wear off for years. Decades if it's a strong dose, and this was! If I hadn't been distracted I might have noticed something, but—"

"But we were arguing." Kelsa pushed guilt aside. "What's the cure, and how do I get it to you? Bake you a cake with the antidote in it? I'm pretty sure they'll analyze anything I bring you, and they might have a rule against prisoners getting food from the outside."

For the first time, Kelsa saw genuine fear in Raven's eyes.

"Don't tell me there is no antidote," she said sharply.

"No, it exists. An inhalant, like Fenesic. But it's in the sap of a tree that grows only in the Southern Hemisphere, so you couldn't possibly get it and get back here before I was transferred to some larger facility. And Fenesic . . . it doesn't wear off. They could leave me here to die!"

He sounded panicked. Kelsa couldn't blame him.

"I'll get you the antidote," she promised rashly. "Even if it takes years." Assuming the tree plague didn't kill the trees he needed before she could reach them. And after years of plague, even if she saved Raven, it might be too late for her planet. Kelsa had no more desire to die than he did, and even less to see her world die with her.

But she was getting ahead of herself, letting his terror infect her.

"Tell me about this tree," she said. "My father was a botanist who specialized in forests. Maybe there's a sample of

Fenes-whatever in some arboretum, and since I've got his com pod I might be able to fake my way in."

Raven's face brightened slightly. "It's found in Australia. It grows very tall, very rapidly, and has long dark green leaves and . . ."

A few sentences later Kelsa was sure. She began to laugh.

°   °   °

Deese Lake was too small to have a megastore; it barely had a grocery store. But like many small-town stores, it stocked a wide variety of goods. It had a very decent selection of herbal and natural medicines, including a big squeeze bottle of eucalyptus chest rub.

Raven had been startled when Kelsa told him that his exotic foreign tree was common in California and other places as well. It probably hadn't been imported when he was learning words like Jehoshaphat, so the enemies who'd poisoned him wouldn't have known about it either.

It shocked Kelsa to realize that they were willing to destroy one of their own. Stripping Raven of his powers and landing him in a human prison—and without any way to prove an identity, even in Canada, that's where he would have ended up—seemed almost as horrific as being kidnapped by a biker gang.

After Kelsa had told him that the scent of eucalyptus wouldn't be any farther away than the nearest pharmacy, they'd worked out the rest of the plan. The window wells above the cells were barred and screened with wire, but the windows themselves opened four inches to allow the prisoners fresh air. Raven's had been open when Kelsa arrived.

Having purchased the chest rub and removed the seal, Kelsa opened the fly on her bike pants and zipped the bottle inside. Bike wear was loose enough that it wasn't too uncomfortable. It was also loose enough to conceal the shape of her body.

This time she parked the bike behind the police station—from the back it could have been a store or a real estate office, almost anything.

She left her helmet on, trying to walk with a manly swagger as she entered the shadowy alley beside the jail. Only one of the barred window wells glowed with light, but Kelsa knew Raven was in the cell closest to the back of the building, anyway.

She turned toward the wall, opening her fly and hunching her shoulders in the characteristic posture—a posture that helped conceal what she was holding from the cameras on the building's eaves. She flipped up the bottle's cap with one flick of her thumb and sent fragrant liquid splattering into the window well. Even if someone happened to be watching the security monitors, they would have no way of knowing what that liquid really was, although they might be a bit startled by the capacity of her bladder.

When the bottle was empty, Kelsa zipped it into her pants and strolled back to her bike.

She rode straight out of town, expecting at any moment to hear sirens behind her—though they probably didn't chase people down with sirens for urinating in a public place.

She was out of Deese Lake in a few minutes, and between the deepening dusk and the rough road it was easy to go slowly enough for Raven to catch up with her. Soon she had to turn on her headlight, and on the potholed surface that slowed her down even more.

How long before the antidote would take effect? Assuming that eucalyptus sap that had been made into a chest rub would work at all.

Eucalyptus might have been imported to this continent, but California was a long way from British Columbia, especially by dirt bike. Kelsa couldn't afford a plane ticket, and if she transferred money from her mother's account to her own, this adventure would come to a screeching halt. Because when she refused to come home, her mother would call the Canadian police to bring her home.

Hell, the police would be after Kelsa anyway the moment they noticed that Raven had vanished from their jail. Assuming he could break out of jail. He'd sworn his beak was strong enough to tear that screen, but if he couldn't . . .

It was almost two hours later when a big black bird swooped out of the night and through her headlight.

Kelsa stopped the bike. There was still no traffic, and her lights would warn anyone who came around the curve. She pushed up the shield on her helmet.

"Don't change," she told Raven, as he assumed his usual perch on her handlebars. "Otter Woman told me the police set up a roadblock somewhere between here and Good Hope Lake. I don't match the description of the girl who ripped off Charlie, but I don't want to push my luck. Can you scout ahead and circle back to stop me if you see anything?"

The raucous squawk that answered was completely uninformative. Kelsa grimaced. "One caw for no, two for yes."

The great wings lifted, almost like a human shrug, feathers rustling. Then he cawed. Twice.

"Thanks."

The wind from his takeoff caressed her face like cold fingers.

⚬ ⚬ ⚬

He flew ahead of her all night, swinging back occasionally to reassure her. It wasn't hard to figure out that when he swooped low and flew down the road in front of her that meant go on, and that flying across her path meant stop. He stopped her twice, near creeks both times, where he took a drink and rested on the handlebars for a while. Kelsa took advantage of those brief breaks to relieve herself and down some water or an energy bar.

He didn't stop her before the town of Good Hope, where the magneto-repellant asphalt resumed and she was able to increase speed, though he did fly back to her less and less often.

The sky was beginning to brighten in the northeast when he swooped across the road a third time.

Kelsa, who really didn't want to encounter a roadblock now, turned off the pavement, rode through a shallow drainage ditch and into the trees.

The mountains had leveled out here and the forest was dry and thinner, very like the Rockies she'd left so far behind.

She turned the headlight off and waited till Raven flapped down beside her. In the growing light of dawn, the change from bird to man wasn't quite so horrifying. Was she finally becoming accustomed to it?

"You're going to need a new set of bike clothes," she said, reaching into the pack. "My spare jeans will be too short, but it's better than running around naked, and we can buy you some clothes in the next town."

"Clothes, yes." Raven pulled the therma knit she tossed him over his head. Her jeans were too short, and also loose around his narrow waist—a fact Kelsa noted with some annoyance.

"But not biker clothes," Raven continued. "Do you have any shoes that would . . . ah, I suppose not. We'll have to buy them too. Give me the highest-denomination bill you've got and I'll copy it."

"Why not bike gear?" Kelsa asked, pulling the spare cash he'd given her out of her pocket. "You need something reinforced, in case the bike—"

"We'll have to leave the bike behind," Raven told her. "I turned off both the lights and the surveillance in my cell, but the moment someone on the morning shift brings me breakfast, the police will start looking for both of us. And this bike. Could you become a blonde? Or a redhead?"

"No," said Kelsa. "But the black will wash out. How can we reach Alaska without a bike?"

"By turning right when we hit Highway One—it's just ahead—then going east about five miles to Watson Lake," Raven told her.

He wasn't exactly well dressed as he swung onto the bike behind her, but no one would report them for indecency. And it felt ridiculously good to have him back in his proper place.

Kelsa turned toward the road. "Isn't Alaska to the west? What's in Watson Lake that we need to go back for?"

"Trucks."

CHAPTER 12

THERE WERE PLENTY OF TRUCKS in the travel center on the outskirts of Watson Lake. Looking over the parking lot behind the long building, Kelsa estimated that seventy or eighty drivers had pulled in to take advantage of the inexpensive hotel rooms—or if they slept in their rig, the chance for a shower and breakfast in the restaurant.

The store attached to the center was twice the size of most charge stations; its clothing selection was limited and cheap. Kelsa left Raven to spend his newly created money and went into the ladies' room. After some thought, she decided to wash off the dark foundation. Now she looked like neither her PID photo nor the mixie who'd visited a prisoner before his escape.

She came out, chose a booth, and told the waitress her friend would join her shortly.

Despite the similarity between this place and the Woodland Café, she wasn't nervous. Sleepy truckers were wandering down the corridor from the hotel, and in from the parking lot out back. Kelsa thought there were already too many human minds for their enemies to control, and more were coming in all the time. Otter Woman might not even be awake yet.

Kelsa was studying a menu when Raven came up to the booth, wearing jeans stiff with newness and a black stretchie with a skull surrounded by rippling flames.

"Charming." Kelsa watched the colors shift and wondered how brightly they glowed in the dark. "Inconspicuous too. Can you turn it off, or is the display constant?"

"They didn't have a big selection." Raven picked up a menu, but his gaze was fixed on the charge bank outside. "I got some other shirts too. Do you think that woman will come in?"

Kelsa looked out the window. The woman he was watching stood beside her charging car, with a wiggly three-year-old girl in one arm and a boy about Joby's age tugging on her other hand. Both kids wore footed sleepers.

"With kids that young? You bet she's coming in."

"Hmm."

The woman unplugged her car and deposited the kids inside it, not bothering to fasten the protective belts, since they were driving only a few yards to park in front of the door.

"When she comes in," said Raven, "can you distract her? For just a few moments?"

"Probably not. And why should I? What are you up to now?"

"Her car has an Alaska label."

Their booth was close enough to the doors for a blast of fresh air to disturb the smell of warm pancakes and oil when the small family came in. In addition to the toddler, the woman carried enough packs to topple a sherpa.

The boy was blond and looked nothing like Joby, but Kelsa wasn't surprised when his gaze shot to the D-game table.

He looked up at his mother and said something, resisting her tug toward the tables. One look at the woman's harried expression told Kelsa all she needed to know about the answer.

The boy's lower lip quivered, then stuck out. He planted his feet on the floor, making his mother drag him. The next act was equally predictable. And whatever Raven was up to, what harm could it do to help them out?

Kelsa rose and approached the woman, who looked like she was about to swear—or give her son something real to cry about.

"Hey, if it's OK with you, I could give him a game." She gestured to the table. "I've got a brother his age, so I know all of them. And"—she glanced at the woman who manned the cash register—"Cynthia here could keep an eye on us while you take care of the little one. What's your game, champ? Lev-car 500? Fighter jets?"

The toddler was squirming in a fashion that looked serious to someone who remembered Joby's potty training.

Cynthia took one look at the boy's rebellious face and decided that keeping an eye on him and Kelsa was better than having a screaming toddler in the middle of her restaurant.

The mother's tight expression eased into a smile. As Kelsa fed coins into the game table's slot, Raven politely relieved the woman of most of her bags and took them to a nearby booth, promising to watch them.

The kid's favorite turned out to be Maze Run, a game that Kelsa liked too. She was so busy trying to maneuver her red rat through the three-D pipes that she barely noticed when the woman brought the toddler back from the restroom, and settled into a booth.

When the game ended, Kelsa led the happy winner back to his mother. The woman thanked her so fervently she felt guilty—and she didn't even know what Raven had done, yet.

"What did you do?" she demanded in a murmur, sitting down on the opposite side of the booth.

"I ordered for you. Trucker's Special, which has a bit of everything, but if you don't like—"

"You know what I mean." Why did rescuing a person make you forget how annoying he could be?

"I do, and I'll tell you later. For now, why don't you tell me what you've been doing these last few days?"

It wasn't as crazy as it sounded. The restaurant was filling up for breakfast, and the clatter of crockery and conversation was so loud the waitress had turned off the sound on the sports screens over the bar.

Kelsa lowered her voice and caught him up on her adventures. And had the pleasure of seeing startled respect dawn in his eyes.

"You actually fooled Otter Woman? And drugged her?"

"She should be waking up by now," Kelsa said, "though the stronger dose might keep her out a while longer. Would they really have left you here, powerless, in jail?"

"Maybe." His expression was sober, but he didn't seem angry. "What's happening with the leys . . . it's as important, as deadly, to us and our world as this tree plague is to yours. Everyone knows that the longer we wait, the harder it will be for us to fix the leys. But they're convinced that letting you humans wipe yourselves out, so you can't do worse harm in the future, is the right thing to do. A matter of principle, no less."

Kelsa understood the grimace that flashed over his face. Her father said more people died from principles than from crime, though he'd admitted he didn't have any statistics to prove it.

"Who are your allies? I don't want to be fooled—"

The flash of red across the sports screen caught her eye, but it was the picture that followed the headline "Breaking News" that silenced her. A picture of Raven, in full three-D mug-shot style, turning to show both his profiles, as well as the front of his face. The black eye he no longer had was dark and more swollen than when Kelsa had seen him in the cell. The police must have treated it.

The face that followed Raven's on the screen was her own, the flat photo from her PID card. The braided brown hair didn't look like the curly black wedges she now wore, but the features were still hers. At least she was listed only as a "Person of Interest."

Unlike her companion who was "Wanted on Felony Charges."

The police probably didn't want to admit that they didn't know how someone had broken out of their jail. But Kelsa would bet they'd really like to ask him.

"Relax," Raven said. "You hardly look like that at all."

"Yes, but you . . ." Kelsa's jaw dropped. His face was now more square than round, the cheekbones lower and flatter, the lips thinner. It wasn't enough of a change to make the waitress, who chose that moment to set plates down in front of them, notice. But no one would connect that face with the bruised boy in the mug shot.

"OK, you're fine, but I don't look that different!" She glanced around nervously, but no one seemed to be looking at the screens. "When they pull up my record in the States they'll learn I'm here illegally. I'm going to be arrested, and I can't shapeshift out of jail!"

"Keep your voice down." He looked far too calm to suit Kelsa. "It may look suspicious, but they can't prove you had anything to do with my escape. Just say that we met on the road, and I told you whatever you told them I told you. In jail, I asked you to call a number, which you can't remember, and you did. Then you decided to move on, since the person you talked to said he'd take care of it. You don't know who I am, or who he was, or how I got out, or where I went. The worst they can charge you with is being here without permission, and that's hardly a major crime."

"Improper entry, they call it." The horrifying prospect of ending up in prison began to look less likely, and Kelsa's pounding heart slowed. "I think in Canada they only deport you, though in the U.S. it's more serious."

"Well, we're in Canada," Raven pointed out. "So that doesn't matter."

"But they'll still get a complete description of my bike. And then they're going to . . . Oh God. They're probably calling my mother right now."

° ° °

After breakfast they took Kelsa's bike and rode it into the woods behind the service center. She rearranged the branches that concealed it three times.

"It will be perfectly safe tucked into these bushes," Raven told her tartly. "It's not going to starve without you."

He was packing some necessary supplies into one of the bike's saddlebags, which Kelsa had unstrapped. They didn't have enough food left to need the other.

"I don't want it stolen. Or damaged." If she'd still had her tent, Kelsa could have wrapped the bike to protect it against dust and weather. "I'll come back for it. It's just—"

Her com pod chirped. She'd been expecting it, but she still flinched.

"Don't answer," Raven said. "Didn't you tell me they can trace your location if those things are live?"

"Not if it's only for a few seconds. And I have to. She'll be worried about me."

Worried? Her mother would be frantic. Kelsa pulled out the pod, and her mother's white face appeared on the screen. "Kelsa! Where the hell are you? I just got a call from the Canadian police, and I called your aunt, and—"

Kelsa's mother never swore. "Mom," she broke in desperately. "Mom, I can't talk long, but I'm fine and I'm . . ." She couldn't say safe, not with Otter Woman and company on her heels. "I know what I'm doing," she finished. "I'll tell you all about it, I promise, as soon as I can, but for now you have to trust me. I know what I'm doing. I'm sorry and I love you. Bye."

"*Kel*—" She disconnected in the middle of her mother's shriek.

"I'm sorry." For once, Raven sounded as if he meant it. He reached out and wiped a tear from her cheek.

"So am I." Kelsa blew her nose, then turned and put the com pod into the bike's remaining pack. She knew it was much harder to trace a pod when it was turned off, but she wasn't certain it was impossible. And she couldn't endure hearing it chirp again and again as her mother desperately tried to reach her.

She drew a shaky breath and turned away from the two biggest links she still had to either of her parents.

"You said something about a truck?"

There were a lot of trucks in the lot, but most of them were closed and locked. Only a handful had open beds, their loads of pipe or machinery covered with plastic tarps or nothing at all. Not all of them had destination stickers.

Raven stopped beside one particularly lumpy load.

"This one is headed for Fairbanks. Perfect."

Kelsa peered through an open triangle at one end of the thick blue tarp. The twisted lumps of metal were so carefully crated that for a moment she wasn't sure what the contorted humps might be; then she recognized the upside-down shape of a clawed, scaly foot.

"It's a statue," she said. "A big statue, in sections, on its way to being reassembled.

"In Fairbanks." Raven cast a swift glance around the lot, tossed their pack onto the truck bed, then heaved himself up after it. "Which means it's going our way. With any luck, we could take this all the way to the border."

He'd crawled under the tarp by the time he finished speaking, leaving Kelsa to scramble up by herself, even though the truck's flat bed was shoulder height for her.

Muttering about alien manners, she pulled herself aboard and followed him into the blue world beneath the plastic tarp. The wooden bracing around the statue's pieces created a tangled maze. Kelsa climbed carefully over an upraised bronze arm holding a neatly cut piece of rope. She didn't dare brush up against the plastic, lest someone see the moving bulge and come to investigate. "I don't know if there are two statues, or if this is a cowboy riding a dinosaur."

"Up here," Raven called softly.

Between two sections of the statue—definitely a cowboy riding a dinosaur—was an open space about a yard wide. And except for a narrow gap where one of the tarp's seams had ripped, it was completely concealed.

"It's perfect," Raven murmured.

"It should work," Kelsa admitted. "Until we either reach the border or have to pee. Then what?"

"As for the latter, the driver has to stop sometime to do that himself," Raven said. "And for the former, back in the United States I saw a number of people walking across the border, with people meeting them on the other side. There were even some buses."

"A lot of buses drop off and pick up at the borders to avoid paying the crossing tax. Because it's based on the value of the vehicle. And sometimes people who drive really expensive cars walk across and have a driver come out to meet them. But you need a ticket to get on a bus, and no matter how you cross, you have to have a valid . . . That's what you were doing! You stole that poor woman's PID!"

"All she has to do is produce a DNA sample when my fake vanishes, and she'll be given a new one," Raven pointed out. "And she probably won't be asked for it till she tries to go back across the border. She lives in Anchorage," he added, handing the card to Kelsa. "But more important, she has permission to travel in and out of Canada at will, just like your legally home-less people. That will show up on the reader strip, right?"

Kelsa stared at the small checked box on the PID card. "It will show up on the strip. It's not exactly like being legally homeless. I bet her parents live in Canada, and she got that permission so she could take the kids to visit them anytime. But it also says she's twenty-nine, and the reader strip will show that too. Not to mention the fact that I don't look any-thing like the picture on this card."

"Give me a minute." Raven took the card back. "I've never done this before, but it should work."

His eyes were on Kelsa's face, but she could tell his attention was elsewhere. His attitude was so focused that she didn't dare interrupt.

He stared at her for a long time, caressing the card with his thumb. Kelsa was becoming bored enough to interrupt him when he finally glanced down and then grinned.

"I really am good."

Kelsa stared at the smooth plastic surface. The name on the card was still Elizabeth Stayner, but the photo bore Kelsa's face. And the age now read nineteen, instead of twenty-nine. The "1" was a trifle blurred, but not enough for a busy border agent to notice. And the reader strip would send her across the border into Alaska with no questions asked.

"But how will you—"

The truck rose gently, startling her. Kelsa had been so astonished by Raven's feat she hadn't heard the driver arrive.

"How will you get across?" she asked. "Do you still have whatshisname, Robert's ID?"

"No." The plastic tarp rattled as the truck's speed increased, and Raven had to raise his voice to compensate. "I managed to drop it into the trash bin at the garage before the police arrived. I'll fly over."

Kelsa nodded. They'd turned onto the highway now, and the noise from the wind-lashed plastic was so loud she couldn't hear anything softer than a shout.

Raven lay down in the flat space between the crated bronze shapes and held out his arms. After a moment's hesitation Kelsa accepted the invitation. His shoulder made a softer pillow than the edge of the crate, and the warmth of his body helped fight the cold breeze that flowed beneath the tarp. With the plastic rattling like a hailstorm and sunlight flashing as the wind tugged at the torn seam, there was no way she would fall asleep. She might as well be comfortable.

o   o   o

Kelsa woke stiff, groggy, and very confused till she remembered where she was. She sat up and looked out through the vibrating gap in the plastic. They were driving along the shore of a deep blue lake.

"What time is it? Where are we?"

"What?" Raven shouted.

He too had sat up, looking almost as stiff and cross as she felt.

Kelsa put her mouth near his ear and repeated her questions.

"It's about noon." With his mouth next to her ear he didn't have to shout. "And we're heading north on Highway One. Haven't reached Whitehorse yet, but if that's Teslin Lake we will in a few more hours. We've been driving beside it for almost an hour, so I think it has to be."

Kelsa's brows rose. She crawled out to the tarp and looked through the gap, ignoring the wind that whipped her hair. The lake was only a mile or so across, but it stretched out before and behind them as far as she could see.

Driving beside it for an *hour?*

"How long is this lake?" she shouted.

"Ninety miles."

"What? I thought you said—"

Raven was nodding. "Ninety miles. The first humans here called it Long Water."

No kidding. Kelsa crouched in front of the rattling gap and stared in fascination as the lake went on and on. Eventually she moved back to sit more comfortably against one of the braces, but another half-hour passed before the lake finally narrowed to a rushing river.

Otter Woman was probably awake by now. But surely it would take their enemies a while to find them and then to catch up with them. And which of the shapeshifters were enemies, and which were allies?

They passed through Whitehorse, slowing down enough that they might have conversed, but there were people on the streets, and Kelsa didn't dare risk it.

She sat on her jacket to ease the growing ache where her butt rested on the hard truck bed, until she got cold and had to put the jacket back on. Then she took out all the squashable energy bars and sat on her pack.

The driver must have been peeing in a bottle or something, because they were several hours out of Whitehorse, and Kelsa's bladder was about to burst, when Raven suddenly gripped her arm.

"What?" she half shouted in his ear. "I'm going to have to piss on the floor if we don't—"

"Be quiet." His grip tightened. "There's something up ahead. I don't know what they're doing this far south, but I think I can coax them . . . Hang on!"

The truck's drop brakes squealed on asphalt as the truck skidded to a stop. It was a good thing Raven had warned her. Kelsa was almost thrown into the next crate, despite his grip on her arm.

Another set of brakes screamed as the car behind them stopped, then another.

"What on earth? Never mind! I'm getting out. Now."

Kelsa crawled to the back of the truck, and despite her urgent need, peered out to make sure the driver who'd parked on their bumper wasn't watching. But the middle-aged woman had climbed out of her car, leaving the door open behind her, and now hurried past the truck, setting her com pod to "record" as she ran.

Kelsa climbed down from the truck and turned to look. For a moment she didn't recognize the circle of hairy brown lumps that blocked the road; then she saw the big curved horns and a round half-buried eye, and gasped with astonished delight.

Raven swung down to stand beside her, staring, and another car added itself to the growing line behind them.

"What are they doing here?" he asked. "I've never seen them this far south."

"Could they be shapeshifters?" Kelsa asked in some alarm. "Trying to stop us?"

"No. I got a good sense of them when I called them onto the road. But they're a long way from their usual territory."

"That's because of the climate change," Kelsa told him. "Muskoxen were endangered by the warming, but they've been doing pretty well for the last fifty years, spreading beyond their original habitat now that they're protected. But they're shy in the wild. I never thought I'd see one, because they only live in the very far . . . north."

She was in the Yukon. In a part of the world where Ice Age survivors roamed wild, and the sun hardly set all summer long. Kelsa had been so busy running for her life and breaking people out of jail, she hadn't had time to realize how far she'd traveled, how much she'd accomplished.

But even the shock of that realization was overshadowed by her mounting physical need. Kelsa hiked into the trees till she couldn't see the road—which fortunately didn't take long— and attended to nature's demand.

The muskoxen were still there when she returned, and the traffic jam on both sides of the road was growing. A man and a couple of teenagers raced past her, pulling out their cameras.

Kelsa was reaching for her own com pod when she remembered she'd left it with the bike.

"Here, take this." Raven crawled onto the truck's tailgate and held out their pack. A truck ahead of them sounded its horn, and several more followed suit. It was hard to see much reaction under all that hair, but Kelsa thought the circle of oxen drew tighter.

They were shorter than she'd imagined, the adults only a bit over four feet. The calves in the center, from what little she could see of them, looked like giant, furry exercise balls.

"They're so cute!"

The pack bounced off her shoulder and fell to the road, and Raven climbed down.

Kelsa picked up the pack, frowning. "Are we getting off? I thought we were taking this truck all the way."

"We still might," said Raven, "if our fuzzy friends can hold the traffic long enough. But I've been listening to the ley for the last few hours, and it needs healing."

Startled, Kelsa took her gaze off the oxen to look at him. "Is there a nexus here?"

"No." Raven's face was sober. "It would be better if there was. Maybe it's damage from the beetle kill, but the ley has gone very deep here, spread wide, and running slow. Sluggish.

Hard to reach. It needs to be healed in many places at once, raised higher to flow more strongly. I think this is where you need to call on animal life."

"Animals?" Kelsa didn't know why she was surprised. Living organisms were a part of nature too. She gazed dubiously at the tight circle of oxen. They were tremendously cute, but their attitude was pugnacious. The tourists who gathered around them, frantically recording, were keeping their distance.

"I suppose I might get close enough to throw some dust over them, but with so many people—"

"Not them," Raven interrupted. "And you can't just sprinkle them with dust, anyway. You need to blow it into the nose of the creature you summon. That's why we're going up there," he added, pointing to the hillside that loomed above the road.

The sign said Glacier Rock Trail, and beyond the trees Kelsa saw a huge ridge of glacial debris.

"How am I supposed to get near enough to any wild creature to blow dust in its face? Especially on that rock field? I won't be able to move fast enough to catch even a butterfly, and I won't be able to move quietly, either."

And if her victim didn't like having sand blown into its nose, she wouldn't be able to run.

"You aren't going to chase it down." Raven's tone was a bit too patient. "You call it with the incantation, and when something comes you blow the dust into its face."

"*Something* comes? I can't call for a small animal, like a mouse or a bird?"

This was bear country.

"You're not afraid of animals, are you?"

"I'm sensibly cautious of wild animals," Kelsa told him. "Especially ones that are bigger than me. Like a moose. Or a bear. Even a deer will fight if it's frightened enough, and they can do a lot of damage."

"Whatever comes to your calling should know you for a friend." Raven took the pack with one hand and grasped her arm with the other, steering her toward the trailhead. "But candidly, that's one of the reasons I want you on the rock field when you call. I'm hoping you'll get a wild sheep—there are several species around here. That way, when the calling ends, it will probably just bound off."

Kelsa considered the implications. "So while I'm calling, it will know me for a friend and approach. But once I blow the dust in its face the spell ends, and then it's a wild animal who suddenly finds itself very close to a human who just—"

"You'll do fine." Raven nudged her in the direction of the trail. "I'll stop here and delay anyone who wants to hike up after you. The animal might know you for a friend, but anyone else would frighten it off."

That didn't sound so bad to Kelsa, but if the ley needed healing . . .

"Couldn't I do trees here instead?"

Raven shook his head. "Trees will work better if you're on top of a nexus. The healing will spread farther."

"But—"

"There are plenty of trees in Alaska. Animals here."

He was the expert on leys, after all. Kelsa shrugged and started up the trail.

Despite her misgivings, it felt wonderful to be off the truck, hiking in the sunshine. The pine and aspen wood was full of unfamiliar bird songs. Maybe she would get a bird with her summoning. A small one would be good.

The trail emerged from the glade and onto the rock field. The Canadian park service had laid the jumbled stones flat, but Kelsa still had to pick her way over the uneven surface. She mostly ignored the informative signs—just looking around she could see that centuries after the glacier had dumped it, almost nothing had colonized this barren moraine.

The trail zigzagged up, and up some more. Kelsa was panting when she reached the end of the trail and turned to look back.

The great glacier-carved valley stretched before her, bordered by big round-topped mountains to the north and ragged peaks with fingers of ice still flowing through them to the east. A glowing, royal blue lake filled the long basin, light rippling on its surface.

A chorus of honking rose from the trucks, their drivers more blasé about wildlife than the tourists who still clustered around the herd. From this height the muskoxen looked like dark tumbleweeds, and showed no sign of moving.

What were the right words for connecting the ley to animals? So many species, such an abundant diversity of life. How to reach them all?

Kelsa sat down on a bench the park service had provided, untied the medicine bag, and removed a generous pinch of dust. She closed her eyes, reaching out with her less tangible senses to this vast, open place in the world. She couldn't sense animals, but she'd always felt the life that hummed within the thin skin of atmosphere enclosing her planet. Life was what she was calling now.

"Swift or slow, strong or subtle. Furred and feathered, scaled, shelled, or skinned. You who wander the surface of the world, forgive us, please, and carry this healing in all the places you go. Heal and be strong!"

All her heart was in the words, and though her mind might question, she felt no surprise when she opened her eyes and found a pair of gleaming dark eyes staring back. Eyes framed by soft fur, quivering whiskers, and round, black-rimmed ears.

Pika were notoriously shy, but this one gazed up at her with no fear at all.

Kelsa almost picked it up, but sensible caution about wildlife intervened. Instead she bent down, opened her fingers, and blew the dust gently into the rodent's face.

The whiskers whirred into overdrive.

Then Kelsa's heart gave a great throb, as if it suddenly beat in tandem with thousands upon thousands of hearts. Some were big and slow, but many beat small and fast, faster than her heart could endure, and she gasped and pressed both hands against her chest to contain it.

On the road below, the oxen threw up their heads and bellowed. The pika whisked into a crack in the rocks and vanished.

Several minutes passed before her heart rate slowed to normal, and Kelsa rose and made her way back down the trail. Perhaps it was only in her imagination that with every footfall, every touch of her hand on rock, a pulse of healing energy sank into the earth. But wasn't she too part of the life of this world?

Raven was sitting on the curb in the trail's parking lot when Kelsa emerged from the trees, a disgusted expression on his face.

"I didn't think it through," he said.

Still enveloped in a glorious daze of healing, Kelsa didn't care. "Think what through?"

"The effect of what you were doing on our current situation." The disgust in his expression spread to his voice. "When you healed the animal life along this ley, the muskoxen suddenly felt strong and good, instead of threatened and fearful. Which might not have been enough, in itself," he added. "Their instinct to circle and hold in the face of danger runs pretty deep. Unfortunately, the truckers felt good too, so they stopped pounding their horns. And since that was what was frightening those furry idiots, they broke their circle and wandered away. So . . ."

Kelsa followed the sweep of his hand and looked at the road. One car whizzed by. After that, nothing. The traffic jam had dissolved. Their truck was gone.

CHAPTER 13

HIKING BESIDE A ROAD WAS nothing new to Kelsa. Even when the feeling that her every step healed the world began to fade, dandelions and fireweed glowed in the road's grassy verges, and magpies flashed their elegant plumage in the brush.

"I still think we need to find someone to give us a ride," Raven grumbled, tramping along beside her. "Otter Woman has probably been awake most of the day. This is taking too long."

Kelsa was worried about that too, but . . . "Otter Woman is almost twenty-four hours' travel behind us. And when your picture is on every newscast as a wanted fugitive, trying to hitch a ride is stupid. The sight of two kids hiking in the summer is so common, no one will think twice. And we don't look much like our pictures, especially with those streaks in your hair."

The red and orange swatches matched the flames around the skull on his stretchie. They looked good on him, but Kelsa saw no need to tell him so.

"But anyone who takes a close look at me will call the police," she went on firmly. "That would slow us a lot more than walking into town where we can rent . . . Is that squirrel watching us?"

"Maybe it is," said Raven. "But that doesn't mean it's a shapeshifter. It's almost four." He was looking at the sun, instead of her watch. "I hope your town comes along soon."

Kelsa had to agree. Without her com pod she had no access to the maps of the net. She remembered the basic route—only one road led to the Alaskan border, after all—but she had only a vague memory of several small towns along the way. They were bound to reach one of them eventually.

They still hadn't hit a town two hours later, when they came to a long curve in the road, and another beautiful north-country lake stretched before them.

"Dinner," Raven decreed. It was his turn to carry the pack, so when he went over to a nearby boulder and began digging out energy bars, Kelsa had no choice but to join him. Even though . . .

"I think I see some buildings on the shore." She squinted against the distance and the reflection off the waves.

"We'll do a better job of negotiating for a vehicle after we've eaten." Raven was already peeling the wrapper off an energy bar, and in truth Kelsa was tired too.

The lake was bordered by low tawny mountains, and the quiet emptiness of this rock-strewn valley seeped into Kelsa's soul. Even the cars that occasionally whooshed by had no power to disturb the silent, wild peace.

"Is this valley connected to a nexus or something?" Kelsa asked.

"No." Raven's voice disturbed the stillness no more than the cars did. "It simply *is*."

Kelsa nodded, and let the silence fall once more.

∘ ∘ ∘

The cluster of buildings she'd seen beside the lake were farther away than they'd looked. It was past seven when they finally reached the turnoff and read the sign: Pinewood Cabins and R.V. Park. Fishing, boating, water sports, and bait were listed in the fine print. It said nothing about vehicles for rent.

"We'd better keep going." But Kelsa couldn't stop the dismay from creeping into her voice. Her feet were tired. She'd have been happy to stop for the night, but Raven was right about losing time. Here in the Yukon it would be hours before the sun set.

Raven looked as tired as she felt and even grumpier. "We'll check it out. Maybe they rent off-road vehicles or something."

"If they did, wouldn't they put that on the sign?"

He was already tramping down the driveway. Kelsa shrugged and followed. When he was in this mood, she was in no hurry to catch up with him. She was several yards behind him when he froze, then slipped into the bushes beside the road.

Kelsa looked around. No animals that might be shapeshifters. At least, none that she could see. They were nearing the first building, and the RV lot, about two-thirds full, was off to the left. The tired chug of a washing machine came from the long building ahead and to the right. There was no reason to hide.

Turning, she made her way into the brush and came up behind Raven, who was peering through a clump of willows.

"What are we hiding from?"

"Shh!" Kelsa followed his pointing finger to the back of the long building, to a three-wheeled ATV parked there. It clearly serviced the campground, with its open bins of tools and cleaning supplies strapped to both the front and back of the vehicle.

"We can't take that!" she whispered. "The people who own this place use it all the time. They'd miss it in an instant."

"Not till morning. I think it's been parked back there because they're finished for the day."

"I'm not letting you turn me into a thief," said Kelsa. "Not more than you already have. The people who own that buggy need it. And it's pretty old. They probably can't afford a new one."

"But it will be returned to them," Raven said persuasively. "Possibly by the end of the day. We can leave them some money as a rental fee. More than it's worth if you like."

"Assuming they spend it before it vanishes," Kelsa muttered. He didn't have to explain why they couldn't try to rent it openly. Anyone who did something that unusual would certainly be examined closely—and the owner would demand to see their IDs. Her feet were throbbing, and the rest of her body ached with weariness. And he was right; even if the money vanished the ATV would be returned.

"The key's in the ignition," he murmured in her ear.

On Kelsa's insistence, Raven left most of the money they had tucked into the bin of cleaning supplies she'd unstrapped so quickly and quietly.

The ATV might be old, but the engine hummed to life with well-maintained quiet. It was only in Kelsa's guilty imaginings that shouts rang out behind them and someone called the police.

In reality, Raven settled onto the long seat behind her, and they rode up the drive and out onto the road with no trouble at all.

"Don't look so grim," he told her. ATVs weren't designed for speed, so they could talk over the wind. The enforced slowness was probably a good thing, since they had neither reinforced clothing nor helmets.

"I'll bet they won't even notice it's missing till morning," he went on. "By the time it's reported we'll be long gone."

"You don't care about them at all, do you? How angry they'll be. How worried and upset. They live in a place where people are so trustworthy they can leave the keys in the ignition, and we're breaking that trust."

Even at thirty miles an hour she couldn't turn to look at him, but she saw his puzzled frown in the rearview mirror. He didn't understand. Either that, or he didn't care.

But the "you don't value humans" fight had cost them too much already. Kelsa sighed and turned her attention ahead. She had to admit, driving was better than walking.

Eventually they left the lake behind, and soon after that the road curved away from the valley between two green-clad hills, wending up to a narrower valley. The asphalt surface, hitherto smooth, began to roll in a series of low waves.

"It's like driving over a giant curling ribbon." Kelsa had heard of frost heaves, but she'd never seen them. Not like this.

The valley eventually widened to more open ground, dotted with long shallow marshes and rocky slopes above. It was past ten, and the sun was finally settling into the northwestern horizon, when Kelsa saw a huge tawny lump in the grass at the roadside and brought the ATV to a stop.

"That's a grizzly bear!"

There could be no doubt about it. Its thick fur was pale gold, the same color as the dry grass on the hillsides above, and its shoulders rose in the characteristic hump.

It was twice the size of a black bear, and Kelsa was very glad that after one incurious glare it ignored her.

"It's not a shapeshifter, either," Raven said. "Why are we stopping? Don't tell me you have to piss again."

"No, but . . . It's right beside the road." And on the open, slow-moving ATV she had no desire to get closer.

"There's something in the grass that it likes," Raven said impatiently. "Go by on the other side. If it wanted to eat you, it would be paying more attention."

The great bear had been keeping an eye on Kelsa between bites, but not with the fixed gaze of a predator. And this was the only road to the border, so she hadn't much choice.

Kelsa set the ATV in motion, swerving over as far as she could without going into the ditch.

The bear's tawny head lifted as she approached. If it charged, Kelsa decided, she would use the lights and horn as her first two weapons, and then the ATV itself. Her heart hammered against her ribs.

But the bear only watched her roll past. Kelsa twisted on the seat to keep an eye on it until they were far down the road and the bear had returned to its meal.

Adrenaline sang through her body. There was a fine tremor in her fingers as she turned back to the road, and her senses seemed sharper than usual.

"Oh, my God. That was a grizzly!"

"I'm surprised we haven't seen one before," Raven said calmly. "They're pretty common in the north."

Kelsa's elation drained away. "You said taking over an animal's mind is hard, because they rely so much on their instincts. A grizzly bear is one of the few animals that will stalk and prey on humans. How hard would it be for your enemies to convince a passing grizzly that human would make a good meal tonight?"

Raven was quiet for longer than she liked. "I don't think Bear would let them overshadow the mind of one of his. Unless he's finally made up his mind which side he's on."

"How very reassuring," Kelsa said. "Your allies . . . Who are your allies, anyway? They couldn't prevent that?"

"Probably not," Raven admitted. "We tend to make up our own minds. And we don't change them easily."

"So your enemies aren't going to change their minds, no matter how many leys I heal? And who are your enemies? I need to know that!"

"Why? It's not like Bear, for instance, couldn't shift into a hawk if he wanted to. Abandoning the form this ley prefers would cost him more energy, but he could do it. And it's the neutrals, like Bear, who I'm trying to convince."

So no matter which shapeshifter she encountered, she had no way to tell friend from foe without Raven?

"Wonderful."

"But keeping control of an animal, even if it might be willing to do what you want, is harder than influencing humans," Raven said consolingly. "I don't think they'd try that. At least, not yet."

o o o

Another two hours down the road, in the rich gray arctic dusk, Kelsa saw a sign and slowed to read it: PICKHANDLE LAKE. CABINS. FISHING. CANOEING.

"We're getting a cabin," she said. "There are too many bears around here to sleep outside."

"You spent all our money on the ATV," Raven complained. "And I really don't think they'd offend Bear by—"

"I'm not going to risk becoming grizzly jerky because you *think* they might not want to offend Bear."

Kelsa turned down the driveway and parked the ATV in front of the office. Through the lit-up window she could see the night clerk, a girl not much older than she was, with a book reader propped on the counter in front of her. "I'll go in and find out how much it is while you make us some money."

She was a little worried that the clerk might recognize her from the newscasts, despite the change in her hair. But Elizabeth Stayner's PID passed inspection, and Raven came in with a roll of twenty-dollar bills as Kelsa was signing them in.

The cabins were on the shore, farther down the drive. The dark lake was small and shallow, compared with some that Kelsa had seen recently. But as it came into sight, Raven stiffened.

"Chetthel Chi. I didn't realize we'd come this far."

Kelsa parked in front of cabin eighteen and looked back at him, startled by the unease in his voice. "What's wrong with Chettie . . . Pickhandle Lake? Is it off the ley, or an antinexus or something?"

Raven snorted. "There's no such thing as an antinexus. And we are off the ley's main current, but that doesn't matter. This lake, though, it's at the confluence of three rivers. It's been a human rendezvous for thousands of years. That kind of energy . . . It wants people to gather here."

"*I* want people to gather here," Kelsa said. "The more humans, the fewer bears!"

Raven shrugged, but his eyes still searched the dark woods that surrounded the shimmering water.

"I'm not camping with the grizzlies," Kelsa told him. "I got practically no sleep yesterday, and we're both exhausted. Come in and go to bed."

The cabin held four narrow bunks, so there was no negotiation for who slept where. But it was chilly, and Kelsa was so tired she simply kicked off her shoes and curled up under the blanket with her clothes on.

Even as she slid into sleep, she was aware that Raven lay with his eyes open, listening.

o   o   o

When Raven's hand gripped her shoulder Kelsa came awake all at once, like a soldier in a combat zone. If it wasn't an emergency she would kill him, but for now . . .

"What?" She whispered the word, as if someone in the cabin might overhear.

His voice was almost as soft when he replied, "Come here. Tell me what you make of this."

He led the way to the front window, which looked back up the road toward the office.

Through the relatively thin forest, Kelsa saw half a dozen shafts of light burning in the dark gray twilight of the northern night. At different angles. Bike headlights.

"The biker gang." It could have been an innocent group of travelers, but Kelsa knew in every atom of her terror-chilled flesh that it was them. "How could they catch up with us so quickly?"

"You lost two days with Otter Woman, and breaking me out of jail." Raven's voice was grim but calm, and Kelsa took heart from that. "If they were guided . . . Well, clearly they could catch up with us because they have. What now?"

"The police!"

Kelsa was moving to the cabin's com board when Raven said, "The same police who want to question you about a jailbreak? Who under these circumstances will run the DNA attached to that identity and discover that you're not Elizabeth Stayner?"

"I'll lie." Kelsa pushed the power button. "Say they're trying to break into . . ." The com board remained dark, even when she pushed the button again.

Every horror vid Kelsa had ever seen flashed through her mind. Her knees felt as if they were turning to jelly. "Have they cut the power?"

She was reaching for a light switch when Raven's warm hand closed over her cold one.

"If they haven't, the light will bring them straight here. Get your shoes on. We've got to get out. They're coming."

The long shafts of light were swinging down the road to the cabins now, turning together like a hunting pack.

Despite Kelsa's tug on his arm, Raven stopped to close the cabin's back door behind them, and then hurried her into the shadowy trees. Fortunately, the ground around the cabins was relatively clear.

"It will take them a few minutes to find the right cabin," he said, steering her toward the water, "and a few more minutes to break in, search the place, and realize we aren't there. Then they've got to figure out where we've gone. Though they'll probably have some help with that."

His voice was grim, but being out of the confining walls and moving had broken Kelsa's paralyzing fear. She was still terrified, but her mind was working again.

"We should go into one of the other cabins. Wake someone. They could call the police on their com pod."

Raven shook his head. "Everyone around here has been pushed into sleep. That was what alerted me. You won't be able to wake them. We're better off running."

They were moving steadily away from the ATV, which couldn't outrace a drug gang's bikes anyway. "Run how?" Kelsa demanded. "On foot in the woods?"

The grizzlies were looking better to her now.

"No." They emerged from the trees as he spoke, only a handful of yards from the cabins' dock. Half a dozen sleek dark shapes were lined up on the sand. "We're taking the old road out."

Kelsa's father had been a botanist. She'd gone canoeing only once in her life, at the age of seven or eight, but Raven claimed he was an expert. Remembering his smooth leap onto the back of that horse, maybe he was.

Kelsa dragged one of the canoes into the lake, indifferent to the cold water that filled her shoes. One of the few things she remembered about canoeing was that the person in front steered, so she climbed awkwardly in and settled herself on the back bench. Raven picked up a big wedge-shaped rock and proceeded to crack open all the other canoes with the methodical calm of a cook breaking eggs. Only a lot louder.

"They're coming," Kelsa said. "They don't know what they heard, but they're following the sound."

"Just one more." Raven turned the final canoe over, lifted the rock over his head, and smashed it down on the keel. Fiberglass cracked once more, and several bikers shouted. The headlights were turning toward the dock.

Raven splashed out and climbed into the canoe, setting it rocking. He snatched a paddle, and with several deep strokes pulled them farther from the shore.

"Do you know how to handle these things at all?"

"No," said Kelsa. "But I think I can paddle if you tell me which side."

She could almost hear her father's voice shouting, "Paddle on the right. Paddle on the left."

"Good," said Raven. "First, let me turn us around."

He did so with a smooth speed that made it look easy, though Kelsa was pretty sure it wasn't.

The moon chose that moment to rise over the trees. It was only half full, turning the small waves to rippling silver on the far edge of the lake. Soon it would light up the water like a stage.

Raven muttered something in a liquid tongue Kelsa didn't recognize, but she had no doubt of its general meaning. She wanted to swear too. She gripped her paddle, trying to remember. One hand over the top, and the other went . . . ?

"On the left," Raven ordered, digging his own paddle into the dark surface.

After a dozen or so strokes it began to come back to her, the smooth rhythm of sinking the paddle's edge straight down, pulling it toward her, and circling around for the next stroke.

In the front, Raven switched sides. Kelsa twitched, but when no further commands came she went on paddling on the left side of the canoe. Paddling was easier than steering, and Raven's claim that he knew what he was doing must have been true, for the canoe drew swiftly away from the shore.

Focused on their progress, Kelsa didn't look back till the snarling shout rang out behind them.

"You can't run from us forever, bitch! And when we catch you, you're gonna regret like hell you even tried."

The bikers had reached the shore, their rides gleaming in the moonlight. Two of them had dismounted to check the broken canoes, but most were still perched on their seats. A chill ran down Kelsa's spine. There were nine of them. The original four must have sent for reinforcements.

"If you come back here," the leader yelled, "maybe we'll leave you and your pretty boy alive when we've finished with you. But if you don't come back . . ."

Kelsa thrust the paddle in once more. "That encourage you?" She wanted to sound dry and ironic, but her voice cracked on the words.

"Not in the least. Any chance you can keep them talking?"

"What good will that do?" Did Raven have some clever plan?

"Probably not much. But if they're talking to you, they're not trying anything else. On the right now."

Kelsa switched hands to paddle on the other side. It wasn't much of a plan, but . . .

"I called the police on my com pod," she shouted back. "They should be here any minute. You're all going to jail!"

Several more of the bikers had dismounted, milling at the water's edge, but it didn't look like they'd found a way to follow her. Kelsa's heart began to rise.

"Your face is on every newscast in western Canada," the biker shouted. "Accomplice in a jailbreak. You don't dare call the cops."

So much for that bluff. But as they made their way farther and farther out, it looked like Raven's basic plan was working. If he could get them a few miles down the river that drained this lake, they'd be safe in the forest.

Grizzly bears seemed almost irrelevant now. The fact that her back and arms were tiring meant nothing at all. Paddling with a will, Kelsa was beginning to feel almost hopeful—until an icy wind eddied around them.

Raven stopped paddling and looked around. "What was that?"

"Just a cold wind?" But even in the cool night it had felt like the breath of a glacier. Then it vanished, in a way no natural drop in temperature ever did.

A biker's astonished cry drew her attention back to the shore. It was several hundred yards away now, but the moonlight gleamed on the rim of white spreading out from the muddy banks.

"Tarnation!" Kelsa had never heard that word spoken with so much force. "They're freezing the lake!"

"That's ice? But how . . . ? Who . . . ?" Both answers were obvious. "It's the beginning of June! How could they freeze a whole lake?"

The white was spreading.

"They don't have to freeze the whole lake." Raven dug his paddle into the water once more. "Just enough to close the mouth of the river and trap us. Some help here, please. Left!"

Kelsa fixed her gaze on the dark opening at the far end of the lake, paddling with deep hard strokes as he went on. "And they only have to freeze the surface hard enough for those thugs to reach us. It may not be a *clear* violation of the physics of this world, but they're drawing a lot of power out of the ley. Maybe enough to tip some of the neutrals in our direction. They're gambling a lot here."

"But that's a good thing, isn't it? If more neutrals go over to your side you'll have more allies, right?"

"Only if I survive long enough to recruit them." Raven's voice was grim. "That's what they're gambling on. If they can kill me—"

"Then the fact that they bent the rules hardly matters."

The first biker stepped tentatively onto the ice, and Kelsa felt as if the ice was spreading into her heart as well. The white rim that encircled the lake was slowly closing the gap that opened into the river. She couldn't see the ice sheet grow, but if she looked down for a few moments and then back, she could see a difference.

"How long do we have?"

"Not long enough." Raven was watching the closing river too. "I'm going to try to slow this down. You're on your own for a while."

He set down his paddle, then bent forward and thrust both hands into the water.

Kelsa looked back at the bikers. They were too distant to shout at her now, but all nine of them were mincing carefully across the ice.

Kelsa swore under her breath and turned her attention to paddling. When she paddled on the left side the canoe swerved right. When she paddled on the right it went left. She could control it fairly well, except when the shifting breeze shoved it sideways or set it spinning.

She thought the ice was growing more slowly, but she couldn't be sure. It hadn't stopped. Every time Kelsa looked up the rim of white had crept farther out, closing the river's gap. She heard a crack and a yelp as one biker pushed his luck a little too far, but no splash followed and she didn't look back.

Sweat slid down her back, despite the cold air that made her lungs burn. Her hands were blistering, but that didn't matter. Nothing mattered but the sweat trickling down Raven's taut face and the two edges of ice creeping out to meet across the river's mouth.

Raven swayed, and a shudder shook him. He sat up and ran wet hands over his face. "I can't stop it. Not alone."

Kelsa had known that for the last three minutes. She turned and looked back. The ice covered more than half of the lake's surface, and the bikers were now closer to the canoe than they were to the shore. They'd stopped a dozen yards from the edge of the ice sheet, sensing—being told?—that it was still too thin to bear their weight. They waited in silence now, like the predators they were.

Kelsa took a tighter grip on her paddle. She could stab with the edge and split a skull if she was lucky. She could swing it like a baseball bat, breaking arms and ribs. And with Raven fighting too . . . They would be overwhelmed in minutes. Nine men were too many, even if none of the bikers was armed. Which didn't seem likely.

"I'm afraid," Raven sighed, "that it's time to call in some help."

"You *think?*" In the few moments she'd hesitated a thin skin of ice had formed around the canoe's bow. Kelsa leaned forward and cracked it with her paddle, then turned the canoe back toward the unfrozen center of the lake, working by herself. Raven had turned around on the seat, and now he sat perfectly still in the front of the canoe, his hands and face lifted toward the moon.

Perhaps it was her imagination that the light seemed to gather in his hands, intensifying before it poured into the rippling water. Even when she wiped the sweat out of her eyes, Kelsa couldn't be sure.

All she knew was that eventually a really annoying smirk crossed his face, and he opened his eyes and said, "There. That should do it."

"Do what?" Kelsa's voice was ragged with fury and fear. They'd almost reached the center of the lake. She couldn't go much farther.

Raven finally looked at her, taking in her terrified exhaustion and the ice that walled them in.

"Forget the bikers," he said. "Look at the shore."

It was hard to look away from her enemies as they picked their way carefully closer, but Kelsa dragged her gaze away and focused on the nearest shore, just in time to see dozens, hundreds, of small black dots slither onto the ice. They were so tiny, if they hadn't been moving she wouldn't have spotted them.

"What's that?"

"Frogs."

Kelsa had no idea why he sounded so smug about it.

"Frogs can't fight men, no matter how many there are. We need a wolf pack."

"If a wolf pack shows up we're going to be sorry, because Wolf's on the other side. Frogs are exactly what we need."

"How can frogs help us?"

"Watch," Raven said. "What do you see?"

Kelsa looked at the bikers, who were still waiting for the ice to thicken a bit more so they could close in to rape and kill her. No change there. She looked at the frogs and frowned.

The dark dots seemed bigger now. She could see them, even though they weren't moving.

"Are they growing?"

"No. What you're seeing is water around them. Or to put it another way, holes in the ice."

Holes in the ice that were expanding even as she watched. "They're melting it? How? Frogs are cold-blooded."

"Well, Frog People is giving them some help. He sees no reason to let the leys get worse if we can make the situation better instead. And he owes me a favor. This pays it back, I'm afraid."

Kelsa cared nothing for his karmic balance sheet. "Frog People? He?"

"Frog People is a many-in-one kind of guy." Raven's voice was absent. "But he's good at balancing."

Kelsa didn't think he was talking about physical balance. There was a ring of water all around the shore now, and the ice had stopped reaching toward them. She leaned down and put a hand in the lake. The water wasn't exactly warm, but it wasn't as cold as it should have been.

A crack rang through the night, like a big branch breaking. Or an ice sheet. The bikers, focused on their prey, paid no attention.

"Who are your other allies?" Kelsa asked. "And what can they do?"

"It's complicated," said Raven. "Are those bikers likely to be good swimmers?"

"Stop trying to distract me!" Kelsa said sharply. "I need to know this stuff. Who are your other allies?"

"Ah . . . besides Frog People, well, Goose Woman is leaning my way. Though she's mostly a seductress," Raven added.

"Not as useful as Frog People. Unless you want someone seduced."

Kelsa waited.

Raven said nothing.

"That's it? Frog People, who no longer owes you any favors, and maybe Goose Woman? *Everyone* else is on the other side?"

"There are a lot of neutrals," Raven said. "More neutrals than people who've declared themselves. If I can—"

"This is why you kept putting me off when I asked about your allies, isn't it? Because you don't *have* any—"

This time the cracking of the ice sheet was too loud to ignore. The bikers looked around, yelped in alarm, and started running toward the shore . . . or more accurately, toward the growing rim of dark water that now lay between them and the shore.

Kelsa picked up her paddle and began pushing the canoe slowly back toward the dock. "I'm going to enjoy this."

The melting ice was slippery. The bikers skidded and flailed their arms as they tried to run. One fell, and the ice broke beneath him sending up a great splash. He bobbed up in the hole and threw both arms onto the ice sheet, yelling for help. One of them hesitated but didn't go any closer. The others ran on.

"They'll all be in the water soon." Raven had taken up his paddle too, guiding them through the rapidly dissolving ice. "Pity it's not cold enough to . . . There! We can get through there."

Kelsa's hands burned with broken blisters, but she ignored the pain, paddling hard while Raven steered.

They bumped into several chunks of floating ice, but it wasn't enough to impede their progress, and only once did they encounter a piece of the ice sheet large enough that they had to maneuver around it.

No bikers were visible now, but Kelsa knew they were there. When a hand rose out of the water and curled over the side of the canoe she was ready, bringing up her paddle and smashing the blade down on the gripping fingers.

A man's voice screamed and the hand vanished. The swimmer splashed away, swearing and choking.

Kelsa kept watch after that, paddle raised at ready until Raven had pulled them well past the point where a swimmer might overtake them.

Then she returned to paddling. Raven put in a steering stroke occasionally, but he wasn't pulling his weight.

"A little help here?" Kelsa said. He was supposed to be the expert, after all.

"Sorry." But he didn't lift his paddle. "I put too much energy into trying to warm the water, and it's turning into a physical drain. I should have known better. I'm not a balancer, not at all."

"Is that a fancy shapeshifter way of saying you're tired?"

"Yes." He turned to glare at her. "I'm tired."

Kelsa stopped paddling. Raven's face was no longer the one he'd assumed in the diner, but the one she thought of as his real face. The face she'd first seen. The face of the boy in the newscasts, wanted on felony charges.

"Oh, carp."

She brought them in by herself, saying nothing more as he slumped wearily on his seat, though he did put in a stroke now and then to correct their course.

Kelsa kept working till her paddle hit the bottom, then she shoved the canoe forward till she heard mud rasp under its hull. The shallow water was almost warm as it splashed around her ankles. She turned to the leafy brush around the shore and spoke with all her heart, "Thank you."

Raven, climbing out at the front without his usual grace, snorted. "The magic is gone now. They're only frogs."

"Even so."

If he could make snide comments, he could walk on his own. Kelsa waded past him and went up to the biggest, fastest of the gang's bikes.

"We can't outrun anyone on that wimpy ATV. How much time do I have before the bikers swim ashore?"

Raven looked back at the lake. "Several minutes, at least. And they're headed for the nearest land, which is a ways from here. Why?"

"Because I'd like ten minutes," said Kelsa. "But if I've got less, that'll have to do."

She was already kneeling, reaching up under the compartment cover, groping for the wire that ran from the ignition keypad.

"My dad taught me how to jump-start a bike, and made me practice it at the beginning of every summer before we took our first trip. He said that sometimes keypads fail, and I needed to know what to do. I can charge the bike with solar sheets, change a bad battery, and replace a tire too."

"You're stealing that bike!" Raven's face lit with delight. "Can I help? I don't know these machines, but sometimes a strong will to open something can make other things happen. I don't have much energy left, but opening takes only a wisp of power."

Hand on the wire, Kelsa hesitated. If he could start it without her having to break things, that would be a much better solution.

"Go ahead."

Raven laid his hands on the engine cover and closed his eyes. The hard shell of the rear storage compartment popped open.

"Darn it," he muttered.

"That's OK." Kelsa gripped the wire and yanked it loose. Some of the fine strands broke, remaining on the welded connection points, but there was enough for her to work with. She unstrapped the battery cover. "See if there's anything in there that can puncture a tire. A screwdriver or something. And make sure it doesn't lock again when you close it."

Raven dug into the storage compartment and pulled out a knife with a seven-inch blade. "Will this do? Why do you want to puncture tires? Don't we need them?"

"Not our tires. Theirs!" Kelsa gestured to the other bikes. "Just stab every tire, hard. In the side, not the tread. The side is thinner."

She was afraid the tires might explode when punctured, but only soft pops and the hiss of escaping air followed Raven's progress through the row of parked bikes.

By the time he finished, she had uncovered the battery terminals. Kelsa split the wire far enough to stretch between the poles, and applied one wire to the positive head and one to the negative, as her father had taught her.

The engine hummed to life.

Love and gratitude made her heart ache as Kelsa swiftly re-coiled the wire and covered the battery. Would her father keep on rescuing her, teaching her, for the rest of her life? Probably. She prayed that he knew it.

Raven was already seated on the back of the long saddle when she swung her leg over the bike. Kelsa could feel the extra charge rushing to the wheels as it worked its way around the curves, past the silent cabins. This bike was far more powerful than hers, or even her father's. A gangster's bike. A road hog. And it would probably take the bikers half a day to get new tires.

She and Raven had gained a lead. She had a few minutes to spare.

Before turning onto the empty highway, Kelsa stopped the bike and turned to look at Raven. He still wore his real face, pale and tired in the moonlight, and he'd been leaning against her more heavily than usual.

"You said they were gambling on killing you back there. But you've been alive for centuries. Can you be killed? Really?"

"Yes." For once he spoke without hedging. "I can be killed. If I was, in a few more years, or centuries, there would be another Raven. But it wouldn't be me."

It made no sense, but Kelsa knew truth when she heard it. It was probably the clearest explanation he could give. She turned the bike onto the main road and accelerated into the night.

CHAPTER 14

THE ROAD CURVED THROUGH flat-bottomed glacial valleys, over rivers, and up through the hills, twisting back on itself. The frost heaves became more frequent, the bike rolling over them like a ship in a stormy sea. Even the modern, crack-resistant road surface began to give way, with pothole after pothole flashing up in her headlights.

Sometimes Kelsa could avoid them, but often she was on them too quickly, and the bike slammed over them, rattling her teeth.

She should slow down. Neither she nor Raven had a helmet or any kind of protective gear. If she slid out they could be badly injured or killed. But it wasn't till the fourth spine-jarring jolt that she finally slowed, and she still had to pay close attention to the road. It almost distracted her from the red bar creeping slowly up the gauge in the corner of the bike's display screen—but there was nothing she could do about that except pray.

The adrenaline created by running for her life gave out, leaving her more tired than she'd been when they pulled into Pickhandle Lake. The flat gray twilight of the northern night was giving way to sunrise when the battery died. The engine shut down, and the bike rolled to a stop. Kelsa took it onto the shoulder at the last minute. They'd passed a few all-night truckers, and after they'd slowed several trucks had passed them. In a few hours the RVs would take to the road—not high traffic by city standards, but being stalled on a blind curve was never a good idea.

She'd hoped to make it to a station before this happened, despite the rising red bar on the gauge. What kind of moron set out without enough charge to make it to the next town?

The moron who'd owned this bike, apparently.

Raven lifted his head from her shoulder, where it had settled for the last half-hour.

"What's wrong? Why are we stopping?"

"The battery's empty. We have to recharge it before we can go on."

"But couldn't you tell it was wearing out? Can't you just let it rest for a while?"

Kelsa's eyes were burning. With weariness, she decided firmly. How much sleep had she gotten in the last three days? Four hours? Five?

"Letting it rest won't help. I did know the charge was running out, but sometimes there's more depth in a battery than shows on the gauge. Unfortunately, it looks like this gauge is accurate."

Raven looked around, and Kelsa followed his gaze. They'd been riding around the base of a hill, and a bog dotted with scraggly pines lay on the other side of the road. The trees' silhouettes looked odd, with thin bottom branches and heavy drooping tops, but it was too dark for Kelsa to see them clearly.

"We can't stay here," Raven said. "If my enemies find us, they'll send those bikers after us again."

"How did they find us at the lake?" Kelsa hadn't had time to think about that before. "How could they possibly know we'd pulled off there to spend the night? You said they couldn't use birds and things to spy on us."

"They can't," Raven said. "The thing is . . ."

Kelsa waited in grim silence. She was too damn tired to put up with his stalling now.

"The thing is, I'm afraid they might be tracking you the same way I have. Following that." He gestured to the bulge the medicine pouch made under her shirt.

Kelsa's heart sank. The medicine pouch was the one thing they couldn't leave behind. "If they can track the pouch, why didn't they find us earlier?"

"Until you started using it, they couldn't know what it . . . smelled like, for want of a better term. But that scent, the unique feel of its magic and yours working together, have been dumped into the ley several times now," Raven said. "And Otter Woman spent too much time with you. Thank goodness you were smart enough not to let her touch the pouch. They probably only have a vague sense of its magic. But the song of your human magic mixed with it is very distinctive. From now on, staying in one place for a long time is probably a bad idea."

"Wait. Are you saying that Otter Woman, all your enemies, are going to be able to sense me? Wherever I go?"

"Yes. So how do we charge this battery?"

Kelsa rubbed her eyes. She wasn't going to cry. She was tired, that was all. It only felt like they were going to be stranded here forever.

"Ordinarily, in a situation like this, I'd pull out my com pod and call for a mobile recharge. We can stop the next vehicle and ask the driver to call it in for us."

Almost any driver, and any professional trucker, would stop for a stalled vehicle.

"We can't," said Raven. "Even the bikers have seen those newscasts. We don't dare let anyone get a good look at us."

"So change your face again. I don't look a lot like the picture they're showing, and if I were traveling with, say, my grandfather, most people wouldn't look at me twice."

Raven's silence lasted too long. Kelsa was turning to face him when he said, "I can't shift. Trying to warm that lake, with half a dozen strong molders working against me . . . I won't have enough power to change my shape for days."

He sounded cross, almost arrogant. Kelsa was beginning to suspect that was how he dealt with fear. She was plenty scared herself!

"Couldn't you . . . I don't know. Use some power from the ley to do it?"

"I'm not your stupid battery," Raven snapped. "It doesn't work like that."

"Then how does it work? I'm sick to death of your not telling me things!"

Raven sighed. "To use the power of the ley, you have to use your own power to call it forth and control it. Exhausted as I am, I couldn't begin to touch it. And a power drain isn't like physical weariness, either. Mostly, if you retain some part of your magical energy the rest comes back pretty quickly. But when you drain it completely it takes a lot longer to return. Unlike your battery, resting will restore me, but it will be three or four days before I can shift shape."

Kelsa remembered other times he'd become tired, how shifting had taken him longer and longer. And he wasn't the only one who was exhausted. A tear ran down her cheek. She fought to keep her voice steady.

"How come you could do the opening spell on the bike's storage box?"

"That was only a nudge for the compartment to do something it wanted to do anyway. It didn't take more than a wisp of will. Molecular manipulation takes real power."

"So no money either?" The tears were falling now. Her breath began to catch.

"Not for days," Raven confirmed. "Though that doesn't need as much energy as changing a whole body does."

"So we're stuck here. We're fracking stuck here, and you're helpless, and those bikers are coming, and . . . and . . ."

"Are you crying?"

"Of course I'm crying, you moron! I don't want to be murdered by bikers! I want . . ."

She wanted to heal the ley. She wanted to heal the whole world, and her relationship with her mother, and—

A pair of warm arms came around her from behind. How could this grip be so different from the one that let him hang on to the motorbike?

"I can't do it," Kelsa wept. "I don't want to get killed! I can't save the world. I couldn't even save . . . save . . ."

"Save what?" he asked.

"My father."

She was crying so hard, she barely felt him lifting her and turning her so she sat sideways on the bike. Leaning against his chest she cried for fear, for exhaustion, for her father, for the whole damn mess.

He held her till her sobs began to subside.

"I can't do everything, either," he finally said. "I'd never have gotten this far without your help. So if you're finished, could we get moving again?"

A giggle interrupted the sobs. No matter how solid and warm his body felt, he wasn't human. And she was beginning to accept that. Even to be all right with it. Some of the time.

"Get moving how?" Kelsa fumbled in her pocket for a tissue.

"Didn't you once say you could charge these things with sunlight?"

"Maybe." Kelsa blew her nose. "Assuming that pack holds solar charge sheets. And that the sun comes out. And that you're willing to wait a full day—a sunny day!—for a charge that will take us about a hundred miles."

"Do we have another choice?"

They didn't.

o   o   o

Thrusting her hand past various lumpy objects to the bottom of the bike's storage compartment, Kelsa's groping fingers finally encountered the crinkly mass of solar sheets. By the time they'd walked the bike past the swamp, to a place where they could pull off into a drier stretch of forest, the sun was rising.

"We can't stop here," Kelsa said. "We've got to find a sunny place that can't be seen from the road."

On the assumption that the bikers would be at least several hours behind them, they pulled the bike onto the road's shoulder and set out exploring. It didn't take long to find a place where the denser woods gave way to bog once more.

By day, the mop-topped pines Kelsa had noticed before appeared even more sickly. Not only scraggly, but a yellowish color that looked like the early stages of tree plague.

"Are they supposed to look like that?" she asked.

"What? Oh yes. The Russian settlers in this part of the world called that kind of boggy forest taiga, 'land of little sticks,' because the trees are so spindly."

"They still call it taiga," Kelsa said. "I didn't know it looked like this."

At least the thin trees that covered the ice-bottomed bog would let light through to the solar sheets.

They wheeled the bike through the woods, swearing as they rammed it over humps of grass and tree roots. To Kelsa's amusement Raven muttered "carp" several times, as well as "consarn it!"

When they finally reached the grove they'd selected, she looked at Raven with concern. His pale face was covered with sweat, and there were dark circles under his eyes.

The storage compartment also held several gallon jugs of water, and some energy bars that Kelsa was hungry enough to dig into immediately, and without complaint. She even wished the gangster who'd owned this bike had carried peanut butter, but no such luck. There were also three bottles of beer, which she set aside without comment, and a sleeping bag, which Raven promptly appropriated and rolled out on the ground.

"You don't need me for anything else, do you?"

"No." Crying had left Kelsa tired, but strangely at peace. "Why are the solar sheets always on the bottom?" She lifted out a big leather satchel with a magnetic seal, closed by a DNA lock pad. "I wonder what they've got in here?" She set it aside. "Probably their—aha!"

She did need Raven's help to unfold the flimsy black sheets and spread them over the open ground, angled toward the sun. Kelsa plugged their thin cords into the small ports on the bottom of the battery. Raven, who had found the charge meter on the bike's display, stared at it impatiently.

"It's not going up," he said after almost a minute had passed.

"It won't even start going up for over an hour," Kelsa told him. She wished the bike had carried another sleeping bag, but if she unzipped the one Raven had taken and spread it out they could both lie down on it. She might not feel as tired as he looked, but it was close.

"We'll have to wait at least half a day before it charges enough to give us any chance of reaching a town."

Surely there would be some sort of charge station in the next fifty miles, even in the Yukon.

With a resigned expression, Raven watched her take over half his bed. "So what's in that leather bag? It looked heavy when you dropped it. Food maybe? Or some blankets?"

"Not with that kind of lock," Kelsa said. "That's the kind of lock you see on briefcases full of diamonds or top-secret documents. It's programmed to open to only one person's DNA."

"Why would bikers carry diamonds?" Raven asked.

"They wouldn't. I'm afraid it's illegal drugs," said Kelsa. "And that's something I want no part of."

"We should see what it is," Raven said. "There might be something useful in there."

Kelsa wasn't surprised when he knelt beside the bag, examining the lock and seal. Excessive curiosity was one of his many bad habits.

And who knew? There might be something useful in there.

"Can you open it, like you did the storage box?"

"No." Raven ran one fingertip down the magnetic seal. "This is designed to stay closed, not to open. Its energy is all wrong."

"Then we can't open it?"

"I didn't say that." He pulled out the big knife, and before Kelsa could do more than open her mouth to protest, he punched through the leather beside the closed seal and slit the bag with one expert swipe. He opened it, and his brows rose.

"Drugs?" Kelsa wasn't sure she had the energy to go over and check it out herself. That sleeping bag looked really good.

"No." Raven sounded amused. "But now I see why they go to so much trouble to sell them."

He lifted the bag and tipped it so Kelsa could see. It was crammed with neat bundles of money.

"Oh my God!" She was on her feet, with no memory of having risen. "They'll kill us. They'll track us to the ends of the earth, and kill us in a heartbeat, to get *that* back."

"They've already tracked us to the end of the earth." Raven was rummaging in the bag. "Or pretty nearly. And they already intend to kill us, so I don't see that we've lost much by solving our money problem. And we now have this for when they show up."

The solid black shape was something Kelsa had only seen on vids, but she recognized it instantly.

"A plastic gun," she groaned. "That's all we need!"

Raven looked at her curiously. "You don't sound like you mean that. Why is having a weapon a bad thing?"

"Because that's more illegal to carry than any drug," Kelsa told him grimly. "We finally managed to get guns out of criminal hands, because all modern guns have a DNA lock on the trigger."

"What does that mean?"

"It means no one except the person a gun is registered to can fire it. Unless they cut off the owner's finger, and it's hard to aim a handgun while pulling the trigger with a foreign object. A dead foreign object."

Raven studied the gun in his hand curiously. "I don't see a scan pad on this trigger."

"That's because it's an illegal gun," Kelsa told him. "It's made out of plastic, so it won't trip border scanners, or make consistent ballistic marks on the bullets it fires. It will work for anyone, and it's completely untraceable. Which is why being caught with one in your possession means a mandatory ten-year prison sentence, with more time added on if they can figure out why you wanted it. Get rid of it. Break it. Bury it. Right now."

After a moment of fiddling, Raven clicked the load out of the gun's handle and studied it. "Only five bullets? And they're plastic too. To go through border scanners? Are you sure about getting rid of this? With those bikers after us—"

"I'm sure," said Kelsa, "because there's another little problem with plastic guns."

"What?" Raven looked disturbingly comfortable with a weapon in his hand. Guns had been common, Kelsa knew, in the last several centuries of this continent's history. She still didn't like it.

"The problem with plastic guns," she said, "is that they're made of plastic."

"So?"

"A plastic barrel deforms a bit each time the gun is fired. That's why there are no reliable ballistic marks, even if enough of the bullet survives to take them. The first shot will be as straight, as accurate, as with a metal gun. The second shot is almost as good. The third through sixth shots are probably OK, but you'd better be close to the target. The seventh and eighth shots, anyone who isn't standing behind the person firing is in danger because there's no accuracy at all. And on the ninth shot," she finished grimly, "about one in forty of those guns blows up. That's low enough odds that some people are desperate enough to take the ninth shot. Or even the tenth, though there's a one-in-six chance the gun will blow up then. No one ever takes the eleventh shot. Not ever."

"Hence five bullet clips." Raven nodded understanding. "But that still gives us two good shots, and at least three decent ones, so—"

"Unless," said Kelsa, "it's already been fired five times. Or three. Or seven, and just loaded with a fresh clip. We have no way to know how many times it's been fired."

"Ah." Raven eyed the gun more dubiously. "Then we probably shouldn't rely on it. Are you really going to take half my sleeping bag?"

∘ ∘ ∘

They slept all morning, and Kelsa didn't wake till the clouds started blowing across the sun. Some of the hard bumps had poked through the sleeping bag's inflated pad. She sat up, rubbing a sore spot on her ribs.

Raven had already unplugged the solar sheets and was folding the crackling plastic.

"The battery gauge shows a little charge, and it's getting cloudy. I think we have to try."

It was past one by the time they'd repacked the storage compartment. Raven used the point of the big knife to break the latch so he wouldn't have to waste magic opening it next time. And despite Kelsa's arguments, he'd put the plastic gun back into the money bag.

"It must have at least a few shots left, or they wouldn't have kept it. And while we shouldn't use it unless we get desperate . . ."

He didn't have to finish. The police were looking for them, the bikers were hot on their heels, and if Raven's enemies didn't know where they were right now, they would the moment Kelsa healed another point on the ley. She and Raven might well become desperate enough to need that plastic gun.

The clouds were thick, but high enough for Kelsa to see the top of the snow-capped peaks as they moved on down the road. She kept one eye out for the bikers. Who knew how far behind they were by now? Or even ahead? She kept the other eye on the battery gauge.

A little over an hour later, when the indicator was nearing the bottom, they pulled into a charge station at Beaver Creek.

"We don't dare go in," Kelsa said sharply as Raven started for the store. "Not looking like you do now."

She hoped the drivers around them would be too busy charging their vehicles, taking care of their own needs, to pay close attention to the two teens on the bike. At least Kelsa looked somewhat different from the picture they were broadcasting, and the bike was completely different.

Except for the missing black eye, Raven looked exactly like the picture on the vidcast.

"I don't like this." He too was glancing around the charge lot. "They're closing in. We're only about thirty miles from the border and I can't shift. Not for days yet. I don't know what to do."

Kelsa had been thinking about that for several miles, but she still had to hold hard to her courage when she spoke. "If we're that near the border you'd better get off here. When you can change again, you can fly over and find me."

"But what about—"

"It'll take the bikers a while to stash their drugs before they cross." Kelsa tried to put more confidence into her voice than she felt. "Elizabeth Stayner's PID should take me right through."

She pulled out the card as she spoke, just to make sure. The picture still showed her, with her short black hair. Did the "1" in front of her age look a bit more blurred? No matter. It only had to last a few more hours.

"I won't trust any more little old ladies," she added. "I'll find somewhere to lie low, to keep safe, until you find me."

"I don't like leaving you." Raven was scowling in a way that might have attracted attention, but his concern was so sincere Kelsa didn't have the heart to scold him.

"It's just thirty miles to the border. I'll be OK. And I'll get the dust across. I finish what I start. Remember?"

Raven sighed. "I can't think of a better plan. Be careful. And Kelsa?"

"Yes?"

"When you said you couldn't save the world . . . You've already done more than I dreamed a human could."

Before she could begin to come up with an answer, he turned and walked away, past the station store and into the woods beyond. Watching him vanish, Kelsa realized that he'd become a friend—despite the fact that his comments about "humans" were still a little condescending. The fact that she could make friends again was probably another sign of healing, but right now it only added to her worries.

Would he be safe, from grizzly bears for instance, without the ability to change his shape?

He could work minor magic, Kelsa consoled herself. He could probably protect himself from anything but another shapeshifter.

And away from the medicine pouch, he was probably safer from them than she was.

Kelsa unplugged the bike and got back on the road. Despite the gathering clouds there was no rain, and shafts of sunlight lanced through the gaps, illuminating tree-clad slopes and brushy tundra.

The taiga bogs, with their twisted trees, had become common beside the road. Raven had assured her they were healthy, but Kelsa couldn't help but think that this was how all forests would look if the tree plague reached the north.

She had to go on. The ley had to be healed, no matter how dangerous it was for her. But that didn't mean she would try to cross the border with a plastic gun in her storage compartment.

A ten-year *minimum* sentence.

About eight miles out of Beaver Creek, she passed a local road heading away from the highway. There was enough traffic this close to the border that pulling off to bury the gun seemed like a good idea.

Kelsa turned the bike and started down the side road. She hadn't gone a hundred yards when she saw two bikes coming toward her. The riders were anonymous in their helmets and heavy jackets, but all four tires gleamed with newness.

She put her bike into a skidding spin and laid rubber on the asphalt as she raced back to the highway.

Two more bikers were coming up the highway toward her. There were still stretches of potholes, but Kelsa stepped on the accelerator pedal and kept her foot down.

They'd been waiting for her, watching for her. Had Raven's enemies learned to track the medicine pouch?

However they'd done it, they had her now. With power streaming from the newly charged battery, the bike she rode could hold the distance between her and her pursuers. But where were the other five?

Kelsa discovered part of the answer when two more bikes appeared on the road coming toward her.

The darkened helmet shields concealed their faces, but the thought that they might be innocent travelers never even crossed her mind.

The cutaway slope of the hill closed off one side of the road, and if she swerved into the forest the thick brush would stop her in minutes. Was that what they wanted?

Kelsa headed straight toward them. How could they stop a speeding bike? Besides shooting her. Or shooting one of her tires. Or driving her into a tree, or off a cliff, or . . .

Just before she reached the bikers she swerved off the smooth surface, too swiftly for them to intercept her, riding not into the woods, but up onto the slope where the hillside had been carved away.

It was almost a forty-five-degree angle—too steep, the dirt too loose—but she was going so fast that sheer momentum took her several yards up the slope, with rocks and dirt spitting from under her tires.

The handlebars bucked as the front wheel began to turn, but Kelsa fought with all her strength, holding the wheel straight as the bike skidded and slithered back down to the road—beyond the oncoming bikers.

She shouted aloud in triumph, in gratitude at still being upright, in motion. Her heart was hammering in her chest. Her father would have killed her for pulling an idiotic stunt like that.

All six bikers were behind her now, and she sent power screaming into the wheels and shot ahead, ripping around the corner . . .

Then slamming on her brakes as the border post appeared.

It was almost a quarter mile away, so Kelsa had time to slow to a speed that wouldn't trip the sensors. She had little to fear from the bikers here. U.S. state border stations were formidable; the national stations were full of armed, trained guards. She was safe from mayhem, as long as they were in sight.

She was also riding a vehicle that wasn't registered to Elizabeth Stayner, carrying a large bag of cash she couldn't account for, and a highly illegal plastic gun.

She would almost rather have faced the bikers.

Kelsa took her place in one of the five lines of cars waiting for the scanners. The station was busy—there were seven cars in front of her, and the line of RVs and trucks waiting for the big scanners was even longer. Not many people were waiting to pick up walk-across passengers. Whitehorse was a long way back, and there were no large cities near the Alaskan side of the border either, but a handful of cars occupied the designated parking lots on either side of the walk-through gate.

Many of those drivers had abandoned their vehicles, taking advantage of a small park, with benches and a stream, that had been built to showcase the big WELCOME TO ALASKA sign.

That welcoming sentiment was somewhat diminished by the twelve-foot steel-ribbed fence that ran downhill on the stream side and up the hillside to the right, continuing out of sight in both directions.

Two cars pulled in behind Kelsa before the bikers rolled decorously around the curve and took their place in line. Clearly they'd known where the border station was. Had they used the time to ditch their weapons? And where were the other three? Out burying their drug stash in a place that could be reached from the Alaska side of the border? Or were they already on the other side, waiting for her to cross?

Raven had been wrong. Recharging the battery with solar sheets had cost them too much time.

"Hello, bitch." Kelsa jumped, but the low, fierce voice didn't come from behind her. It came from the small screen on the bike's display. "Punch the contact button. We need to talk."

It made sense for the gang to have a bike-to-bike com system. It probably had a feed in their helmets as well. Kelsa looked at the bikers, two cars back. Several had taken off their helmets, like good citizens enjoying the sun that had broken through the shifting clouds.

The one who was looking down at his display was the red-head who'd accosted her at the Woodland Café.

Kelsa's stomach knotted, but they were all locked in by other cars, surrounded by witnesses, and under the omnipresent gaze of the grid—a grid whose cameras were probably being watched by border agents. She would never be safer than she was now. She punched the "com on" button.

"What do you want to talk about?"

The camera's tiny lens distorted his face, making the nose more prominent and the ears recede. The puffy brown patches of fresh burns showed starkly against his pale skin.

She winced, and he must have seen it, for he grinned nastily.

"Yeah, you got me good. So you can't be feeling you owe me any dirt, right? If anything, you owe me a favor."

He was trying to sound friendly, but his voice lingered on the word *favor* in a way that made her skin crawl.

"What kind of favor? And what makes you think I owe you anything? I was defending myself. Creep."

It was only bravado, but it made her feel better, even though his expression didn't change.

"Now that's where you're wrong. You've got something that belongs to us, and we want it back."

"That big leather bag?" Kelsa's thoughts raced. "What's in it? Drugs?"

Could she trade them the bag, and keep them on this side of the border?

A flicker of surprise crossed his face before he realized that she couldn't have gotten through the DNA-locked seal. She wouldn't have, without Raven's creative destruction.

"None of your business what's in it. It's ours, and we want it back. Drugs won't go through the scanners, so you don't want to be carrying it yourself."

That much was true. The cash and the gun would go through, but Kelsa's expression would certainly give her away to a customs guard trained to watch for people with a guilty conscience.

"Just bring it back to us," the redhead wheedled. "And we'll take it, turn around, and go. You'll never see us again. Promise."

It sounded like a lie, but she couldn't be certain. Even if he meant what he said, would Raven's enemies release their human tools now that they had the medicine bag within their grasp?

"Where are the others?" Kelsa asked suddenly.

"What others?" He hadn't expected this question, and his eyes slipped aside. He was lying. He was lying, and he knew it. The others might still be hiding the drugs, but there was an excellent chance they were waiting for her on the Alaska side of the border.

Cold dread gripped Kelsa's heart. She wouldn't be able to get away. Not from the bikers. Certainly not from Raven's enemies, if they could track the pouch she carried.

She wanted to heal the world; she didn't want to die for it.

"The guys who were with you at the lake," Kelsa said. She needed time to think. "There were nine of you. Where are the other three?"

"Just taking care of business," he said mildly. "Our business. Don't worry about them. You know we can't let you get away with robbing us, bi—uh, girl. You gotta give the bag back."

"I could turn it over to the border guards," Kelsa said. "And tell them how I got it."

His narrow face brightened with what looked like a real grin. "Well, if we end up in jail you can tell us how to get out.

Jailbreaker. How did you do that? It ain't so easy to get out of the slam once you get in."

He sounded genuinely curious, and not at all frightened. He was right. She didn't dare approach the authorities. That would put an end to her quest as surely as if the bikers killed her.

"I'll think about it." Kelsa cut the connection. Her face felt cold despite the sun. Her hands shook.

She'd promised Raven to get the medicine pouch over the border. To finish what she'd started.

But if she crossed the border the bikers would be waiting. And even if she could elude them, Raven's enemies would sense her magic. She might be able to keep ahead of them till Raven caught up with her, but he couldn't defeat all of them. The ice had proved that. Sooner or later, his enemies would win and the quest would end.

No, *her* quest would end. Just as Atahalne's quest had ended long ago. It was her magic, not the pouch alone their enemies were tracking. All Raven needed was the medicine bag and a human, any human, who was stupid enough, desperate enough, strong enough to see the truth and take up their duty. It only had to be a human. It didn't have to be her.

I always finish what I start.

Raven was counting on her to finish. The bikers were counting on her to try to finish. To give back their cash and go racing across the border into their trap. Raven's enemies were counting on her to try. And die.

What if she did something no one expected?

The bottom of her stomach dropped away as if she were stepping off a cliff, but Kelsa got off the bike and opened the storage compartment.

She brought out the big satchel. The weight of its load pulled the slit together. It looked more like a fold in the leather than the damage it was. Her heart was pounding, but Kelsa took her time, giving the bikers every chance to see what she was doing. She needed maximum confusion for this to work. Chaos and running crowds. They'd run toward the money, right?

"Hey!" A startled voice came from the bike's com. "What are you doing?"

Kelsa ignored him. Hefting the bag she set off, walking between the lines of cars toward the border station. Toward the border station's guards.

Several of the guards seemed to notice her. Or maybe they were looking at the person whose steps she heard jogging up behind her.

"Hey!" The voice was louder than it had been on the bike's com, and angrier. "What are you doing with my bag?"

Kelsa didn't stop until a rough hand grabbed her shoulder and spun her around. It was Redhead, and his burns looked even worse in person than they had on the screen. Kelsa no longer cared.

"It is your bag," she said. "And the drugs inside will have your fingerprints and DNA all over them, which is why I'm turning it in to the authorities. They're watching us." She nodded toward the guards, since both her hands were clamped around the bag's handles.

A female border guard had started walking toward them.

The gang leader followed her gaze, and his expression darkened. "They want you for jailbreak. You can't squeal."

"They only want to talk to me about it." She hoped that was true. "They can't prove I did anything. All they're going to do is deport me. You plan to kill me. I'd have to be crazy not to turn myself in."

He didn't even bother to deny it. An angry flush flooded his face as he reached out and grabbed one of the handles. "Give me my bag, bitch."

The approaching guard quickened her pace, but she was still too far away. A man two cars back opened his door, looking concerned, and she could see the worried face of the woman in the car next to them. The woman was turning on her com pod.

"No." Kelsa pulled back, letting the guard see her beginning to struggle, letting the cameras record it.

The soft click of a cocking gun was familiar only from vids, but Kelsa froze, staring at the biker.

Only one of his hands gripped the bag now. The other was concealed beneath it, pointing the gun at her.

"Let go or I'll shoot."

But his gaze flickered toward the guard, who was jogging now, and frowning.

Kelsa met the biker's cold eyes. "There are dozens of cameras recording every move we make. Recording your face. You don't dare."

She gave him several seconds to think about that, to realize its truth, before she let go of the handle he still held and pulled on hers, opening the slit in the leather wide and putting distance between them.

"Gun!" she screamed at the top of her lungs. "He's got a gun! He's trying to rob me. Help!"

She twisted her wrist, flipping the gaping bag. Money tumbled into a growing pile, and the plastic gun skittered across the pavement.

Not everyone in the nearby cars could see it, but the guard did. She tapped on her com button, then pulled out her own gun as she ran forward. "Hold it right there! Both of you. Freeze!"

Kelsa let go of her handle and turned to run. The bag swung down revealing the gun in the biker's hand. The woman in the car behind the biker began to scream.

The boom of the shot almost deafened Kelsa; it wasn't at all like the mild bang she heard on the vids. She spun to look back, staring in horror, wondering where the pain was.

But the biker had fired at the guard, who had dived behind a car and was yelling at the people in it to get down.

Was Redhead insane? Every second of this was being caught on the net. Kelsa hadn't dreamed he'd actually shoot at someone.

But he had. Horns sounded, and people yelled and jumped out of their cars, running away from the shooting—except for a foolish few who were creeping in on the money.

Redhead looked back, toward his gang, his bike. The gun in his hand was a clear warning. Kelsa heard the hum of a swarm of bikes drawing near. She turned and ran, weaving through the parked cars.

Shouted commands were followed by shots as more border guards ran forward. If anyone got hurt in this mess it would be her fault—though she'd never dreamed the biker gang would be crazy enough to try to shoot their way out in full view of the net!

The penalty for possessing an illegal gun was ten years. The penalty for firing one was much, much worse. Thank goodness she'd refused to touch the gun in the bag! She hoped the plastic bullets wouldn't penetrate a car.

As a fusillade of shots rang out behind her, Kelsa dodged around a final bumper and reached the park where the sign welcomed everyone to Alaska.

She pressed her hands over her ears and dived behind a concrete planter, praying that everyone survived. This had gotten totally out of hand!

But she still had a job to do. Looking around, she saw that most of the people who'd been waiting for walk-through traffic on this side of the fence had taken shelter behind the welcome sign. At least, there were a lot of feet beneath it.

On the other side people were crouching behind whatever cover they could find—planters, benches. Who to choose? One boy, who'd taken shelter behind a tree that looked too small to protect him, caught her gaze.

He was clearly a full Native American, with cheekbones higher and broader than Raven's. His shining black hair was cut in modern wedges, and he wore what looked like a business suit and shiny black shoes.

No teenage boy dressed like that voluntarily. Someone's driver perhaps? He looked too young for that, but he also looked like someone who would understand Native American magic far better than she had. And at least she could be certain he wasn't a shapeshifter, because not even a supernatural being could have anticipated this!

Like everyone else, he was staring toward the gun battle. The shooting had stopped, and the guards were shouting demands that the bikers surrender, while the bikers were yelling for the guards to back off.

It didn't sound promising, but Kelsa had to get the boy's attention. Now. Somehow.

The planter that sheltered her was filled with dirt, covered by a layer of smooth stones.

The first rock she threw over the fence clattered on the ground several yards from the boy. He glanced at it, but he didn't look at her.

Another shot was fired, and the shouting grew louder.

Kelsa gritted her teeth and took careful aim. She wasn't good enough to throw anything through the fence's tight-spaced ribs, but . . .

The next stone banged off the tree over his head, and the boy jumped as if it were a bullet. This time he had the sense to look around.

Kelsa waved frantically at him. Once his gaze was fixed on her, she pulled the medicine pouch from beneath her shirt and held it up for him to see.

It took only moments to wrap the cord around the pouch. The leather was warm from her body. Her father's ashes were mixed in with its dust. She'd given her heart to completing this quest. But it was Atahalne's quest as much as hers. Humanity's quest. Humanity's duty.

Love and death and duty didn't seem quite as clear-cut to Kelsa now as they had a few months ago.

It was time to pass it on.

She threw the pouch over the fence. She'd intended it to fall at the boy's feet, even into his waiting hands, but the pouch wasn't as aerodynamic as a stone. It landed almost six feet short of the tree.

The boy's brows rose, questioning.

Kelsa gestured impatiently for him to pick it up.

He seemed to make up his mind all at once, scrambling to snatch up the pouch and then diving back to shelter as still more shots rang out—though that tree really was too small to protect him.

Kelsa prayed once more that no one was hit, that no one had died, because the bikers had created so much more of a diversion than she'd intended.

She was still praying, with her eyes closed, when the sound of applause and honking horns signaled the bikers' surrender.

The sudden relief sent weakness shooting through her, and her knees gave way, dropping her to the ground beside the planter.

The Native American boy was staring at her, curiosity and concern on his face. She made a little gesture of shooing him away, hoping he'd realize he should stay where he was and do nothing. The less contact between them the better.

In a few days Raven would track down the pouch, and a shapeshifting stalker would appear in the boy's life to explain. He would probably cope with it better than Kelsa had.

If the cameras had caught her strange behavior, she'd say she'd been trying to warn the boy that the skinny tree he'd chosen wouldn't stop a bullet and he should find somewhere else to hide. It wouldn't be any more suspicious than the rest of the story she'd have to tell—though when she added the bikers, Raven's wild creation almost made sense.

She could say she'd wanted to be alone, to camp and travel to get over her father's death, which was pretty much true. She could tell almost all of the truth about the bikers trying to assault her in the Woodland Café, and her escape.

She could say she'd picked up Raven for protection against the bikers, that she'd been afraid to travel alone. She'd tell the story he'd given her about making a pod call for him, and having no idea how he'd gotten out of jail.

Would she ever see Raven again? If he had any decency, he'd at least come land on her windowsill and tell her how it had worked out. He wouldn't. She'd come to like him, but she'd also come to know him, and that kind of human understanding wasn't part of his nature. If the tree plague ended, that would be her answer.

She could tell the authorities most of the truth about the bikers tracking her down—at a campsite, since the clerk at the cabins had seen Raven that night. She'd say she'd run off into the woods, circled back, and stolen one of their bikes to escape on. She'd come to the border intending to turn that bag in to the authorities there. She didn't even want to go to Alaska. She didn't have any desire to go on healing her world, to feel the brimming rush of life-giving magic—

"Miss, are you all right?" The urgent question was accompanied by the pressure of a gentle hand on her shoulder. Kelsa looked up into the concerned face of a border guard and realized that her face was wet with tears.

"Are you all right?" he asked again. He carried a first-aid kit, and his gaze was already straying to the shaken people emerging from behind the sign.

"I'm fine," Kelsa said huskily. "Was anyone hurt?"

"Not that we've found so far. If you're all right, would you mind staying here for a bit? We're sorting this out, but it's going to be a while before anyone can move on."

"I'll stay here," Kelsa assured him. She rose to sit on the planter, and had just enough time to slide Elizabeth Stayner's betraying PID down into the dirt before the guards who were looking for her showed up.

"Would you please come with us?" It wasn't a question, despite the polite phrasing. "We have some questions for you, Miss . . . ?"

"Kelsa Phillips." They'd get the information from her DNA scan anyway. And soon after that she'd have to face her mother, who'd be harder to lie to than the cops.

She wasn't just going to be deported, she was going to be grounded forever.

"Yes, I'll come." Kelsa rose to her feet, careful not even to look over the fence at the Native boy.

It was in his hands now. And he was probably the right person to finish this healing.

Her mother had believed that the hospice staff were the right people to deal with her father's death. Had she been right, after all? Wrong?

All you could do was the best you could do. No one could do more. And unlike the shapeshifters, Kelsa could change her mind.

"I'll come," Kelsa repeated. "And I'll answer your questions. I'm ready to go home."

EPILOGUE

HE SHOULD HAVE GONE ON. The moment the pouch left her hands he'd felt it, the dissolution of the energy song that Kelsa and the catalyst had created between them.

Separated, their signatures were so different, so much less, that he couldn't have sensed either of them. But he'd found the pouch before, in the museum. He could find it again.

He doubted his enemies could.

So he had time. A few days, at least. And if she hadn't broken him out of that human jail he'd still be there. It seemed . . . rude to abandon her before he knew that she'd go free.

He'd found her by following the bike. It wasn't long after he'd regained the ability to shift that two uniformed humans had arrived, bundled the motorbike into a van, and driven away. A longish drive. The nearest airport was in Whitehorse.

Half a dozen black birds were tearing at trash in the airport parking lot, so no one looked twice at him. Even Kelsa, after a swift glance at the hovering flock, had shrugged and gone back to fussing over her bike as it was loaded into a shipping crate. If it hadn't been for the hovering policemen he could have approached her, but it sounded like their orders were to keep their eyes on her till her plane was in the air. They didn't have enough evidence to charge her with the jailbreak, but they were taking no chances with "young Houdini's" deportment.

In this form he couldn't laugh, but delight bubbled up and he flipped his wings to display it.

Even if he'd been able to speak, he wasn't sure whether he'd have praised her or berated her for abandoning the pouch in that spectacular way. Probably praise. If she had crossed the border, sooner or later his enemies would have killed one or the other of them. Maybe both. Now he had another chance, a little more time. But whoever was carrying the catalyst now hadn't connected with it at all, and that worried—

Raven had never seen the woman who hurried across the parking lot toward Kelsa, but there was something familiar about the mouth, the tilt of the eyebrows. He had gotten better at reading human faces.

Kelsa looked up and her jaw dropped. She took a slow step toward her mother. Then another. Then she ran straight into her mother's outstretched arms.

They were both crying, Raven observed critically, a state that seemed to reduce even sensible humans to incoherence.

The two policemen wore the smug look of humans who'd known this was going to happen.

"This is stupid," Kelsa finally said, her voice muffled against her mother's shoulder. "I'd have been home by tonight. They're going to put me on a plane in just a few hours."

"It's only the cost of a ticket," her mother said. "And Mrs. Stattler agreed. Worried doesn't begin to cover it! You're really all right?"

"I told you I was." Kelsa pulled out of the embrace just enough to see her mother's face. "You didn't have to come."

"I didn't have to." The older woman's voice was firm now. "And Jemina said that as long as you were all right I should let you cope with the consequences yourself. But she was wrong about that. Kelsa, we need to talk."

The girl's expression was serious, but sure. "You're right. It's time. And now, I'm ready to listen."

She looked up as he launched himself into the sky. She had no way of knowing it was him, but her hand still rose in the beginning of a farewell wave.

She had no further need of him. Just as he no longer needed her—though for a human she'd done amazingly well.

He would actually miss her.

But time was rushing on, and it was the healing that mattered. Raven circled once and settled into flying, north and west, toward Alaska.